W9-DIN-658

For Fucks Sake

by
Robert Lasner

PUBLISHING
New York

For Fucks Sake

Copyright 2002 by Robert Lasner

All Rights Reserved.

This is a work of fiction. Any similarity to persons living, dead, or otherwise, is purely coincidental, totally accidental, and shows what a bunch of fucked-up people the author used to know.

Published in the United States of America by
Ig Publishing
Brooklyn, NY
www.igpub.com

10 9 8 7 6 5 4 3

ISBN 0-9703125-1-2

Cover Art & Design by
Joseph Tullman

For Fucks Sake

For EC

I

We almost froze to death in Alabama. "Twenty-one degrees" said with a southern drawl over the loudspeaker at the Alabama Welcome Center was mighty funny tawk to these northern ears, especially after twenty-one straight hours spent in a Mercedes without heat. But then we came out of the frozen swamps, and bang, this great expanse of unbelievable water was upon us, like an exquisite gaping wound in the landscape. In a matter of minutes, the temperature rose about forty degrees as we crossed over a narrow bridge that stretched out into the invisibility of the water. Where were they hiding that?, I silently wondered to myself, as Ray and Dan slept in the back of the unheated car, now heated by the rising sun and the steamy vapors of the thick Cajun air.

To the sounds of Jan and Dean we crossed over the lake into the Crescent City. Could I be happier? I don't remember—I think I was just exhausted and relieved. I shouted for Ray and Dan to get up—"The Lake! The Lake!" They mumbled and barely stirred. In we went, with a big smile on my face and a song in my heart—

"Two Girls for Every Boy!" Or at the very least I hoped, "Some Chick to Talk to." We didn't hit our hotel immediately, but drove straight into the French Quarter, right into the heart of the pig.

The February streets of the Quarter were warm-blooded and sun-dazed, filled with the expectations of fucking, drinking, and vomiting. At least our expectations. We could see it through our sunglassed eyes, feel it on our Southern-heated skin, and taste it on our as-yet-unkissed (but soon to be kissed we were sure) salt-wet lips. Through the ancient streets we drifted and turned, guided by the simple movements of my hand at the steering wheel, left and right past wood-frame houses attached to empty balconies that meant nothing to us yet, right and left past unopened cartons of alcohol piled high on the sidewalk that would mean plenty to us soon.

At some point during our dream-lit drive, a girl standing on the sidewalk smiled at me. Or at Ray. Or at Dan. Depends on your perspective. She looked Filipino or Hawaiian, or something exotically brown like that, with long shiny black hair and eyes that shined like summer pearls. I knew right at that moment when she looked at me (or Ray or Dan), that she was the most beautiful girl in the world. I also knew right at that moment, driving through the warmth and un-

3

opened booze, smiling back on the perfect smile that was thrown our way, that the three of us were blessed to be young, alive, and full of mind and heart, awaiting the forthcoming night when the magical city of New Orleans would consume us and take our furtive unwritten souls and make night music of our deep unrooted and unruly desires. The beauty of it all! The warmth of the sun! The girls with lights in their eyes! We were dreaming of places unbuilt, of women untouched, of words untold. We were as of yet undrunk. "We dream of you, New Orleans! And tonight, we will drink of you!"

We left the Quarter and drove to our hotel, which was in a filthy slum section right outside of general New Orleans. Our room cost $150 a night for two beds and three roaches. The sign in the lobby said that a room with two beds (and no roaches) was usually $25 a night. Mardi Gras room tax was now in effect!

After checking in, we went straight to the local liquor store and purchased some items for the "prepping" portion of our evening—Jack Daniel's for me, Bacardi for Ray, and Dewars for Dan. A little while later, after we had all showered, shaved, shat, and prepped, Dan announced, "Well Robbie, I think on our first night in New Orleans we should have a fine meal at a top-of-

the-line eatery!" Ray and I agreed wholeheartedly
and most drunkenly already with Dan.

~

    Ray was a brilliant jazz musician, capable
of playing every instrument imaginable
unimaginably well. He was Japanese, with long
black hair that would hit the back of his ass as he
walked. The chicks loved that. Back home in
Philadelphia, there were many who mistook him
for the local Tae Kwon Do instructor. I always
joked that he looked like a 2,000-year-old man.
He wore a thin goatee, wire-rimmed glasses, and
was of slight build and slighter height. A good
friend he had been to me the past few months.
We bonded from the first—he taught me about
jazz, I taught him how to drink excessively and
pick up women. We were comrades in sax and
cunt.

    Dan was in his mid-thirties, a decade
older than Ray and I. He was six-foot plus in
height, with short blonde hair and bloodless
white skin. He made a nice color contrast to the
well off-white Ray, if mixing and matching companions based upon hair and skin color is your
thing. He waited tables in an expensive restaurant, but had apparently been a college professor in the past. Apparently, in the past he had
also been married to some woman whom I never

met but heard was a crazy bitch, and he apparently had never gotten over her, so, in the present, he only dated teenage girls. I say apparently in reference to all this information because I don't know if any of it was true (except for the stuff with the teenage girls), because while he was supposedly an intelligent sort, revealing the details of his life was never his strong point. Often, you would ask him a question, and in response he would grunt a few times and smile vapidly, not quite sure what to say. But, he liked to have fun, and would rub his hands together in excited anticipation whenever something wild and wacky, like the taking of drugs or the fucking of women, was about to occur. It never usually happened the way he hoped, at least with the chicks, but his hands were red from trying.

~

We took a bus into the French Slaughter. Since we had "prepped" in the hotel, we were crocked and rocked even before we hit the streets of cum and cock. The restaurant we dined at made things worse. Wherever we went to eat, it was good, real good, with real tall (like a foot tall) drinks. After our liquid supper, we put on our dark shades and hit the Quarter. From what I could see through my blackened eyes and bourboned mind, the streets seemed blurry and

6

red, filled with reel-to-real people. I felt like I was in the red-light district of Hamburg, though I had never been in the red-light district of Hamburg. Around us swirled a lot of whirl and whiz and scream and cream and hump and jump. Lots of frat boys, fat boys, flat girls, rat faces and no tail. Sucky fucky for everyone, except us.

We quickly realized that this was not our kind of scene. What was our kind of scene? Dan told us he wanted to go the bars where the "girls with the nose rings hang out." Now, *that* was our kind of scene. Someone told us we would find such girls on Decatur Street.

We headed toward the street Decatur, which we found at the edge of the river Mississippi. Unfortunately for Dan, we didn't encounter any pierced women there, but we did discover a bunch of the Deadheaded, who lived in vans on Decatur unwashed and unspayed during Mardi Gras. At some stoned point I was sitting on the street with these hippie typos, smoking weed and getting my hair braided, when all of a sudden, from above, I felt a soft hand on my cheek—a girl's hand was touching my cheek! She said, "You have the most beautiful face!" I looked up. She had a beautiful face too. Tasty full lips, red like everything in this night scene, a large bosom that I could just rest my face in, and tight jeans framing firm taut buttocks. Finally, what I had come to Mardi Gras for, a girl, a beautiful girl, a girl who wanted me! And I didn't even have to get up off the sidewalk! And I immediately knew that she was different from every other girl I had met in my whole life up to that point. How did I know such a thing so quickly, so absolutely, with such certainty? As they say, it's all in the eyes, my eyes in this case. I looked straight out in front of me where her left leg should have been. Instead of a leg, I saw a man urinating on a storefront across the street. Why did I see such images of the pre-heated Cajun night where flesh and blood and tendon should have been? Because my beautiful admirer, the love of my night, the woman who had chosen me on the street corner above all the other Mardi Gras minions, had but one leg! Yes, one stump, no waiting, one leg, no dating! No hopscotch for her when she was a kid, I imagined, unless the de-legging was an event she hadn't celebrated until later in life. I thought of some joke I heard once about a drowning person with one leg. I couldn't remember the joke, but I remembered that the punch line was Bob.

I now had a stinging dilemma in my dope-dreary mind. How would she and I do it? How would Bob and I become one, successfully? The beast with two backs, and three legs? If I were fuckin' her good, real good, would she wrap her *leg* tightly around my ass? I guess doing her from behind was sort of out of the question—an issue of balance, unless there were some kind of pulley system available. Or maybe a stack of phonebooks would suffice. We chatted for a bit, but she seemed rather empty-legged, I mean headed. So, there was to be nothin' doin' with this chick on a stick. Besides, I must admit that I was not really into one-legged stands.

~

We quickly discovered that in New Orleans the night was the morning, which was the afternoon, which was forever, which was the night again. Meaning that it really didn't matter what time it was. We continued to continue our wanderings far into the night, about as far as the darkness would take us. We stopped everywhere, talked to no one but ourselves, made sure all limbs we encountered were real, and drank our minds into a depressive funk, surrounded by flashing lights, swinging hips, exposed tits, and chanting cum-caked men.

As the daylight of our first night arrived and tripped over the drunks spilled all over the narrow streets, we were looking for something to break us out of the mildewed party-funk of Mardi Gras, something better, something unusual, something different. On Chartres Street (pronounced *Charters* in New Orleans, as Carondolet is pronounced *CarondoleT*—the first time I used these words I thought I was a big deal with my proper French pronunciation, and I wondered why the hell nobody understood what I was saying), we managed to find some *thing*. Here, in the urine-stenched morning haze, we discovered a frat boy—at least we assumed he was a frat boy because he had all the usual markings of one (overweight, baseball cap, baggy T-shirt with a Greek letter on it)—with his pants down around his ankles, trying to throw himself through a plate glass window. Now, this was certainly something different. We viewed this inspiring spectacle for several minutes. But after watching the frat boy repeatedly throw himself *against* the plate glass, but not *through* (to our great disappointment), we got bored and decided it was time to go and get some breakfast at the Shoney's down the street.

While enjoying a wonderful meal of sausage, bacon, and eggs, we heard that some guy had been arrested by the police after throwing himself through a plate glass window (success!). Now, however, wasn't the time to celebrate, as our drunken bones needed some place to pass out, I mean sleep, in the French drawn and quar tered, since we were too tired and drunk to make it back to our hotel.

At first we tried to sleep at our table, but were quickly informed by Shoney's management that this was not a fuckin' bedroom, and shown the door. Then after conferring for a few minutes in the brightening light of the morning, Ray and I reached the logical intoxication conclusion that it would be swell to sleep on the docks on the banks of the Mississippi River. So cool, we thought, didn't Mark Twain sleep there, in Hump Finn or something? Dan, however, disagreed with our decision to dock, and said he was going back to the hotel room 'cause he was paying $150 a night and therefore he was sleeping in a bed. Whatever. He left and we fell onto the wooden planks by the side of the river.

There were humans everywhere around us, some sleeping with vomit beside them (hopefully belonging to them), some sitting in circles singing Dead songs, some staring at the rising sun and the receding waters, some smoking weed, some muttering silently into their souls. Some pissing into the river. All the leftover remnants of the night were here, and that night, that morning, we slept among them.

We must have slept until about noon. Then, as the midday sun reached full bore, melting the vomit and piss and whiskey remains into the Earth, Ray and I were awoken by the piercing sound of a ship's whistle. As this painful noise shrieked through the hanging noon, I opened my eyes and was immediately blinded by the combination of sun and last night's spirits. Luckily, I had fallen asleep behind some large wooden pillars on the dock, so the majority of my mortal flesh was protected from the wrath of the pulverizing Southern rays. Before I had a chance to re-orient myself to where the hell I was, the whistle sounded a second time. At this second attack upon my drunken eardrums, I rose up and yelled at the whistle, at the ship, at the whole world to "shut the fuck up!" Then I closed my eyes again, and heard a lot of people laughing.

Ray and I ambled back to the hotel. Danno was asleep. He could not constitutionally awaken before four in the afternoon. Look it up. We joined him in sleep for a few more hours, and then we all woke up and got some food from the local gas station convenience store sewer, since there was no place else to eat in the human latrine that we were staying in. After "lunch," we drank some more of what we had purchased for the "prepping" portion of our evenings, and after the usual showers, shaves, and shits, we headed back to the bus, back into the 1/4.

It was the same as the night before. Things happened, unremarkable things that we had seen before and didn't want to see anymore. Nothing different. Well, one thing different—a man fell on me. We were walking down Bourbon Street, near Canal, when I felt a hand on my back like someone wanted me. Then I felt another hand, as if two people wanted me, then an ever-increasing amount of weight and pressure, as if a small group was trying to get my attention. As I turned around to see what they wanted, a finely-dressed gentleman in suit and tie fell right past me, straight to the ground, like a rock falling through the air. $150 a night for a room, hmm? Or, nothing for a wee catnap on a pillow of shit on the cream-covered sidewalk of post-Confederate fornication.

Later that same evening we were walking down Bourbon Street again, merging and melting with the masses, when the crowd suddenly parted. Being Jewish, my first thought was that Moses was coming. But this was not the time for religion! Down the now-open middle of the street came a horse, a police horse. Behind it was another police horse. Between these two fine equestrian specimens were two gentlemen, chained to the horses. I don't know what they had done to end up in such a predicament, but whatever they had done, they had apparently gone too far. How you go too far in illegal activities in New Orleans during Mardi Gras I didn't know, (do I hear "plate glass window?"), but apparently they had broken the imaginary barrier that separated acceptable decadence, marauding, and molestation from wicked, sinful, unwholesome and thoroughly un-Mardi Gras-like behavior. And now they were being made an example of for the rest of us. The authorities were showing us what happened if one crossed the line. I tell ya, don't ever cross the line. "Because you're mine, I walk the line."

After witnessing this, Dan, Ray, and I held an emergency alcoholic meeting on the corner of Bourbon and Toulouse to discuss what we had experienced over two days and nights in the city of the menstruating hurricane. We quickly and unanimously reached a decision—New Orleans fuckin' sucked! "Maybe we should just get the fuck outta here. Ray, don't your parents have a place in Florida? We could lie on the beach for a week. Anything is better than this shit." It was agreed. This was to be our last night in New Orleans. We would get up tomorrow and to Florida we would go. Goodbye New Orleans, city we loved for an afternoon. You were just a cheap thrill, and not too thrillin' at that. Goodbye, and good fuckin' riddance!

After our meeting ended, we were about to proceed down Toulouse Street to take one last look at the Mississippi before our departure, when I stumbled over a crack in the sidewalk and fell down, clutching my ankle. As I lay on the ground in the garbage and Mardi Gras beads, I looked up and saw a round black wooden sign with red lettering. The letters seemed to spell *The Cage*, albeit a bit blurrily. The Cage? "Dan! Ray!" I shouted, "didn't our good buddy Mike in Philadelphia say, 'When you guys go to New Orleans, you have to go to this bar called The Cage!' Well, doesn't that sign that we are walking by on our last night in New Orleans *ever* say The Cage?" Dan grunted and rubbed his hands together, while a wicked smile of evil-minded rummery crossed Ray's face.

We walked through a maze-like area that was indoors, yet outdoors, which was confusing to my alcohol-infested thoughts. There were windows overlooking us from all directions, and there may have been a fountain, but as I write this I can't remember for sure, so I'll say...yes, there was a fountain, a big fuckin' fountain, with a large sculpture of a naked woman with whiskey shooting out of her nipples and twat. We waited on a line filled with idiotic drunken overweight pimple-faced shit-for-brains kids from Southern colleges, and their equally drunk shit-for-brains bimbette companions with questionable blonde hair and unquestionably open cunts.

We didn't have to wait on line for very long. Within a few minutes we were beckoned in through a large wooden door by a large sweaty hand belonging to a large sweaty man. Upon entering the dark and woody bar, we were immediately hit by the stench of human sweat and cigarettes, as an infinite number of people were stuffed into a finite area. The door closed, and we were trapped among them. They were pressed against us, against each other, dancing, falling, grabbing at each others' privates (at least the men were trying to grab the women's), staring, drinking, and contemplating. Mindless mid-seventies Kiss was blaring from the speakers. The place was so crowded, hot, and noisy that within seconds we had turned around, and were about to leave. However, before we even had a chance to push toward the door, the crowd suddenly thinned out, and we were able to breathe, and even better, get seats at the bar.

Since my ankle was starting to bother me, I decided to take off my boots and set them atop the bar. Within seconds, some drunken imbecile grabbed them, tied the laces together, and announced that he was going to wear them as Mardi

Gras beads. Before I had a chance to react, the bartender came over and told him, in a stern and husky voice, to put my boots down. Our eyes met for a second. She was pretty, with long curly hair and a thin but overly made-up face. She greeted me in the friendly way bartenders usually do, and quickly took notice of the Guatemalan shirt I was wearing, which I had purchased at some neo-hippie shop back in Philadelphia. She excitedly told me that she used to live in Guatemala, and that my shirt was authentic. I thanked her for complimenting my shirt, and ordered a Jack and Coke. She put the drink in front of me, and then stared at me for much longer than most friendly bartenders do, and left without asking for any money. I put a ten down on the bar, figuring she would take it later.

I don't remember much about the rest of the night, except that Ray and Dan kept telling me that the bartender seemed interested in me. I guess their judgment was based on the fact that she gave me free drinks all night long. When I left at the end of the night, I took the ten that I had put on the bar off the bar.

Based upon the priceless quality, and proficient quantity, of my drinks that evening, I decided to ask this as-yet-nameless bartender out for breakfast as the night ended and the morning began. She replied that she couldn't because she had to work early the next day. Mardi Gras, you know. "What day?" "The next day." "Then, what day is today, in relevance to the day not being today, but the day of our date, which specifically could be today, if today is the day that we are talking about? Breakfast *today*?" "Sorry, no." "How about maybe tomorrow night, then?" Couldn't. She wasn't working tomorrow night, but she was going to spend the night in, sleeping. "Tomorrow night? What night?" "Can't." "All right. Good night."

That was that. Back to the streets at dawn, well into the day. Back to the one-legged women, and the dope-smoking morons living in vans, and the well-dressed business suit pricks passed out on side streets. Back to the high priced hotel of hellaciousness. Back to sleep, for one more night. Then, tomorrow, it would be pure flight, further into the sun, to the beach and the sea, lying on the sand ogling the bikini line. So long, No Holeans, salivation city of pubic nonsense. Good luck at the bottom of America, the bottom of the world, the top flight of shit.

~

We didn't leave the next day. I don't remember exactly why, but it probably had something to do with the friendly bartender, even though she had rejected my advances. You see, back in those days, I believed that if a girl rejected you the first time, you still pursued her a second, or even a third time, until she hated you, dated you, or the two of you found some kind of codependent middle ground. Try, try, and try and try and try again! That was my gospel. So, even though she had rejected me, I had to see her again, had to try again. Tomorrow to Florida! But tonight, I had to find the girl of my rejection dreams.

We, of course, went back to The Cage to begin my search for the girl who said she wouldn't be there. And *she was there!* Not working. Just *there*, seated at the bar. I ambled up to her. "So, I thought you were going to stay in tonight?" "I changed my mind." As I was about to question her further, she suddenly got up from her seat and ran from me, full speed, into the night. For a few moments I was in shock. What the hell? I had been rejected by women before, but they didn't usually sprint away from me. This unexpected and unpleasant rejection caused me to cry for a moment, in the shadow of the screaming bass drums and the steaming vapors of sex that poured over the bar yet washed away from me. Then, just as quickly as they had come, my tears vanished, and I was back, with a little less of myself inside myself. I straightened my mind back into arrogant normality, and put on a face to face the rest of the night that I no longer wanted to face.

I, we, everyone, drank heavily that night. The local economy was booming! I'm sure we left le Cage aux fornication soon after my rejection, but I do not remember doing so. I'm sure we drank and drank and drank some more, but I do not remember doing so. I know I cried a bit more because I remember doing so. What did I feel towards this girl that had brought me back again, to be rejected again? Was she attractive? Yes, but not any more so than a thousand other women I had seen. Was she intelligent? I didn't know, as we hadn't had a real and sober conversation. I didn't even know her fuckin' name! What was it then? I didn't know, but there was something about her, something about me, that made me unable to leave this place, that made me come back to her again, to be rejected again.

As dawn approached, Ray, Dan and I finished our last night of imbibing and headed to the bus to go back to the hotel, back to the end of this trip that had never begun. We walked through the leftover ruins of the Mardi Gras massacre—a swamp of plastic cups, plastic beads, human waste, and wasted humans. As we boarded the bus that morning, I was sure that we had spent our final moments in New Orleans. I sat in the back, alone, staring absently out the window at the pink sky that was sizzling with the first rays of the morning sun. As we rode over the river wet with my unremembered memories, I dozed off, and must have slept for an instant, for an hour, for an eternity, in her arms, in her empty memories. I was awoken by Ray's voice. "We're here."

~

Even though she had rejected me in such a dramatic manner, we decided to stay in New Orleans for yet another night. Why not give her a *third* chance, I thought, one more opportunity to prove that what she had done was an aberration, that despite her actions and statements to the contrary, she was in fact interested in me.

We returned to The Cage. She was behind the bar. And, unlike the previous night, she was friendly and flirty toward me, much like she had been on the night we met. I could see her eyes shining toward me again, even in the dark of the bar. And the drinks were still free! So, my philosophy about coming back over and over again had paid off after all!

"Your name. What is your name?" I asked. "My name is Annabel Lee. Annabel Lee Plurabelle. Or just Anna. Some people just call me ALP." She lived in Arkansas, she told me, and came from a prominent and wealthy family. She ran her own store back home, making and selling hand-crafted goods, and came to New Orleans every year to make a few extra bucks during Mardi Gras.

Since I did not know the geography of this part of the country, nor had I cared until that moment, I asked, "Is Arkansas far from here?" "About eight hours, but it's a beautiful drive, alongside green fields, across gentle rolling hills, and past peaceful streams." "And past poverty, and cute men in little white sheets burning the skin off their Negro neighbors," I said out loud—all was permissible to be said in The Cage, especially late at night, especially early in the morning, especially after the fifth fifth of Jack. She laughed and poured me another drink. Meanwhile, Dan had taken a liking to the other bartender, a tall, attractive, dark-haired beauty of the mysterious South named Donna. Love for him too? But none of that mattered, Ray said defiantly, because we were definitely leaving for Florida first thing tomorrow. "I'm going back to the room after this drink. Or, maybe one more, and then definitely I am out of here, and tomorrow we're definitely off to Florida. You guys can stay here all night if you want, but I'm going back to the hotel and getting a full night's rest. I'll drive, and you guys can sleep in the car. But we're definitely going to Florida!"

My mother always told me that people died in threes, especially celebrities. If Dan, Ray and I were about to discover death, or celebrity, with the ALP's and Donna LP's of the untamed night, then there must be a third. The father, the son...the holy whore. Her name was Debbi. With an I, not an E, after the B's. She was a friend of Annabel Lee's, who had once worked at The Cage herself, but was asked to resign because she used to trip on LSD while on the job, which made the booze hard to pour and the walls start to melt. I could identify with those problems, especially the former—once I had been on acid, sitting in a bar trying to drink a beer, and each time I took a sip, it seemed like the level of the beer in the bottle went up instead of down. Later on the bagel store turned Irish, but that is for another time, another story. Annabel Lee told me that Debbi had a thing for Asian men, particularly the Japanese. Later, we found out that Debbi had had many things with Japanese men—four children with three different Japanese men to be exact. Or close to Japanese—she would approximate the ethnicity if she were unsure.

Debbi was sitting cross-legged on top of the bar. In the semi-dark haze of Jack Daniel's and Deep Purple, she looked attractive to my whiskey-soaked eyes. She had a decent face, with deep-set dark eyes, and an ample bosom pushing out of her tight rock n' roll T-shirt. Her hair was long and straight, and seemed to be blonde, or some color from a bottle approaching or approximating blonde. She was staring at Ray, who was sitting at the bar, one seat away from her, and one level below. Between them was a fat guy wearing a Houston Astros shirt, siting alone and mumbling to himself. Debbi began throwing ice at Ray from her perch on high, to get his attention. He thought she was throwing the ice at the fat guy in the Astros shirt. So wonderful he was when he had no ego, no confidence. Confidence is a killer. Best to be innocently clever instead of smart; cute instead of devilishly good-looking.

After a few minutes of ice tossing which failed to spark Ray's attention, Annabel Lee pulled me aside and told me that her friend Debbi wanted to talk to my friend Ray. I went over to Ray to inform him that the ice might be meant for him. "Go over and talk to her," I said. "What about the fat guy?" he responded. Whatever, Ray. Minutes later, or it could have been hours, after he and Debbi had had a conversation of apparently some merit, Ray pulled Dan and I aside and told us that if he got laid that night we could stay in New Orleans another day, and he would pay the entire cost of the hotel room!

Everything was now in perfect order. Dan and Donna were sitting at the end of the bar with one another, all cuddles and glances. ALP was merrily preparing drinks for the denizens of Mardi Gras mayhem around us, keeping her eyes always on me. I was sitting at the bar, sipping my Jack and Coke, keeping my eyes always on ALP. Ray and Debbi were huddled together atop the bar, chatting and smiling and longing and groping. There was water on the floor all around us, as if someone had been throwing ice. I suddenly began to cry to myself, this time out of happiness! I felt like god! I was the first, the leader, the seer! I had had the first chick first, the chick from which all the other chicks came. The chick that begot the chicks. I felt like a war hero making my men happy before the big battle. Sergeant Lasner! Tonight though, there was no blood, only bourbon; no war, only shore leave; no loneliness, only a fuckin' free hotel room! Tomorrow, there would be no Florida, and there would never be! Tonight, tomorrow, the next day, the day after, and all the days after, there would be three, for the three of us. We were all one. Cubed!

~

Mardi Gras officially ended the following night when a fleet of municipal trucks came marching down Bourbon Street at midnight, clearing away the trash both human and plastic. That is how they end it. The fun is over, and now it is Lent, and now we pray. Makes perfect sense to me. After witnessing the driving of the trucks, Ray, Dan, and I returned to The Cage for a few more hours of Mardi Gras marauding. By this time I had fallen for Annabel Lee. After the first few nights of confusion, I had thought that we were not to be, and that she would just be another forgotten face from my forgotten past. In the last twenty-four hours, however, it had all changed. I had gone from reject to accept, from dejection to redemption! I was so happy as I sat at the bar that night, drinking my usual share of Jack and Cokes, staring at ALP, thinking of ALP, dreaming of ALP! At dawn, we shared a cup of tea, to warm our shared heart from the cold night of drinking. We sipped together out of one plastic cup, and looked at one another out of one shared glance as the morning light streamed through the half-open shutters on the bar windows, illuminating this dark hole of New Orleans with the clear light of renewal.

As last call was called and we were about to leave the bar, I leaned over to say goodbye to

Anna. She told me she would be done in a few minutes, and that I should wait outside for her. Then, she grabbed me and kissed me full on the lips. I turned and left the bar without saying another word.

Out into the blinding sunlight I went, the streets filled with five-foot high piles of trash and the accompanying smells. I could still feel the oiliness of her lipstick upon my whiskey-flavored lips, and the heat of her breath on my tongue. I found a big pile of trash at the corner of Toulouse and Bourbon and danced around it like a child ringing around the rosy. I leapt in the air several times, shouting "She loves me, she loves me!" The sun was strong on my alcohol-dipped flesh, and the brightness of the morning illuminated all that was around me, from the dried vomit and stale piss on the ground to the unborn outline of my life that ALP had awoken. It was the happiest morning of my life, the beginning of a day that I felt was the beginning of all days.

By the time ALP came out of the bar, I was sitting on the ground, on a little step right outside The Cage. She jumped into my lap before I even realized she was there. I had never seen her in the clear natural light of day. I looked at her face, and she looked at mine. I saw her eyes for the first time. They were green, so incredibly green, as if the sea was flowing through them. Her eyes I drank like time! She stared at me with an intense expression of no expression that expressed it all. We didn't speak. We didn't have to. We knew.

She took my hand and put it down her shirt. What was this, I thought, I didn't want to touch her breast; it wasn't time for *that* yet. As I looked into her eyes, I saw that she knew it wasn't time for *that* either. She wanted me to feel something else, something more perfect than the randomness of lust. She wanted me to go in, all the way in, past the shape of a breast, or the moisture of a vagina. All the way in, to where she had let no man go before.

I touched her chest. Through her soft white skin I could see the red hue of her blood pumping, strongly, deeply, through veins and capillaries, through mountains, and years, and lives. I felt her heart. It was beating fast and sharp, alive, oh so alive, like a city by itself, as if we weren't there, weren't in New Orleans, but in a world of our own construction, of our own shared wordlessness.

We sat on the concrete, among the urine and vomit, among our looks and glances, and it was all happening, without a sound between us, without the unnecessity of language. I saw her green sea eyes, I felt her warm red heart, and I felt as if she had taken me out of the universe, away from the flesh and skin of living and breathing, to a world of noiseless absolution and voiceless joy. As the sounds of the street disappeared into the sun, we shined upon the passed out drunks and blood-splattered streets of the French Quarter, guiding the lost, the confused, the fucked up, and the forgotten, toward the end of it, the beginning of it, all of it, throughout all time from this time forward.

Then I grabbed her, touched her cheek, and ran my fingers over the outline of her eyes, those sea eyes, wondrous and full of life, a life I had never seen before. As the sun burned high in the sky, between us, among us, I reached over with my lips toward hers, she reached back toward mine with hers, and we kissed, and merged together as one under the brilliant flame sky.

~

We sat on the street for a little while longer, gazing into each other's eternal memory. Then we got into a taxi with Dan, Donna, Ray, and Debbi. We were all going to stay at Debbi's house, deep in the Quarter, our $150 a night hotel sojourn a thing of the past. Look mom, we're moving in!

Annabel Lee and I were whispering to

each other in the back of the taxi, drunk with delight, drunk with bourbon, and I think a little bit stoned. This was certainly a joyous cab ride through the streets of the French Quarter, the first cab ride of my new life with my new love in this new city of fucked-up brilliance. I don't remember how it got started, but Anna said she had something that she had to tell me. "Sure, whatever," I said happily, "you can tell me anything you wish!" She was nervous at first, so it took a little while for her to get to the point. And, I don't remember the exact words, so I can't quote her directly. But, the general gist of her statement was that she had been in a relationship for seven years, and that she lived with someone back in Arkansas, eight hours away through green fields and rolling hills.

I listened. I absorbed. I evaluated. I reacted. I burst out laughing. "Relationship! Seven years! Living with someone!" I loved her even more now. I told her that this was lovely, great, wonderful. "Anna, this is lovely, great, wonderful! I want to be with you, more than ever now! Who the fuck cares about your man back in Arkansas! Break it off with him!" But somehow I had misheard part of what she had said. No sleep and lots of drink will affect your hearing in strange ways. She repeated her statement to me, but it sounded remarkably different the second time. "I live with a *woman* in Arkansas. We are lesbians. I haven't been with a man for seven years!"

I listened. I absorbed. I evaluated. I reacted. "Hmm?" I leaned over to Dan who was seated beside me. "Annabel Lee is a lesbian. She lives with a woman in Arkansas. She hasn't been with a man for seven years." Dan smiled a big smile of surprise and delight, rubbed his hands together, and exclaimed in a sort of mocking Scottish drawl that he often used when addressing me: "Ah, Robbie!" Robbie thought it was funny too. "This is interesting, Anna. I love you," I said. She then looked at me with those eyes that were as green as my experience with lesbian women, took my hand, and placed it down her shirt, unto her beating heart. That was the way she told me she loved me. Pretty cool. In the happiest times. During the heterosexual season between winter and spring.

The taxi let us off at Debbi's apartment. She lived, with two of her four children, deep in the Quarter, on the same block where Paul McCartney owned a hotel. At least that's what Anna told me, and she always knew about such things. We went down a tree-lined courtyard surrounded by large iron doors. I asked ALP what

31

was behind these doors, and she said that today they were extra rooms, but in the old days they had been the rooms where the slaves lived. I laughed upon hearing this. "Hey Anna, maybe one day we can get some slaves ourselves!" Instead of laughing at my attempt at black humor, she got this serious look on her face, and told me that she knew people in New Orleans who still kept slaves today. I responded that I thought that was illegal, especially after the Civil War. She told me that it didn't matter. "This is New Orleans!" Oh!

Upon hearing her say, "this is New Orleans," my mind immediately drifted back to the old days, days that I had only read about in history books, the days of slaves and masters and plantations and cotton. As I walked down the courtyard that smelled like ancient concrete and Spanish moss, I though of the slaves who had once lived behind the iron doors, their dead bones and anguished cries extinguished over a hundred years of progress and bloodshed. Then I thought about the people who ALP told me still kept slaves today. I imagined black people living in the condominium closets of today's New Orleans, being let out to vacuum the rugs and wash the dishes and clean the toilet, with a white man masser in a business suit holding a whip over their bruised backs and broken lives. Finally, I thought about what a strange place I had entered, and what a strange city New Orleans was, filled with a despicable past that in some unexplainable way the city was proud of.

Once we entered the apartment, Ray and Debbi fell unto the couch and began making out. Donna led Dan by the hand into some room, and the door closed behind them. Then I felt ALP's hand in mine. She led my love-weary body up a flight of stairs, into a large blue room that was filled with children's toys strewn about aimlessly. We found a small stained vinyl couch in the corner, and fell unto its filthy cushions. It was barely large enough to fit our two bodies, so we had to lie tight together, compressed into one ball of living warmth. Though we were drunk, stoned, and a bit tired, we started to talk. And talk. And talk. And talk. In the light of that morning, that afternoon, we had a nine-hour conversation. I don't remember a single word of what we said, but the energy, the synergy, the fuckergy, the cumery, that the two of us shared was breathtaking, even to an insider such as myself.

As time passed, we slowly started to remove each other's clothing—one hour the shirt, the next hour the pants, the next hours everything. Afterwards, she turned me onto my stomach and started to massage my back. As her hands pressed against my skin, blasts of pleasure shot through my spine. In one movement of her hand, in a single concurrent movement of her fingers, I could feel it all—love, sex, connection, trust, and want—crushed into one continuous sensation. I had never been touched like that, never felt as I felt on that couch. I was so ecstatic that I couldn't imagine what life had been like before her, before I had entered the insane domain of the Crescent City.

After our nine-hour conversation, we made love. Then we playfully wrestled for awhile, before the whole gang of us went to the bayou to canoe amongst the gators and snakes and marijuana trees in my face. The bayou is the most perfect place on Earth, at least the Southern Earth. Still waters, strange-colored trees, quiet gators lurking in the murky water, looking for a hand, out.

~

I remember the next several days or so not as if they were complete, with a morning, an afternoon, an evening, a beginning, an end. Rather, I recall them as moments that are separated from existence, that have memory, but no substance, no reality. Event after event that happened with no logic, no timeline, no stopping, no starting, just endless never-ending time never counting itself, no measurement, only remembrance.

The next day, or one day, or someday, or Sunday, sometime in the wee small hours of the early morning, or late afternoon, after a night, or day, of partying, Anna and I were chasing each other through the streets of the Quarter. We ran, we charged, we stampeded, we caught one another, we hugged, we kissed, we fondled, and then we ran and charged and stampeded some more, right into this coffee shop where Dan, Ray and Debbi were eating breakfast. Like a tornado of insobriety and romance we swirled into this eating establishment, and then right into everyone's food. First it was Dan's pancakes. Into thin air they went: batter, butter, oil, and flour. Then it was Debbi's bacon and toast. Swoosh, into the morning light they flew. Next up in my mind was Ray's omelet. However, he was one alcohol-infected thought ahead of me. He grabbed my hand before I could grab his plate. Well, I thought to myself, this won't do at all. So, I picked him up and put him, with some difficulty due to his resistance, into a garbage can. Then Debbi grabbed me from behind 'cause she was angry at me for messin' with her "man." Then Anna grabbed Debbi. Then two big black men grabbed all of us, and into thin air, swoosh, we went into the street.

Life continued on like that for the next several days or weeks or forever, crazy times, magical times, boozing times, fucking times, loving times! Each day more incredible than the last, my imagination soaring with the amazement of how each moment with my ALP was better than the last, each second better than the last minute, each hour better than the last day. I had found my other half, a wild woman-genius of the deep South, and I knew we would spend the rest of our lives together.

And, it wasn't just moi! We were all in! All three of us! In the Quarter! In love! Three guys had come down to New Orleans for Mardi Gras, as billions of ape-brained, pimple-bursting inbred college kids did every year, and what had happened? We had hooked up with the locals! Ray, the man who taught me all about jazz and was the perfect second banana in hedonism, was fornicating with the big-breasted, man-lovin' Debbi. Dan, a possibly educated yet often inarticulate man, was all cuddles and glances with Donna, a possibly educated yet often inarticulate woman. And, of course there was me. I had the best one of all, the belle of the balls, ALP, the MVP of late night hooch-enhanced relationships.

~

While life was in general quite good, there was one dark breeze blowing around us from within—Debbi! While she had always been a little on the loud and Southernly stupid side, we were all initially quite indebted to her for letting us stay in her home. However, as time went on, our feelings of gratitude turned to feelings of inquietude as certain things she said, certain things she did, began to at first annoy us, later concern us, and in the end, horrify us.

First, there were the simple annoying things she did, such as the day she started to demand that Dan change the radio station on her stereo every time there was a song on she didn't like. "Dan, can you get me some *tunes?*" became her mantra, repeated every three or four minutes, and while the easygoing Dan was at first obliging, by about the tenth tune change, his patience was at an end. While this was no doubt irritating to Dan, and to the rest of us who had to hear it repeated over and over again, that word, "tunes," every four minutes, "tunes," "get me some more tunes on the radio, Danny," tunes, fucking tunes, get your own fucking tunes Debbi, it was still no reason for us to launch any negative judgments against her, our generous post-Mardi Whore host.

However, there was more.

Such as her way of earning a living.

She told us that she worked as a bartender. One night she left for work at about midnight. Seemed a late time for someone to go to work, but this was New Orleans. About two hours later, she returned home with several hundred dollars in cash. Hmm? Dan and I wondered about this, but said nothing. The next day she went to work, again around midnight, and returned a couple of hours later with several hundred dollars in cash. Hmm hmm? After a few more days of this, Dan and I decided we'd better voice our suspicions to Ray. Unfortunately, he was off in fuck-fuck land and didn't take our concerns seriously. "She told me that she works in a real busy bar, that's all," he told us with a smile of distracted fuckability on his face. Very busy, I was sure! Still, while this wasn't the best thing for Ray, it was still no reason to condemn her, no moral judgements here please—live and let live we said to ourselves!

But, there was more.

One morning, we all returned to her house around nine in the morning after a heavy night of drinking. Debbi's two children, ages eight and four, were still in bed, as unattended children are wont to do. She immediately started screaming at them, demanding that they get up and go to school, and best of all, wondering why they hadn't figured this out on their own. Then she passed out. Dan and I took her kids to school that morning.

And more!

She fucked Ray on the couch, shouting in ecstasy with every thrust from his cock, while her children slept in the next room, lost in innocent kiddie dreamland.

More?

No more!

The straw that finally broke the whore's back and permanently separated our heroic band happened early one morning, late one evening for us, when I completely lost my mind. It began when I could not comprehend why there were no restaurants open at seven in the evening, when I wanted to have dinner. "Well, Robbie, you see, the problem is, the reason that none of the restaurants are open now is because, well, it's four o'clock in the morning!" "Get out of town!" I had now drunk so much alcohol as to become unfamiliar with the concept of time.

Later that evening, that morning, at some time, whatever time it was, we all wound up at The Cage. While I was at one end of the bar talking with Dan, Anna was at the other end, talking to some fat Creole-looking woman, who I presumed was a friend of hers (we were never formally introduced). At some point during their conversation, Anna became enraged and stormed out of the bar. For some reason I was not too upset at this, but Debbi immediately came up to me and told me that this was a very serious situation, and that I'd better go outside and find Anna before something happened. "Sure, whatever." I left, and walked around the block. I couldn't find her. I returned to The Cage. However, when I tried the door, it was locked tight. I knocked loudly for several minutes, and finally, one of the white trash fucks that worked at the bar opened up a little peephole in the door to inform me that everyone had left. Before I had a chance to ask him where they had all gone, he slammed it shut in my face.

I completely lost it. Filled with feelings of rage, murder, decapitation and castration, I stormed through the Quarter, toward Debbi's place, cursing out loud to myself. Now, it is quite difficult to draw attention to yourself in the Crescent City, real hard to stand out in the crowds. That morning, I stood out. All I remember now is that people were staring at me as I walked like Richard Nixon on acid through the ancient streets. "Fuckin' this," and "fuckin' her," and "fuckin' them," and "fuckin' everyone," are, I believe, an accurate representation of what was coming out of my mouth.

I made my way like an angry reptile through the Quarter, marching toward Chartres Street, in search of vengeance and justice. As I reached Debbi's block, I saw her, Ray and Dan standing in the street around a car that was parked in front of a fire hydrant. Dan approached me first, the stupidest of smiles on his albino face. "Hey Robbie!" "Hey Danny, where the fuck did you assholes go?" I shouted. Then Debbi spoke, a mistake at that moment, or at any moment. "Hey man, we waited for you at The Cage, but you like didn't come back." She then handed me my leather jacket, which I had left in The Cage, thinking I was going to return. I tossed the jacket clear across the street. "Fuck that!" "Now look," she said, "you're going to lose your leather jacket if you do that." "Idiot!" I screamed back at her, while she smiled at me with an uncomprehending look on her Southern shit-face.

I then walked over to the car parked in front of the hydrant. The car looked familiar. I looked inside. The driver looked familiar. It was ALP. She was passed out behind the wheel. "This is fuckin' great!" I shouted, as I pounded my fist on the driver's side window. I then turned and walked away. Within seconds, I felt a hand on my shoulder. I was going to punch whomever it was. I turned with my fist clenched. It was Annabel Lee! My fist melted, my eyes softened, my body yielded. God I loved her so!

She led me by the hand back into her car and sat on my lap. By now, I was like a little spoiled kid who had had his temper tantrum and just wanted his mommy to make things all right again. "I wanna get away from Debbi!" "Yes, sweetie." "I wanna go somewhere else." "Yes, darling." "Just me and you." "Yes, honey." "Okay, we can bring Dan along too."

Dan, who had no driver's license to speak of (suspended years before), drove. We were heading to the Garden District, I was told, where there would be peace, harmony, sleep, and no Debbi. I don't remember much about our arrival, except walking along a long balcony to the back of a white wooden house, which was badly in need of a paint job.

Once we entered, I was introduced to some people, who I assumed were the inhabitants of the house. There was Jan, a heavy-set blonde woman of fairly normal (for New Orleans) sensibilities, who apparently was a friend of Anna's, some Southern belle-ish chick whose name I never learned, and Lawrence Ferlinghetti. No, not the actual world-renowned beat, but some grungy-looking, chain-smoking, unshaven, tattooed sleeveless T-shirt-wearing, quite moody and quite affected guy, who was apparently Jan's boyfriend. Dan bestowed the world famous moniker upon him. All that really needs to be known about him, for purposes of this tale, was that he had the most hideous hacking cough in the history of consumption. All we heard from him all night, all day, was "hack hack aacccchhh ka ka ka spit swallow yiiiiiccchhhh bleeeeeeeeeehhhhh bllaaaacccchhhh."

Ferlinghetti was sleeping in the master bedroom on a four-poster bed when we arrived. After all that had happened with ALP, I had become rather full of myself, arrogant on the wings of love, so I decided that I was much more deserving of the four-poster bed than Mr. Ferlinghetti. And, since Annabel Lee was really into me, my whims were her commands. So, she cleared out the bedroom, as per my orders, and we were in! Livin' large in the four-post era! Larry wound up sharing the living room with Dan, who truly got to experience the joys of "hack hack aacccchhh ka ka ka spit swallow yiiiiiccchhhh bleeeeeeeeeehhhhh bllaaaacccchhhh."

Eventually, after someone brought in some pizza (Domino's was damn good that morning in New Orleans), Jan, Larry, and the nameless Southern belle left, leaving ALP, Dan, and I alone in the house. Dan went off to sleep in the living room, while ALP and I went into the sunny four-postered bedroom. We spent the rest of the morning/afternoon in an antique iron bathtub, talking, groping, licking, and fucking. We hadn't slept in two days. After finishing our fucking, we were about to doze off in each other's arms, two exhausted and happy bodies in a four-poster bed, when Dan entered our bedroom to goto the bathroom (it was the only bathroom in the house) and casually, totally matter-of-factly, announced, "Wally called. He says he is coming to kill us." "Who the hell is Wally?" "I don't know, but he is coming to kill us."

~

Apparently, Wally was Jan's ex-husband (Writer's note: the term "husband," despite what it says in a dictionary near you, has a completely different meaning in New Orleans. Basically, any relationship between a man and a woman that has moved beyond the one-night stand stage is considered a "marriage" in New Orleans. Later on, when I lived in New Orleans with a different woman, we were considered "married" just by virtue of living together. The electric man, the bank teller, the local Councilman all would refer to my girlfriend as my "wife," and to me as her "husband." Therefore, in this story, when I call Wally Jan's "husband," I use the term in the strictest New Orleans definition of the word, which means I don't know what the hell their relationship really was.) ALP told me that he could be a dangerous man. "One time when he was mad, he took all of Jan's paintings off the wall, slashed them to pieces, and threw them off the balcony." So, based on such information, I guessed that "Wally is coming to kill us" was a potentially valid and fatal threat.

Dan came out of the bathroom. "What the fuck did you say?" "Wally is coming to kill us." With that, I burst out laughing. I thought that this was the greatest thing to happen to us yet. "Anna, you take the back door. Dan, you take the side door. I'll take the front. Wally is going to kill us, we'll see about that. Are there any guns in the house?" Annabel Lee seemed concerned. To her it wasn't a joke. It wasn't to me either. I was dead serious. We were going to get Wally before he got us. I meant it. New Orleans and Jack Daniel's had made me strong. I had shed my wimp Jew boy exterior and was now an outlaw of the Deep South, lawless and ruthless.

Like a good deputy, Anna filled me in on the details of the situation that would be unfolding. She told me that there was some sort of vicious love triangle or something between Jan, Wally, and Ferlinghetti. "Ferlinghetti? Didn't you tell me that Jan is dating Ferlinghetti? "That's right" ALP told me. "Great, we'll kill him too." But no matter how heroic I was, or how much I assured Anna that I had the situation under control and that I had all the doors and windows covered, she was still quite upset. "Don't worry honey! Wally is only one man! And I'm from New York!" Nothing reassured her. A beautiful girl I loved, but not very brave. Good thing I was there to protect her, to slay this interloper, this rude drunken jealous New Orleans sot.

I was already making plans as to where to bury the body when the phone rang. It was Wally. He was still coming to kill us. "Everyone get to your part of the house and await further instructions. It's us or him!" However, there would be no dying that night, by my hand or Wally's. Over the phone, Annabel Lee was able to calm Wally down, and convince him that everything was all right, that Jan wasn't here, that she wasn't dating anyone, and that everything was fine and dandy. Wally never did come to kill us. Lucky man! His life spared by chance. If it had been up to me... To this day, I know I would have won the gunfight.

~

We were now ready to go to sleep. Finally! Wally was not coming to kill us. Dan was asleep on the couch in the living room. Ferlinghetti was nowhere to be seen or heard. The curtains were drawn, the room was dark, and the time for sleep was at hand, weekly sleep in the land of Puerto Rican rum and open racism. "Good night, Anna, I love you!" "Good night, Robert, I love you too." One minute of slumber went by, then a second, then a third, then a fourth, then...rrriiiinnngg! Telephone time. Anna picked it up. "Oh god, yes, we'll be right there!" "Right where?" "It's Donna. Remember her sister, the junkie? She's having the baby. We have to go to the hospital right away!" Donna? Sister? Junkie? I didn't even know she was pregnant!

I went into the living room and woke up Dan. "The baby is coming, the baby is coming." Birth! Life! Death! Infinity! Ben Casey! Dan, who was the most difficult person I have ever encountered when it comes to waking up, jumped up swiftly and without complaint. I think that by this point in the trip he had just accepted the fact that the normal rules of Earth and existence no longer applied. Sleep? Forget about it. Babies? Anytime, anywhere. Love? Here, there and everywhere.

Donna was already there when we arrived at the hospital. She informed us her sister was up in delivery, but that according to hospital rules, only two of us could go up at a time. Anna and Donna went up first, telling Dan and I that they would be back in a few minutes, and then we could go up. Why we would want to see this junkie sister we had never met was beyond me, but I hadn't slept in over two days, so I figured there must be a damn good reason.

ALP and Donna disappeared into the elevator. Ten minutes passed. Dan and I sat silently and stared at one another. Fifteen minutes passed. Stare and stare alike. Twenty minutes passed. No more staring! "We're going up Dan." A trick I had learned in high school was that when you are doing something blatantly wrong, do it loudly and openly. For example, when I would cut class, I would usually hang out in front of the Dean's office. So, they'll want to see our passes at the front desk? We'll walk by like we're the head surgeon! We walked by the front desk, and went into the elevator, up to maternity. No one stopped us. No sleep fifty-one hours.

It seemed like a good idea for Dan and I to go into the delivery room, to assist with the birth or something. First, however, we needed scrubs. "There's the supply closet—over there, Dan, past the 'Hospital Personnel Only' sign." We tried the door. It was locked. "Dan, do you know

48

how to pick a lock?" Just then, we heard an unhappy voice in these happiest of times, an angry shriek smashing my well-thought-out plan. "What are you two doing? Where are your passes?" No sleep, no mind, but a quick thought. "Why nurse, I'm so sorry. You see, his wife (I pointed to Dan) is having a baby, and we don't know where she is, and we're from out of town, and we're so confused and excited and scared. He's going to be a father. Right Dan?" Dan grunted his infamous grunt of confusion that he grunted whenever events were going too fast for him. The nurse, who had been ready to castrate us, softened upon my declaration of Dan's impending fatherhood. "Why honey, it's okay. Just go down the hall, make a left, and you can wait in delivery. We'll call you as soon as your baby's born. What's your wife's name sugar?" Never mind, we ran. "Thank you, thank you so much!"

When we arrived in the waiting room, ALP and Donna were there, surprised as hell to see us. "How did you guys get up without a pass?" Anna asked as she gave me a big hug. "We got connections!" I whispered into her ear as I returned the hug. Dan and Donna were in the corner all cuddles and glances again. Perfection had returned to the Southern-fried universe. I think Donna's sister had a girl.

~

After the hospital, the four of us went back to Donna's house. Anna and Donna went in for a moment to get something, while Dan and I waited in the car. While waiting, my mind finally snapped from what I would estimate was now about fifty-three hours of consecutive non-sleep. I went into an angry tirade against everyone and everything in New Orleans, cursing and spewing in a breathless rage. Dan later told me it was the most venomous tirade he had ever heard uttered by anyone ever, at least since my last venomous tirade of twelve hours previous. At one point, I was complaining about ALP's excessive drinking, and kicked the front seat of her car for effect. A bottle of Old Grand-Dad fell out from under the seat. That was the end of the first part of my tirade.

I went into the house to find Anna, since I thought I had been waiting far too long. She was on the phone, speaking to her mother. While she talked to mom, I marched around impatiently, cursing under my breath. When she finally got off the phone, she informed me that she had to return to Arkansas immediately. What the fuck bullshit was this? "I see. Why?" "Well, it's my mother. We are having a (pick one: family reunion, cow-tipping contest, lesbian lickoff, KKK meeting), and my mother wants me to come back.

I was supposed to go back days ago, and she really wants me to come home now. I love you though!" "But," I responded, "isn't there a big snowstorm or ice storm or some kind of storm between here and Arkansas? (I had somehow seen a weather forecast—or I just made it all up, I don't remember which, though I do recall radar, so it must have been true.) You can't drive in that!" "But, Robert, it's my mother!" "Listen Anna, it's snowing everywhere, we haven't slept in three fuckin' days, we've been drinking non-stop for weeks and you are absolutely not going anywhere at all 'cause everyone is a fuckin' idiot and I'm not having you be another fuckin' idiot and drive on those fuckin' icy roads until you kill your fuckin' self and everything." "But, Robert, it's my mother!" "Well, your mother is a fuckin' idiot too!"

Anna didn't go anywhere that day. She made another phone call to her mother, told her that there was a terrible storm, and said she would try to come home tomorrow. I then ordered her to drive back to Jan's house in the Garden District. When we got there, Wally wasn't there to kill us, Ferlinghetti wasn't there to cough on us, no one was there to bother us. Dan went to the couch, Anna and I went to the four-poster bed, and we all finally, mercifully, were able to sleep, sleep, and sleep! We slept for eighteen hours total, until early the next morning. When we woke, we were back on a regular schedule, ready to return to the regular world.

~

After enjoying warm weather during the entire trip, the temperature dropped into the thirties (Fahrenheit) the last day we were there. Like the trip had begun, in ice age Alabama, so it would end here, in the frozen city of Creole cunnilingus. All of us reunited in front of Debbi's apartment, ready to say our goodbyes. I really don't remember much about the goodbye between me and Anna—I was probably too sober! I remember we were on a street corner. I remember we talked quietly and hugged. I remember it all feeling oddly impersonal. Because of the events that had occurred between us, the thought of a separation seemed unfathomable. We were inseparable! So, since this parting made no sense to my emotions, I became detached and emotionless. Besides, I rationalized to myself, this wasn't the end, only the next step in our beginning. So, there wasn't really a need for goodbye. I said, "I'll see you soon, Annabel Lee." She cried. We told each other we would call each other as soon as we arrived at our respective homes. We told each other "I love you." That is all I remember.

The next part, I do remember quite clearly. After ALP left, it was time for Dan, Ray and I to depart, to head back to Philadelphia, the cracked city of underlying indigestion and the leading city of heart attacks (I read somewhere) in the United States. But first Ray had some news for us. "Debbi is going to go with us back to Philadelphia." "What?" "Yeah, she's gonna come up and stay with me for a couple of weeks." My mind was racing, grasping at anything realistic or impossible to say, as was Dan's, only he wasn't too good at expressing it—mostly a lot of grunts and "wells." "But," I argued, "What about her kids? Who's going to watch them?" "No problem. You remember Dave?" "The homeless man?" "Yeah him. Well, he has agreed to watch 'em for a couple of weeks. No problem." Problem, problem, problem! I thought. I thought some more. I looked at Dan. Spittle was coming out of his mouth. No help from him. There was no other choice—the truth, I must tell Ray the truth. It was time, it was the moment. I must confront him, to touch the depths of his soul and reveal the common bonds that bound us, that made us such good friends in the first place. The truth! Yes, the truth would set him free. It would set us all free, free of Debbi. "Ray, man, the truth is that I think honestly, well, that, umm, well...truthfully...I'll blow my brains out all over the highways of America, blood everywhere, blood and more blood, spurting from my shotgun-blasted head, if I have to spend twenty-four hours in a car with Debbi." Ah, the gentle truth! "You don't like Debbi?" he said, as if he wasn't really hearing me. "It's not that I don't like her, it's just that she's so damn fuckin' annoying, and you know, the blood on the highway stuff." "Well, we're all annoying at times." End of discussion. Satan's shredded cunt would be coming north with us. I wondered where I could get some Advil for my head. Or a gun for my head!

Actually, the trip back to Philly wasn't as bad as I had envisioned. Ray and Debbi slept in the back under the blanket most of the trip, out of sight, and fortunately, sound, and the only time Debbi really spoke up was when Dan was driving and she wanted him to find her some "tunes" on the radio. I was half-asleep for most of that, so I just ignored the whole thing. Other than that, she was quiet. She and Ray even drove for part of the trip. However, I noticed from the backseat of the car while I was dozing off that his driving seemed erratic, so I sat up to see what was going on. When I peered into the front seat, I saw that Debbi was giving Ray a blow job, and as a result, he was veering all over the road. I did the driving for the rest of the trip. She was quiet the rest of the way. I did consider abandoning her at a rest stop in South Carolina, but that would have been cruel—to the residents of South Carolina!

~

When I got back to my house in Philadelphia, one of my roommates told me that some mysterious woman had left a message for me— something about calling her in Arkansas. It was true! Everything that had happened was true, real, and alive! And now it was moving out of New Orleans, into the rest of the world.

Things began long-distance-like between ALP and me, and they were much as they had been in New Orleans, intensely passionate and all-encompassing, with frequent phone calls and daily love letters. We would speak on the phone at night until we fell asleep, in each other's ears, a thousand miles apart. Then she would call the next morning, which was the next afternoon for us, and demand that one of my roommates wake me up. She had broken up with her girlfriend soon after she returned to Arkansas, and except for a fight one night in the bar, and some resultant bruises and cuts on her body, the break-up had gone fabulously.

After about a month of our phone calls,

and my letters (she only wrote back once), she drove from Arkansas to Philadelphia to see me. The visit was more low-key than our marathon in New Orleans had been, but just as beautiful. As we were getting to know each other, it seemed as if deeper shades of love were developing between us.

We spent the first few days after her arrival in my house, talking, sleeping and making love. While she slept beside me, she would frequently have the most terrible nightmares, letting out loud cries of pain and despair. She would address me angrily during the night, out of her dreams, and the next day not remember a thing. I wanted to help, to understand. But she said I shouldn't worry, so I didn't.

One day she told me she wanted me to show her the Atlantic Ocean, so we drove to the coast of Maryland, and tried to camp on the ground of the National Seashore. However, since it was too early in the season to camp legally, the park ranger kept chasing us away. We kept coming back. Eventually we parked right on the beach, beside the ocean, in the darkness, so the ranger couldn't find us.

The wind was violent that night, throwing the sea to and fro, throwing my 1976 Plymouth Volare to and fro. We laid in the back seat of my car, drinking wine, eating cheese, and talking easily, while the car windows shook and threatened to break from the destructive gusts. Inside, we were warm with wine and the future. Anna told me she wanted us to get married. She said I should come to Arkansas to visit her next month, and during the trip I could ask her mother for permission to marry. That would be interesting. "Mother Plurabelle," I would ask, "could I have your beautiful lesbian daughter's hand in marriage? I promise to love, honor, obey, and stick my dick inside of her everyday, for all the rest of days." "Why sure, honey, sugar, chitlin, son-in-law with the penis," she would reply, "take my baby, and make her a woman, penetrate her cunt that no man has known, and bring it back to the fold, back to the land, back to the function that god intended for it!" "Yes, ma'am!"

Now, I wasn't against the idea of marrying ALP—not at all...one day. However, we had only known each other for six weeks. And, she had told me that while she couldn't imagine living her life without me, she physically wanted to be with women. Seemed to be a contradiction somewhere in there. I figured, however, that with a little more time to get to know one another, plus a little psychotherapy, we could indeed one day be man and wife.

As we fell asleep in each other's embrace, I whispered into her ear that I would love to come and live with her—in the fall, once we had spent a little more time together. She seemed content with what I told her, and closed her eyes happily upon the stormy night, to dream of calmer times, of me and her, together, as husband and wife. The next morning was sunny, and when I awoke, the first thing I saw was the face of a wild pony, staring at me through the car window.

Two days later, it was time for her to go back to Arcansore. She cried as she got into her car. I followed her out of the city in my car, bumping her rear end at every light. Bumping and grinding through the streets of Philadelphia! Like god had intended it! After the final bump, she disappeared down the highway, to her home, to my future home, down the road of forever that I was about to follow her on. Just a little more time and this circle of love would be completed. In the fall!

~

I was unable to speak to her during her drive home. She never called from the road, and never called when she returned. I became worried. Finally, after a day and night spent trying, I got hold of her, a little more than forty-eight hours after she had left Philadelphia with tears of love and hope streaming down her face. Her voice was flat, even, and emotionless, and she recited the details of her trip as if she were reading the weather report. She mentioned something about stopping on the way to see some friend somewhere, but didn't go into details. I felt like I was bothering her, and she acted as if it was unusual for me to want to talk to her, to want to know anything about her drive, about her life. What had happened? I asked her what was wrong, and she said nothing, that everything was fine. Did she still love me? Yes, of course she did. But she couldn't talk now, and would call me later. Then she hung up. She didn't call me later.

This pattern continued for the next few days—phone calls from me, curt responses from her, "I love you," from me, "I know," from her, followed by "I gotta go" from her. What had happened? I didn't know, but in the space of twenty-four hours, as long as it took her to drive the distance from Philadelphia to Arkansas, something dreadful had happened, something that had changed everything. I felt as if she no longer loved me. Why?

Because I was afraid to confront her and find out the truth, I pretended for awhile that nothing was different, that we were still in love, and that it was just a matter of a few short months until we would be together, forever. However, everything was different.

I started to call her less and less. She already called me never and ever. I tried to convince her to let me come out to Arkansas for a visit. She said no, now wasn't a good time, maybe later, in the summer. I told her I loved her a lot. She said she knew a lot. Spring fell into summer. I left Philadelphia and moved back to New York, back to my parents' house, because I was lost and didn't know what to do without the guarantee of her in my future. I started to take baths instead of showers, because that is what she did, and I figured that if I did what she did, it would bring us back together even though she no longer seemed to care what I did. I listened to Monk. I listened to Sam Cooke, especially "Cupid, draw back your bow, and let your arrow flow." I wore my blue bathrobe and combed my hair straight back and looked at myself in the mirror and wondered about her. I cried a lot. I wrote her incredible, vibrant love letters, the best work of my generation, that she never answered.

Finally, after about a month of silence, I called her one afternoon in July. We talked about the Los Angeles riots that had happened two months before. She hadn't heard about them. Riots? Current events? Me? We talked about gardening, since she planted vegetables and flowers, and my father had done the same since I was a child. While we were talking, I brought the phone into his garden in the backyard. I looked at the cucumbers and tomatoes, and thought of her, of her garden, of her flowers, her creations. It was a perfect humidless sunny summer day. I stood with the phone in my left hand, wearing my blue bathrobe, the sound of Monk's music wafting through the house, the sound of a filling bathtub punctuating the quiet parts of the afternoon between songs. We spoke about vegetables and fertilizer and watering and earth and land and sea. Not about us. We hung up after a few minutes, and "have a good day," and "a good summer too!"

Now I was standing alone in my father's garden, the breeze blowing restfully through the trees, vegetables and tall grass, my long blonde hair flying in the afternoon wind, the disquiet of my interior warmed by the summer sun. It was only July. The garden wouldn't be ready for another six weeks. Things were just beginning. The land had accepted new life, but was not yet ready to yield new life. I looked at the plants with small buds on them, the ungrown growth stretching as far as my eye could see, to the fence that blocked off the other small squares of land. There would be no vegetables until the end of summer. August at the earliest. I went back into the house and cried.

~

She continued to maintain no contact with me over the rest of the summer. I, however, would still call her occasionally, waiting for her to come back to me, as I knew she must. One night, in August, during a surprisingly good middle-of-the-night conversation with her, I managed to finally ensure myself a trip to Arkansas, the great state of castrate. At my own insistence, she had "invited" me to come down and surprise her whenever I wanted. Surprise! What an idea! I surmised that she was trying to recapture the initial power and excitement of our first days together, the crazy hazy days of Mardi Gras. What a woman, I thought. She still loved me! After I hung up, I drank half a bottle of Jack Daniel's, and woke up the next morning projectile vomiting all over my bed, my room, and myself.

She told me the next day that she wouldn't pick me up at the airport, and that I had to get to rural Arkansas on my own, where the buses and trains didn't go. Another surprise. How to get to rural Arkansas, where the trains and buses didn't go? Fortunately, my best friend Stephen had just moved to St. Louis with his new wife Mona. St.

Louis was only about four hours from where Anna lived. I called Stephen, and he told me that if I flew into St. Louis, he would drive me to ALP's little town in the Ozarks. When we got there, I would surprise her.

~

I got so stoned on the drive that I could hardly walk or talk when we arrived. We showed up late at the bar where she worked, right before closing. When she saw me standing at the bar, she poured me a Jack and Coke without my asking. I didn't offer her any money, and she didn't ask for any. She told me that the bar was closing in a few minutes, and that I should wait outside for her.

While Stephen and I were waiting for her, two people sitting next to us on a bench had a fistfight. Already there was violence around me! After the fight ALP came out, hugged me tight, and proceeded to show Stephen and I around her town, which she was evidently very proud to live in. It looked like the Old West towns you see in movies, with dirt, horses, a general store, a saloon, a sheriff, and some desperadoes. Except that there were no horses, no sheriff, and no general store. But, there was dirt and saloons, and, as I had seen up close, plenty of desperadoes. In short, it was a tourist town, where people went to pretend they were in the Old West, when in reality, they were just paying inflated prices for overpriced crap.

ALP's store fit right in with the rest of the town. It was tacky, and not at all the little down-home artistic type of place I had expected from someone like her. Everything she sold, from strange miniature wood carved horses, to denim jackets with the town name embroidered on the back in diamonds, was real cheesy, a kind of high-class white trash.

After showing us around, she took us to get a drink at some after-hours place she knew. I wasn't talking much, as I was still trapped in my marijuana stupor. Anna, on the other hand, was talking a lot, but saying little. She was acting like a tour guide, showing Stephen and I every conceivable part of this town that I didn't give a fuck about. She did seem happy to see me, but in an old-friend-had-come-to-visit sort of way. Not what I had hoped for, not at all!

At about three in the morning, we left the bar and drove to her house, the house where I would live with her for the rest of my life. During the drive, she kept saying that someone was following us. I looked behind us, but couldn't see anyone or anything following us. Stephen looked behind us, but couldn't see anyone or anything following us. The road was pitch-black all around us. "Who is following us, Anna?" She wouldn't say, but she was scared. At one point she veered off the road, stopped the car, and shut the lights off for a few minutes. Stephen whispered to me, wanting to know if this was normal behavior for her.

Eventually, we reached her house safely, having seemingly lost whoever or whatever was following us. But, this little incident concerned me. Stephen wondered if maybe we should just say our good-byes and get the fuck out of there. I told him to calm down and wait.

ALP's house was, again, not what I had expected. The house was well kept, but felt as if nobody actually lived in it. Everything seemed covered in plastic, whether it was or not. A house filled with things to have, not to use. While the furnishings looked expensive, they were all thrown together in a tacky, mass-culture style, as if one day she had bought the most expensive stuff out of the Sears catalog. It all looked like the kind of shit that a wealthy person in a place such as Arkansas might purchase. Or, as I thought later, the kind of shit that someone's middle-aged parents in Arkansas might buy for them.

After a few minutes, Stephen went to the

bathroom to take a shit, leaving ALP and me alone for a moment on her front porch. As I sat down to rest my pot-weary bones, she suddenly jumped into my lap and told me that she was happy to see me. In a second, all my fears and doubts were gone, and everything was wonderful again in the star-tipped universe, me and ALP, happy and content everlasting! She gazed into my eyes, just like she had on that street corner in New Orleans all those months ago, and the distance between us, the midsummer night's separation, fell to pieces in the blink of her seashell eyes, and in the thumping of my cannabis-laced heart.

That night I slept on the couch with Stephen. He left early the next morning, informing me that he could pick me up in a few days if things went badly, or else I would have to wait until the end of the week for him to come back. He asked me if I was sure I didn't want to leave with him right then and there. I told him I would be fine. He left, and I went back to sleep, dreaming of the rest of the week, the rest of my life, with ALP at my side. It was a warm late summer morning, the breeze blowing restfully through the mountains, rolling hills, and tall grass of Arkansas, through the windows and white lace curtains of Annabel Lee Plurabelle's living room, onto my naked chest, upon my half-closed sleepy dreamy eyes. It was September, the summer was dying, and the fall would soon be alive with the smells and sounds of new life, of my new life with the magical queen of the Ozarks by my side, us, together, under the clear eternal Mardi Gras blue-sky fantastic!

~

The first few days we were together were peaceful, but nerve-wracking. I attributed the anxiety to our reacclimating to each other after the long summer separation. But soon it would be fall, the season when I would be moving to Arkansas. I still had hope! She made me sleep on the couch the first few days I was there, with the promise that maybe tomorrow night I could move into the bedroom with her. We had no sex, no physical contact, except for a few strokes by her on my bare chest one morning while I was three-quarters asleep on the couch. After a few days, Stephen called and wanted to know if he should come and pick me up. I told him I would let him know later that day.

That afternoon, Anna and I walked into the woods behind her house. She told me she owned all the land around her house, acres and acres worth. I looked around at the thick foliage and tall trees, which hid the sun from view. The forest felt serene and a little bit dangerous to me, just as she had been when I met her in New Orleans. We sat on a huge rock and talked, about us, about what had happened, about what was happening. She told me how special it was to talk with me again, and how glad she was that I was around. She was happy again. We had seemed to work things out, and I was looking forward to spending the rest of the week with her. I called Stephen and told him that I would stay until the weekend.

The following morning, without warning or reason, ALP descended into madness. She became contemptuous of my presence and disgusted at the sight of me, when she looked at me at all. What had happened over the span of twelve hours, from our pleasant talk in the woods the previous afternoon, to her fireball of hatred for me the following morning? I didn't know, and she wouldn't tell me. She wouldn't talk to me at all.

Over the next several days, things got worse. She brought a woman home with her one night, and fucked her in the bedroom with the door open, so I could hear all the declarations of love and want and grunts and squeals of pleasure of the dykes of the deep mountains. The next day she locked me out of her house so I could walk around the Ozark woods and three gentlemen in a pick-up truck could ask me where the monthly meeting of the John Birch Society was held. I didn't know. Another day I was walking by the side of the road, going to nowhere from nowhere, when she drove by me, glared at me through the closed window, and drove on.

I still talked to her, even though she wouldn't talk to me, trying to negotiate my release from this mountain menagerie. I would ask her if she could at least be sane enough to drive me to Little Rock where I could grab a train or bus or something since there was no public transportation in this dead horse town of hers. Two hours in the car, and I would be gone, and it would be all over! Her response was, "Leave, leave, leave me alone!" Stephen suggested that I try and find someone to have a one-night stand with, as that was preferable to staying with her, but I didn't have any luck with that, even though someone shouted out "nice ass" one day as they drove by while I walked on the side of the road.

While I was upset, and understandably curious about the hots and colds of her behavior toward me, I was also concerned for my safety and well being. I wanted to get out of this place alive! On the night we had arrived, ALP had shown Stephen and I her gun. It was made out of gold, and she kept it in her bedroom, under her pillow. I commented that I had never seen a golden gun before, let alone any gun before. She told us it was a family heirloom from her great great grandfather, Humphrey Chimpden Plurabelle, who had used it to kill eight Yankees in the Civil War before he had been shot himself, right through the heart. She had never fired it herself; she told us she hated guns, hated violence. I asked her why she had a gun in the house if she hated violence. She looked at me incredulously, and told me that this was the *South*! So, as the week went on, and ALP's behavior became more erratic toward me, I became concerned that my presence might cause her to fire that gun for the first time. Whether or not this was an adequate reading of the situation I don't know, but it made me realize how little I really knew about this woman I claimed to love, and who had once claimed to love me. So, rather than confront her, I decided to lay low for the last few days of my trip, and avoid her as much as possible. There was nothing else to say or do.

Finally, the weekend came, and Stephen was able to retrieve me from Dyker's Island. We left and spent the night in a town a few miles down or up the road which I later found out was the national headquarters for the Ku Klux Klan. The next day I left Arkansas for good.

II

It was the fall. I was living in my child-hood bedroom, which looked exactly the same as it had when I was sixteen; the same rock n' roll posters taped to the walls, the same thick blue carpeting that my mother had put down when I was in high school, the same single bed. I thought I had left it all behind when I struck out for Phila-delphia the year before, but after everything with ALP went up in flames, I lost interest in moving my life forward toward the unexpected and new, and instead looked backwards toward home. I had no motivation to get a job, no motivation to go back to school, no motivation to get out of bed, no motivation to try anything. I was home again, in the house that I had grown up in, with the people who had raised me. But now I was fully formed, a mature man with an erect dick that had been used to fuck, to hope, to connect. Being back in my parents' house I felt like a newborn adult, in a womb of my own making, a cloistered infant with an ancient memory and an aversion to each and every thing uncertain and living. I was back home, and I was alone.

I don't remember what I did during the

day to amuse myself, but each evening I would watch basketball games on television with my father, who would constantly tell me how terrible basketball was today and how good the Knicks championship teams of his youth had been. After the game was over, at ten o'clock or thereabouts, my high school friend Nick would pick me up in his latest discombobulated BMW, which would chug loudly like a mad moose outside the house while my father shook his head in disgust at the car and at my life. Nick was a mechanic by trade and a pathological liar by practice. Being a mechanic, he would buy ten-year-old European import cars that were in dubious condition, and "fix them up." Since he never had enough money to completely restore them, these cars were always a mess, with wires hanging everywhere, and weird ways you had to drive them—usually real fast and no stopping for lights—so they wouldn't stall. He would move every six months or so, and his apartments were much like his cars—big plans, wires hanging everywhere.

Fifteen minutes after he would pick me up, (he drove those cars real fast, too fast), we'd be at our favorite bar, Angie's, in the East Village, which Nick had dubbed "the fatherland." Beers from the tap were a buck, and many more were given to us for free by the best bunch of bartenders a shot of Bushmill's could ever find. There was Jack, the English gent with the martini wit who liked to ply me with Jameson's until one night when I spat up all over some girl I was making out with. There was Shawn, the Irishman with a fetish for Oriental chicks, who was by far the best in terms of giving out free beer. And finally, there was Harold, who had a classics degree from Harvard, and who would often speak in a foreign language to the patrons of the bar whether they understood it or not. One night he refused to speak anything other than Italian, which confused the less literate and more anglicized bar dwellers. He and I would have these long involved discussions about all things literary, and I always seemed to impress him, even though most of my ramblings came after I had consumed upwards of ten mugs of cheap McSorley's Dark and didn't know what the hell I was saying anymore. He was a strange guy, but I liked him, and he liked me. I liked 'em all at Angie's!

The bar itself was a total freakin' hole, the whole of holes, the king of the bottom of shit and despair. The men's room had one window right over the toilet which was always broken, so if you went to take a piss in the stomach of winter, you were hit with an icy blast of Manhattan hospitality right in the balls. Adjacent to it was the ladies' room, separated only by a thin decaying wall. At some point in the course of natural alcoholic lower Manhattan events, the wall between the two bathrooms was damaged, so that while the top half existed, the bottom half didn't, which made for many interesting goings-on (and under) when one needed to take a leak.

The rest of the place was equally representative of this type of post-apocalyptic shit chic. The front of the bar was comprised of two huge windows surrounding a glass door, the bottom pane of which had a crack in it that was never repaired. I was there the night the crack was made; one of the regulars smashed someone's head into the glass. Another night Nick and I came in and one of the front windows was completely boarded up. We asked Jack, who was working that night, what had happened, and he told us that another one of the regulars had gotten upset and thrown one of those metal New York City garbage cans through the front window. Jack told us that the guy was banned from the bar for a month. Many of the regulars at Angie's were like that—friendly and intelligent alcoholics who would occasionally become violent after too much booze and a long ridiculous argument over nothings such as religion and politics. Nick and I had gotten into several fights at the bar ourselves, usually over a woman who wanted him when I thought she should want me. After our fights, whoever was bartending would give us even more free beer, as if that wasn't a significant part of the problem already.

One time, however, I starred exclusively in the mayhem. It was late on a Monday night, in the dead of winter, and I was sitting around a table with a group of classic late night drunks, contemplating the world and the cute blonde with the tight ass who was sitting next to me. Suddenly, I realized I had to take a piss. The only way for me to get around everyone to get to the bathroom was to climb over the next table, which while devoid of humans, was filled with glasses that the bartenders had been collecting to wash over the course of the night. Fifty, sixty glasses easy on this table. I got up, put my leg on the table for support, and...bababadalgharghtakammina rronnkonnbronntonnerronntuonnthunntrovarrhouna wnskawntoohoohoordenthurnuk. The table had split in two, and I had a great fall, right upon my back, in the midst of broken glass everywhere that could never be put back together again. As quickly as I fell, however, I sprung up, and announced to the shocked crowd "No Mah-Jongg tonight." The crowd cheered my non-sequiturian

utterance. A few minutes later, as I was returning from the rest room, the cute blonde with the
tight ass came up to me and said that what I had
done with the glasses had been, like, the coolest
thing she had ever seen. Ever! But then she left
the bar without me!

By three in the morning, the only people
left in the bar were Nick and myself. While we
were drinking, and eating late night pizza, two
women came into the bar out of the frosty night.
I caught them out of the corner of my eye, but
paid them little attention, as I was so drunk either the bar was spinning, or the bar was standing still and I was spinning. During the course of
the intense drunkersation that I'm sure Nick and
I were having, a woman's voice from the other
end of the bar shouted out something about boxer
shorts. Upon hearing this, Nick pulled his pants
down to expose his boxers, and then disappeared
toward this faceless female voice, leaving me behind.

About five beer minutes later Nick came
back and dragged me over to his new group of
friends. He told me that this girl (pointing to a
tall blonde, seated) liked jazz, and since I liked
jazz too, we were made for one another. I asked
her, "So you like jazz?" She responded, "I work
in a jazz bar. I don't know too much about the

music." I then asked her a follow-up. "Can I ask you a personal question?" "I guess." "Are you a lesbian?" "Sometimes." Nick and I high-fived one another. You see, at that time, in the post-ALP era, I would often ask women this question as a sort of icebreaker.

~

Nancy and I had our first date a few nights later. We went out to dinner at a little haunt we both liked a few blocks from Angie's, and afterward went to some gay bar in the West Village, to meet her roommate, Glen, and his boyfriend du jour. Among the booze, sniffly noses and smiling big-bellied men of the night, Nancy told me about herself. She had been a wild party girl most of her life, living in several different places across the U.S., but was now sick of the wandering lifestyle, and wanted to settle down and have a normal life with a white picket fence and a distillery in the backyard (yuk, yuk). Like me, she seemed to like to talk and talk and talk, about all things real, mundane, and insignificant. We thus hit it off immediately (I could tell because she kept rubbing her leg against mine under the table). After last call, the four of us went back to her apartment, where her roommate and his Goodbar boy disappeared into the bedroom, while Nancy and I made out on the couch, until I

had to leave at seven in the morning to go back
to my parents' house before the city towed my car
away. No parking after seven!

Within two weeks, I was spending five to
six nights a week at her apartment, a decrepit
fifth-floor one-bedroom walkup on the Lower
East Side. The building had no front door, and
was thus open to all of the colorful and varied
street life that pre-gentrification downtown New
York City had to offer. The neighborhood kids
sold heroin in front of the building (Poison, they
called it. "Poison! Poison!"), and at night the
junkies slept in the hallway. Nancy's apartment
was filled with roaches in the kitchen, in the living room, in the bathroom, in the bedroom, in
the bed. It also contained the height of NYC high
rent luxury, a bathtub in the kitchen, where
Nancy and I could bathe for all the world and any
visitors to see! There was a huge hole in the bedroom ceiling, and a boarded-up window in the living room, which had been a gift of the New York
City fire department (who also stole a few hundred dollars in cash during a false alarm). The
"hardwood" floors of the apartment were comprised of rotten splintered wood, which were so
covered in dirt that if I made the mistake of walking around without my shoes for even a few minutes, the bottoms of my socks would turn dust

black. Instead of trying to wash them, I would just throw them out the window.

To add to the neighborhood shriek aesthetic, the gentleman who lived below Nancy periodically showed up at her door brandishing a baseball bat and complaining about noise, even if we were fast asleep. (Nancy's usual response was to ask him if he wanted to fly us around the apartment like Tinkerbell.) Above lived a band of middle-aged Hispanics who played salsa music non-stop twenty-four hours a day. This group was a mixture of fedora-wearing men and middle-aged women with thick legs. They would often get locked out of their apartment, and would have to go up Nancy's fire escape in order to get back in. Thus, about once every two weeks the following would occur—a timid knock on the door, followed by a few words of Spanish, followed by a procession of fat legs, yellow smiles, and tipped hats, while I usually sat on the couch in my underwear smiling politely.

During the early stages of our courtship Nancy shared the apartment with the aforementioned Glen, who was the first HIV-positive person I had ever met. He was a longtime friend of Nancy's from way back when, and she told me he had had a bad childhood, including a father who sat on the couch crazy wearing an Elvis wig. Because of that, as well as some belief about the perfection of youth, he wanted to die young, preferably before he was thirty-five. He would get his wish. Glen earned some extra cash as a male prostitute, but before too long he disappeared from the scene into a drug-induced inferno with some rich chick named Spike.

After Glen's disappearance into syringeland, Maria moved in. She was a sweet Spanish girl with a charming smile, an agreeable disposition, and a tall, well-toned, model-like body. Her two chief attributes, as far as I could tell, were the ability to compose the worst poetry I have ever had the horror of hearing, and the inability to work or pay her share of the rent. Her bedroom was the couch, as Glen's had been before her.

The bisexual Maria had two regular companions; a pudgy blonde chick named Nico, who was her most-of-the-time on-and-off girlfriend, and Greg, a drug dealer from New Jersey. Nico was a talkative sort, and among the things she spewed within my earshot was that she was HIV-positive, had been a cop in Detroit, drove a motorcycle, was homeless, was eighteen, nineteen, and twenty years old, was a stripper, was a prostitute, was a model, etc. She had a lot to say. Greg, on the other hand, was a quiet sort, but really gave Nancy the creeps. His most interesting quality was his skin, which had an ever-present dark hue about it, as if he bathed in coal. We could never figure out if he was just very dirty, or if the sleaze of his soul, his black bile so to speak, was spilling through his skin.

After a few months of bad poetry, bad liars, and filthy friends, Maria "moved" out, owing Nancy hundreds of dollars in back rent. Fortunately, she left behind two expensive Cannondale race bikes chained to the radiator. Nancy and I cut the chain and sold the bikes. Thus, Maria's debt was paid in full! Months later, she called and asked if she could have the bikes back. Funny.

Nancy and I were now alone in her pad of squalor and sympathetic sin. We spent most of our time fucking and drinking and taking Valium and sleeping and fucking and drinking and taking Valium some more. Eventually, the fucking slacked off as Nancy didn't seem to particularly enjoy it, and the Valium ran out. But the drinking continued unabated and uninterrupted. As quickly as we had become lovers, or to use a better term, "likers," we had also become co-dependent cellmates, spending day after day with one another, not out of any particular feelings of passion, but out of emotional necessity. Our relationship had not evolved past the "hanging out" stage, and would never evolve past it, but we stayed together, and I clinged to her like a junkie to a candy bar, because I needed her, anyone, to solve the things that I found unsolvable, to be my new ALP in the post-ALP era. And, to get me away from my parents' house! Luckily, or sadly, she needed me as well, to fill in her own mysterious emptiness. We filled in each other's gaps as poorly as any lovers could—instead of filling in the empty parts with love and trust, we brought out the worst sides of despair and self-loathing in each other.

The only thing that stopped me from spending *all* my time with Nancy was "the break!" About once a week, usually around Wednesday or so, she would get sick of me, need what she called "the break," and send me back to Queens, where I would stay in anxiety-wracked anticipation and perspiration at my parents' house. Then, after about a day or two, she would call and tell me that she missed me real bad and that I should come back to her side. I would then jump into my '76 Plymouth Volare (eight cylinders—all right, hold tight), speed across the Williamsburg Bridge, find a parking spot, and run up the five flights of stairs into the roach and filth heavens and her waiting arms and loins. Or usually a hug and a hello. This was what my life had become, barely a year after ALP had given me her heart forever—"break," home to mom and dad, puke, phone call, highway, bridge, stairs, Nancy, roaches, dirty socks.

~

Sometime early in the summer, Ray and Debbi came up to New York for a visit. After the ALP situation fizzled out, I had stayed in touch with Ray, who stayed in New Orleans and shacked up with Debbi, having the baby that they had conceived for all the world to hear on the couch during those halcyon Mardi Gras days of yesteryear. Before they came to town, I warned Nancy about Debbi, telling her that she was about to meet the most indescribable human being to ever walk the earth. Nancy nodded in absent-minded agreement, but I don't think she was adequately prepared for what she was about to encounter.

The night of their arrival, the four of us went out to this real cool (and quiet) jazz bar on Avenue A that Nancy and I liked to frequent. They had a piano player, no cover, good margaritas, and were never very crowded. So far, Nancy thought that Ray was nice, and Debbi a bit stupid in a Southern sort of way, but not half so bad as I had described her. I laughed to myself in expectation of what I knew would come.

During the pianist's performance, maybe Monk, maybe Coltrane, it happened. A quite intoxicated Debbi started shouting out what she was going to do to her "man" later that evening, the sucking and fucking and screaming and creaming. Needless to say, it was an embarrassment to everyone except Ray, who sat with a stupid and contented smile on his face, and acted like this was the most normal human behavior, the way that every young woman expresses her love for her man in public. Nancy whispered to me that she now wholeheartedly agreed with my assessment of Debbi.

Later that night Ray and I were alone in some apartment somewhere that belonged to a friend of Debbi's. Nancy had gone to the store to get some Doritos and to get, she said, "the hell away from Debbi!" Debbi was passed out on the bed with her new baby lying beside her. While we were chatting aimlessly and half drunkenly, Ray informed me that he and Debbi were going to move from New Orleans to Kentucky. "Kentucky, Ray? Why Kentucky, Ray?" Well, it seemed that Debbi wanted to reunite all the children she had had over the years with different men, children that were scattered all over America unloved and unwanted without their natural birth mother whore. Debbi's plan was to gain custody of all these kids, have Ray adopt them, and then live as one big happy family forever. The first child they wanted to reacquire lived in Kentucky, and according to the law they had to live in the same state as the child for six months in order to have a chance at obtaining custody. Ray informed me that Debbi wasn't real happy that they had to move to Kentucky 'cause it was real cold in the winter, but that he had convinced her to do so for the sake of her children.

I sat listening to all of this with an open mouth and spittle running down my chin. "This is all very nice," I said to Ray, wiping my chin. But, he had more and even better news to reveal to me. If we wanted, Nancy and I could go down to New Orleans and live in the house they were currently living in while they were away. I was rather surprised by this bit of news. Was this the chance I had been waiting for, I wondered to myself, the chance to have Nancy all to myself, to start life with her anew, and leave all the fear and anxiety and lack of passion behind?

I asked Ray if he was sure about all this. He told me it was a done deal. I asked him who owned the house? He told me that Debbi owned the house, well actually this guy who was the grandfather of one of Debbi's children owned the house, but he didn't care about it, so as far as Ray was concerned, Debbi pretty much owned it, almost, so there was no need to worry. Then I asked him about rent. Well, he said, though he didn't actually own the house in name or anything else, he wouldn't dream of charging rent to such a good friend as me. Maybe we could just pay the electric and such and sort of act as caretakers while they were away. I told him that this all sounded good to me, but that I would have to ask Nancy first.

When we were alone in bed later that night I mentioned Ray's plan to Nancy. She responded that she didn't think our relationship was strong enough for that kind of commitment, and that it would be a great mistake if we moved to New Orleans together, or anywhere together. Since I knew she was right, I didn't argue with her at all. In fact, I respected her for having enough sense to speak the truth and avoid the easy way out. There was no mention of New Orleans from me again. But, I still kept Ray's plan, and my secret hopes to execute it one day, buried in the backyard of my mind.

~

One night, about two weeks after Ray and Debbi's visit, Nancy and I were lying in bed when she told me something that she had kept from me during the entire four months of our relationship.

She told me about *him*! She had met *him* about ten years ago, when she was barely out of her teens, and had just moved to Florida. *He* was a decade older than her, and was from another country. She was a taxi dancer when they met. *He* came in one night for a dance. But *he* was not like the other middle-aged sleaze that wandered into those types of establishments. *He* was different. She told me that despite an initial language barrier, *he* wound up being the most passionate man she had ever met, and when they had sex, tears of joy would well up in her eyes at the point of orgasm. In short, *he* had been the love of her life, and nothing, and no one, could ever compare to *him*.

I asked her what had happened between them. She told me that despite their great passion, or maybe because of it, they fought terribly all the time, and after about six months or so, she could no longer take the arguing, so she left him, left Florida. But, she had never forgotten him, and would never forget him.

She went on to tell me that since we didn't share this kind of passion, she found it difficult to enjoy intimacy with me, and even though I was very good in a technical sense in bed, she didn't enjoy fucking me anymore. That explained why we hardly ever fucked anymore. Furthermore, she went on to say that because of the way she felt about me, which nothing and no one could ever change, we should no longer see each other. Or at least not as much. But, she added as a carrot, we could still hang out and be friends and drink together sometimes and eat together sometimes and rent movies together sometimes and who knows still fuck sometimes, even though it wouldn't be passionate like it was with *him*. Still, our relationship as it is, was, will be, was over, or at least different on a very substantial not-boy-friend-and-girlfriend level any more.

Being in a codependent sort of mood, I naturally disagreed with her interpretation of our relationship. I spent the rest of the night trying to talk her into coming back to me, explaining to her what passion really meant, and how she needed to get over *him* so she could move on with her life (and fall in love with me). However, since she really had no intention of leaving me in the physical sense, only in the emotional realm, it was easy to talk her into staying, as she was never really going. She just wanted to tell me the truth, she said, so I would now know. I now knew.

After her confession that night, our relationship became even more intense on my side, my anxiety, dread and mistrust hitting new heights I was unaware I could ever reach. I now could never leave her side without having a complete emotional breakdown. Our weekly one-day breaks became even more torturous for me than they had been before, as I paced around my parents' house talking to myself non-stop in fits of singsong desperation.

When she would inevitably call and tell me to come back to her side, all these feelings would subside, and I would feel a great surge of relief, as if I had never experienced all those negative emotions consuming me just seconds before. My misery would end, like the flick of a switch, the instant she called. But, within a day or two it would all come back, as my mind began the countdown to the next "break" and, consequently, my next breakdown.

It went on like this for months. I wouldn't and couldn't live without her. Was it love? A chemical imbalance? The alignment of the stars? I didn't know. I just knew that I felt dead without her, paralyzed to the world, unable to move, to live, to function, to breathe! I would do anything, anytime, anyhow, to anyone, to be with her, to keep her, to keep this dread and death away. My true feelings towards her—and things like love—didn't matter in the equation. I needed to be able to breathe!

The rest of the summer passed for me in

this semi-queasy, permanently anxiety-wrecked state. However, the cool fall wind was about to bring change to my life, to Nancy's life, to our life together. It all began on a Saturday night in early September. I had seen Nancy the previous evening, but had left to go home because a cousin of mine was getting bar mitzvahed early the next day. I went to the bar mitzvah with my parents. I worshipped with my parents. I became intoxicated by myself.

After the celebration of Jewish manhood was over, I went home and called Nancy. There was no answer, so I left a message on her machine. She didn't call back. I called back a little while later. There was still no answer. This time I didn't leave a message. Hmm, I thought to myself, this is odd. We had plans together, we always had plans together as far as I was concerned, whether we had plans together or not. So, where was she? Already my mind had arrived at thoughts of desertion and isolation, and my innards were a tornado of ceaseless anxiety. The usual stuff.

I called a third time. This time she picked up the phone. I could hear in her voice that she had been crying. I asked where she had been. She told me she had been there. I asked her if she was okay. She told me she was okay. Then I asked what time I should come over. She immediately shot back that I should not come over, that I should never come over again, that it was over, that we were over, and that I should move on with my life and forget about her. I asked her what the hell was wrong. Just forget about me, she told me, over and over again. I told her I was coming over right now. She said no. I said yes. She said no, I said yes...She said okay, whatever. I left for her place.

The traffic was brutal. I remember being stuck in a terrible jam on the Williamsburg Bridge and seriously contemplating abandoning my car on the roadway. I also remember that I was wearing a long-sleeved striped sweatshirt. I remember nothing else. I was beyond frantic. All my fears had been realized, utter and total and final rejection, unexpected, unequivocal, unsympathetic. I felt unmasked, unmade, and undone.

When I finally arrived in the city, I parked my car illegally, and bounded up the five flights of stairs into the roach infested heavens. I opened the door (Nancy had given me the key by this time), and went in. There were no lights on, and since it was dusk, I could barely make out the shapes of objects in the apartment. I could see Nancy sitting on her white mohair couch. She didn't say anything to me when I walked in. I sat down beside her and gently rubbed her shoulder. "So, what's up?" I asked. "Nothing," was the reply. "It took me awhile to get here. Traffic was a bitch." "Oh." Then there was silence.

I noticed that the wind was blowing through the apartment. However, the window wasn't open—it was lying on the floor, smashed to bits. "What happened to the window?" I asked. "It broke," she responded. "How?" "I was trying to open it and it fell out of the support. I didn't clean up the glass yet." "I see." I got up and went over to the window. "You're going to have to call that idiot landlord of yours." I didn't know what to say to her or how to say it or how not to say it. I sat back down on the couch beside her. Of what of her face I could still make out I could tell that she had been crying, as I already knew from the phone. What had happened to bring this about? Suddenly, out of nowhere? Sure, things were always fairly fucked up between us, but not any more so lately than usual.

Finally I asked, "What happened?" "I don't want to talk about it. I told you you didn't have to come over." "But, I love you! Tell me please. I want to know. Why are you so upset? Did someone die? What happened, you're scaring the hell out of me." She said nothing. "Please Nancy, please," I said in a tone of ever-increasing desperation, "tell me what's wrong, please!"

She relented and began telling me the story. Last night she had had a dream about *him*. She wouldn't tell me the details of the dream, she said they didn't matter, she didn't remember, whatever. This morning she had gotten up and called *him*. I told her that I didn't know she had *his* phone number, as I thought she hadn't spoken to *him* in years. She didn't have *his* phone number, she said, but she had *his* parents' number, from the old days. She had spoken to *his* mother, asking for *his* number. She was informed that *he* was married, *he* was living overseas, and that she should leave *him* alone, always. Silence. She went on to inform me that since we didn't have any passion in our relationship, and certainly nothing approaching what she had had with *him,* that we should no longer see one another.

I sat there on the couch for awhile staring straight ahead into the darkness, saying nothing. She asked me what was wrong. I said nothing. It was all churning in my head, in my belly, what, where, how? "But, I can't live without you. I need you!" That was all I said. She hugged me for a few minutes. We then went into the bedroom and fell asleep for a few hours. When we awoke, we went to the supermarket to get some food and ate, as we had a hundred times before, on top of the coffee table in her living room. Then we went back to bed, holding on to each other through the night. The next day we got up and went to some peculiar fair with my sister where grown men and women dressed like medieval citizens jousted with each other and sold overpriced beer they called mead. Nancy cried a lot, I cried a lot, while the knights fought. The kingdom appeared to be threatened the whole time. My kingdom was threatened the whole time.

The following Friday night, five days later, Nancy and I were drinking in a restaurant on Avenue A that we both hated, but we were bored of our usual haunts. We were sitting at the bar, sipping our beers, when Nancy looked at me and said, "I think we should go to New Orleans. Do you think Ray still has the house down there?" My body turned into pure light, shining in on myself like the first eye opening of the first baby ever born to the first person ever. "I don't know. Do you really want to go to New Orleans with me? Didn't you turn me down when I asked you a few months ago?" "I changed my mind." That was enough of an explanation for me.

I called Ray that night. Sure, the house was still ours if we wanted, that would be great, we would love it down there. Kwan, the Chinese gentleman who owned the house, was a great guy, we would really like him. He owned a Chinese restaurant next to the house and his wife, Ma (that was not her real name, but her real name was something unpronounceably Chinese, so we all called her Ma, Ray told me) was a great cook. Ray told us he would take care of everything.

It was all set. We would leave the day after Halloween. Since Nancy's brother worked for a shipping company, we were able to ship all of our stuff down to New Orleans for next to nothing. Since we couldn't afford plane tickets, and couldn't rent a car because we had no credit cards, we bought tickets on Amtrak.

We departed on All Saints' Day. We were running late for our train that day, and encountered the only cab driver in New York City who stopped for yellow lights and obeyed the speed limit. I was scared as he sped slowly through the clogged streets that we would miss our train, or that Nancy would change her mind, and we would never get started on our descent into Southern-fried madness. Fortunately our train was delayed, so we made it. We put our luggage into the overhead bin, put our butts into the comfy red Amtrak seats, and opened a bottle of vodka we had bought for the trip, to toast our new life and our new future together. Scarcely three weeks after that Friday night in the bar on Avenue A that we didn't like, Nancy and I were seated in a train facing south with a bottle of Vodka in front of us, and a land undiscovered before us! And a life of uncertainty and indecision behind us! New life, new days, new meanings. But deep down I wasn't very happy.

~

Don't *ever* take Amtrak on long trips. Unless you pay extra cash for a sleeper car.

~

I was content and calm with things until we passed Philadelphia. "My old home Philly, I was happy there once," I said to Nancy. She nodded in disinterest and kept staring out the window as we passed through Thirtieth Street Station into the rest of Pennsylvania, Delaware, and many more points south. The further we got from New York and our old life and the further we headed toward New Orleans and our new life, the more fearful and foul my mood became. I realized there was no turning back now. I was really on the train, Nancy was really beside me, and we were really heading together into the southern unknown. I took a deep breath and tried to breathe. I took a few sips of vodka and tried to forget. I tried to talk to Nancy, to share with her feelings I found impossible to share with her.

Nothing helped. I had made my choice, made my bed, and now I would have to lie in it, or in the case of an Amtrak train, sit upright in it.

As night fell and we moved further south, my fear turned into anger, anger at my own life, anger at my own inadequacies, anger that I was on this train with this woman heading down south to nowhere. I began to notice the other people on the train, the stupid fuckin' hicks and hickesses. "Look at that one, Nancy!" "God, did you hear what the one behind us said to what I presume is his wife, must be his wife, they wouldn't let cattle on the train, would they, ha ha ha!" Nancy told me to be quiet, as she was trying to get some sleep. So I steamed alone, boiling at the presence of these fuckshit hicks all around me. Is this what we were heading into? I drank another shot of vodka while Nancy napped and the train pulled into the heroin-fueled city of Baltimore.

After the train left Baltimore, I decided to get some sleep. I tried to adjust my seat and move it back so I could lie flat. It wouldn't move more than a few inches. Hmm, I thought to myself, how will I sleep through the night? The lack of flatness could be a problem. So I tried to sleep sitting up, twisting and turning my body, trying to find a comfortable position for sleeping in a most uncomfortable position for sleeping. After a few minutes, I gave up, downed another shot of vodka, and stared out the window at the black landscape that was whizzing by. I was now moving through the great expansive belly of these United States, through the redwood forests, the purple mountains, and the Gulf Stream waters! Well, on this trip it was the Confederate states, the dank swamps, the muddy streams, and the hillbilly shacks, but you get the overall point.

I closed my eyes and listened to the chug of the metal wheels against the iron and steel below me. America! A train! The girl you love by your side! A bottle of hooch by your side! I had a pad of paper and a pen with me 'cause I was going to write some of those great writins' that can only be composed on the great trains of America. What a tradition, what a beautiful American thing, perhaps the only real beautiful American thing that ever was! America! A train! The girl you love and a bottle of hooch by your side! I was heading down to the mysterious South, the home of the blues and Elvis. "Train, train, sixteen coaches long!" I was feelin' it now—America, the blues, the black experience, the vodka, the poetry, the chick by my side, the vodka, the sixteen coaches.

As the steel and steam soared down the

tracks past a million American lives, past cities and towns and streetlights and swamps and shot-guns and Bubbas and twangy drawls and cotton fields and carpetbaggers and freed slaves and unfreed slaves and masser with his whip lovin' those darkies and fuckin' those hot darkie bitches and lemonade on the porch in August and the drums of battle as brother killed brother and Appomattox and segregation and desegregation and Governor Wallace and Senator Helms and Senator Thurmond and Jefferson Davis and Faulkner and Poe, I thought of me and Nancy heading toward the great loins of Louisiana, to-ward our home now, our undisturbed sweet fer-tile land! I drank one more shot of vodka, and toasted our new life. "God bless us and fuck us and let the vodka flow and let our lives flow here in our new home. To the South—Let it grow!" I drank one more, and the next thing I heard was...

"Eleven o'clock! Lights out!"

"If you do not wish to go to sleep, you may head to the car, I mean to the dining, ah, car, where, ah, if you want, you can get some, ah, I mean, can purchase some, if you need, ah, some chips, I mean, ah, some, yes, definitely, yes, some beverages, are, yes, on sale, in the dining train, ah, I mean, car, for sale, various bever-

ages for your purchase, yes, in the dining car, yes, ah, yes, but, yes, it is eleven, ah, now, lights out, except, yes, for, ah, beverages, in yes, the dining car, for sale"

That was the way all the public address announcements went on this particular train. Some woman made all these long and winding to nosense announcements devoid of grammar and logic and follow this if you can't, I mean can, I mean what? Sleep! At eleven o'clock! Fat fuckin' chance! I woke up Nancy, and carrying our trusty (now half-filled) bottle of vodka, we headed toward the dining car. After stumbling through several darkened cars, we arrived at the only lighted car, which was at the end of the train, or the beginning? There were a few people scattered about, seated at various tables under the sharp florescent light, traveling through the midnight blackness.

Once Nancy and I sat down with our bottle, we became quite popular. The first one to introduce himself was Ralph from Rochester. He was a plain, good-natured fellow, eager to be liked and approved of, dumb, but not dumb enough to be insufferable, yet. He had a perpetual stupid grin on his pale thin face, and wore a baseball hat on his puny head. He told us that he used to work for his brother or something, and was now heading to Alabama because there were plenty of jobs down there. Like ditch digging and lynching! Whatever. We gave him some vodka in a small plastic cup.

Ralph was good for about five minutes of conversation. As we sat talking with him, each word from his simple mouth causing more disinterest in my nerve-wracked and alcohol-filled brain, I began to notice the other non-sleepers who were sharing the dining car with us. Sitting behind us was a Hare Krishna in his full orange robes, smoking a cigarette. When he saw our bottle of vodka, he came up to us and asked for a drink. As I was pouring his glass, I casually mentioned that I thought Hare Krishnas didn't drink or smoke. His response was, "Party on, Wayne!" (he apparently thought I looked like the blonde guy from the *Wayne's World* movies.) This would be the only phrase he would utter the rest of the night, over and over again.

Directly across from us was a gigantic guy with a thick black Chicago moustache, downing can after can of Budweiser in rapid succession. The cans looked so tiny, encased in his large, artery-clogged hands. He looked as if he were trapped in his seat, so tight was his stomach against the edge of the table, the fat within his shirt hanging over the Formica like a horizontal ass cheek dislodged. He was speaking to two equally fat women who were dressed in the usual white trash train uniform (tight jeans revealing huge butts, tight T-shirts revealing huge guts). When he "spoke" to these lovelies, he never fully opened his mouth, so what came out was unintelligible to me. The ladies, however, seemed positively charmed by his garbled utterances, if their smiles and flattered giggles could be taken as the measure of the man's success.

Just as Nancy and I were growing bored with this gaggle of freaks, and were thinking of returning to our seats, a sharp female voice rose aloud in the dining car. "You think my sister's fat? You're a fuckin' pig!" One of the two lovely hefties had risen from her seat and was now screaming at the piece of human blubber with the Budweiser hard-on. Apparently in his mumblings he had somehow insulted one of the whales he was talking to, and apparently they were sisters, and apparently one of the sisters was sticking up for the other. And she was real mad! She went off on him for the next ten minutes , fuck you, and fuck this, and how dare you, and you're the biggest pig, and etc. The whole time he just sat there smiling a smile beyond brain dead, mumbling incoherently under his breath, staring at his beer can.

The commotion between the blimps lasted a little while longer, until a truce was reached and peace and harmony was restored to the dining car, after eleven o'clock, after lights out, as this train filled with discontented souls and discontinued intellects roared down into the praline-pricked South. All aboard were all ab-horred.

Finally, at one of the stops, I believe somewhere in one of the Carolinas, the Hare Krishna de-trained, followed by a parting "Party on, Wayne!" for my memory to hold eternally. We took this as an opportunity to thank Ralph for his stimulating contributions to our evening's dialogue and we were, after a few minute's hag-gling, able to bid him adieu.

~

We stumbled back through several cars of the dark and shaking train, our blood warmed from vodka and the intellectual atmosphere of the dining car. As we found our seats and sat down exhausted and buzzed, hoping for a quick descent into dreamfulness, my earlier concerns about the sleeping arrangements began to come back into alcohol-blurred clarity. I pressed the release but-ton, and tried to push my seat back, all the way back. "Hmm, our seats don't go back very far. Hmm..." What to do? I got on my hands and knees in the pitch-blackness, looking for the button, the lever, the magical switch that would turn my seat into a bed. There was nothing under the seat except for dried chewing gum and some oil-like substance. I sat back in my seat. "Okay, well, maybe it won't be too bad," I thought after a few minutes of puzzlement. After all, I was fairly well liquored up, and hadn't slept much the night before, so even if these weren't idyllic resting conditions, getting to sleep should be no problem. I pressed the recline button, and pushed with my back as hard as I could, getting my seat to go back at about a thirty-degree angle. "This is not so bad. Yeah, this will be fine. Good night, Nancy."

Tick...tock...tick...tock...cough...shift...left...right...chachacha...groan...burp...fart...shift...neck...arm...paralysis. "THIS FUCKIN' SUCKS! Who the hell can sleep like this? What the fuck were they thinking when they built these trains?" I gently shook Nancy, who seemed to be having as much trouble getting to sleep as I was. "I can't stand this. Do you think we should try and sneak into one of the sleeper cars, cutie?" "I just want to sleep!" she replied. "I know you do, so do I, but how?" "I don't know!"

There was no solution. We resumed tossing and turning, turning and tossing. Night turned into later night, me on my side, Nancy on her back. Later night turned into early blue black morning, me on my back, Nancy on her side. Blue black turned into blue haze, me on my stomach, Nancy on the floor. Blue haze turned into bright sun, Nancy and I both seated, staring straight into space, our eyes aglaze in the morning light.

Seven a.m.! Lights on! Breakfast is served! "This is your dining car steward. This is your first call to breakfast."

We decided that it would be nice to have a big breakfast after our wonderful night's sleep in the first night of our wonderful new life together. We thus proceeded to the dining car. Because of our shabby, train-ride-induced dress, the steward at first ignored us, seating only the regal elite of Amtrak. Finally, after we complained and he gave us one of *those* looks, we were shown to our table. As I was mouth-wateringly awaiting our choices on the of course immensely fairly-priced Amtrak breakfast menu (I could smell the bacon already), the train suddenly stopped. Dead. Nothing. A few seconds went by, a few minutes went by. No movement. Finally there was an announcement.

"Ladies and ah, gentlemen, we have momentarily ceased, I mean, ah, stopped, going, the train has stopped. We are having some, I mean, a, ah, problem, and we hope to rectify it, cor-

rect soon, ah, I mean, get going soon, as we, ah, get going, and rectify, the situation, we should, ah, be moving shortly, ah, yes, thank you very much for your patience."

We heard a herd of running feet as a group of Amtrak workers raced by us. I managed to ask one of them what had happened as he sped by. "We hit something" he replied. "It happens all the time. I can't wait to see what it is this time. Usually it's a deer, but we've been stopped for awhile now, so it could be somethin' bigger!" At this I lost it. No sleep, no movement, no bacon, no mind! "Fuckin' deer, fuckin' train, fuckin' can't get any fuckin' sleep. What the fuck is this! Can't they build a wall or something around the tracks to keep the deer out? Damn fuckin' Amtrak!" Need I say more? We stayed frozen for about an hour.

Finally the problem was solved (it was a deer), we ate (I had the bacon omelette), and we were now on our way to the Crescent City, the Big Easy, Nu Awlins, New Orleeens, however the hell it's pronounced. We still had another ten hours to go, through the swamps of Mississippi and Louisiana, and then we would be there. Our new life would begin. All the old problems of New York, the uncertainty, the lack of passion, the complete and total stagnation of our lives and our ambitions, would be washed away in the new waters of the old city of fornication and all-night marauding. Nancy had visited New Orleans many years before and had fond memories of the place. I, of course, had my own memories, remembrances of a time not too long before that seemed so long ago, memories of a face, ALP's face, etched in my mind like mist in the wind, never there, never not, always present. What would this return mean? As far as I knew she was no longer there. I had moved on, in body at least, to a new reality, into new arms, mingled with new flesh, a new voice tearing into my blood, reawakening, reminding, and I hoped to god, remedying.

I never felt as alone with someone as I did with Nancy during those last ten hours on the train. We sat in silence most of the time. I could feel the terror rise in my throat, the holy fear that I felt at being alone with a person who often made me feel very alone. We sat together and stared alone into our own memories, our own expectations, our own hopes for the future, separate memories of two people so together, so apart, of two worlds, two voices speaking to no one. We were alone, and no one remained. We had left behind nothing we wanted to think about and were now moving forward in the breath of a train, the classic American travel story of two souls seeking their fortunes in places unexplored, in vistas unannounced, in dreams undreamt. I felt like I was choking—I couldn't breathe with or without her. There was nowhere for me to go now but down, into the deep, cold South, into the city of my emotional stillbirth, towards a spirit that had already deserted me, alongside a spirit that never had been.

The train pulled into New Orleans. There was no air, only silence, no hope, only fear, no day, only night. I walked with her out into the sticky air, my eyes assaulted by palm trees, my mind by reminders of my own mortality, my own lack, my own inability to move towards or away. We got into a taxi and headed towards the West Bank of the Mississippi, to a house that had been given to us by an old friend of mine. The city felt like a bowl surrounded by smog and strange lights. I couldn't tell where these lights came from. They were not like the lights of pollution on a muggy New York City evening. I loathed New York City at that time and was glad to be gone. However, this was not the New Orleans I remembered. ALP was gone, Nancy was here, and my connection was one of fear.

The taxi roared across the Mississippi, the lights of the city growing dim, the night ripe with death. I wished I was dead—the feeling would have been more comfortable for me. We got out of the cab in front of a Chinese Restaurant. I paid the driver. The cab left and we were alone. I could hardly walk. There was silence. The air was heavy with its own voice, its own agenda, its own murderous force. We stood alone in the Southern night. I could not talk. Nancy said nothing. We stood and stared at the Chinese restaurant for a few seconds that seemed like a few eternities. Then we went inside.

~

The place was a hole. It contained a few ragged wooden tables, and was decorated in cheesy Chinese restaurant Polynesian style, with bucolic pictures of tropical places on the walls. Pictures of paradise! It was halfway between a takeout joint and a real restaurant, with none of the personality of either. Behind the counter was a small Oriental man with his back to us. He was hunched over and beaten, as if he had performed years of backbreaking labor. I got his attention and explained who we were. He initially had no reaction, no smile, no frown, no nothing. He then asked in broken English if we were hungry. We replied in the affirmative. Without a word, he picked up the biggest piece of luggage that we had and walked out of the restaurant. We were presumably supposed to follow him, which we did with the rest of our luggage. He led us across the lawn to the house next door, a Spanish stucco ranch structure with a big wooden fence separating it from the next house on one side. There was no fence between the house and the restaurant. He opened the door and we followed him in.

It was a much nicer house than I had anticipated, quite middle class looking, simply furnished, with a big television set in the living room. It was hard for me to imagine Ray and Debbi living there. Right off the living room was the kitchen, containing a simple wooden table built for four. It would be nice to eat properly at a table again, I thought, after all those times eating on Nancy's coffee table back in New York. There were two bedrooms in the back of the house, one for adults, one for children. As I looked into the adult bedroom, I noticed Kwan, again without a word, putting our luggage beside the bed. We stared and watched him silently.

After he was done he again asked us if we were hungry. We again responded in the affirmative. He led us back silently across the lawn to the restaurant. He silently seated us at a table by a window that faced the house, and then went into the kitchen and started yelling in Chinese. A minute later he came out with a heavyset woman, who looked like she had performed even more backbreaking labor than Kwan over the course of her life. This must be Ma. She smiled at us; she had one tooth, bottom center. Kwan told us she would make us something nice. Nancy tried to explain that she was a vegetarian. After a few minutes, Kwan seemed to understand. Ma smiled a lot and said nothing a lot. No speak English.

I asked Kwan if we could have the key to the house. He looked at us for a moment with no expression on his face. He then gave us his copy, saying that he would have to take it back tomorrow to make a copy for us. The food came. It was mediocre at best. Too much MSG. Not like the home-cooked meal I was hoping for. More like bad takeout that you get everywhere all the time. However, since we were hungry, we ate heartily and quickly as if we enjoyed it. When we were finished, Kwan left us a bill. We paid. I guess we weren't part of the family yet. And, to tell you the truth, I hadn't even been in the mood for Chinese.

We fell asleep around three that night, which was early for us, and must have slept for about six hours, dead like earth under snow, until the doorbell started ringing incessantly at nine in the morning. At first we ignored it. We didn't know anyone in New Orleans, so it must be a mistake. After a few more minutes of excessive ringing, I got up and went to the door. It was Kwan. He asked us if we wanted breakfast. "I guess." I woke Nancy up with some difficulty, and we walked like zombies to his pickup. It was a very sunny morning, much too bright for my eyes. Kwan told us that he was going to take us to McDonalds for breakfast. We explained that Nancy was still a vegetarian. Kwan didn't seem to fully understand. He just kept saying McDonalds, over and over again, as if it was his own personal mantra. We arrived at McDonalds. I ate at McDonalds, while Nancy got a sandwich from the deli next door. Kwan watched us silently the whole time we ate, eating nothing himself.

After we finished, he asked if we needed to go food shopping. "I guess." We all went to the supermarket. While Nancy and I shopped, Kwan followed us around, silently staring at us. Occasionally he would speak, but only to make suggestions as to items we should purchase, what I guess he considered the necessities of life, strange items that we would never purchase even if we were strange, but we were not him.

We loaded up on groceries, bought one or two things that Kwan had suggested in order to appease him, and finally, mercifully, he took us home. In the truck and back in the house he made offers of other services he could perform for us, the bizarre, the macabre, and the fantastic, which we politely declined. He finally left. We now had full bellies, a full refrigerator, and already, our fill of Kwan.

~

The next most pressing concern in our new life in the dank infernal South (after eating at McDonalds) was hooking up the telephone. The following morning I took the bus downtown to visit the Phone Company. Back across the river into greater New Orleans I went, back to where my heart had awakened once, before the illusion and the sanity had dried up. Back to old familiar streets, which now smelled so different, like the change between birth and death. Back to the sidewalks where I had gone mad many times, found love, and lost love. Back to my present, to the Telephone Company, sober and in the pure light of day, to set down roots, permanent and intractable. A telephone, the first step towards freedom, the first cut into this new life, to enable us to communicate with those we had left behind, to tell them that we were now here, in the future, in the new, making it new again. I paid the refundable fee and received a number in my name.

When I got back on the bus, I was feeling pretty good about things. It was a beautiful sunny day, low humidity, light breeze from the south-east. This new life was going to be fine. First the phone, then a job, and then who knew what between Nancy and I. I felt happy and powerful as the bus made its way across the bridge into Algiers and the rest of the West Bank. I was a man, and I was doing what a man was supposed to do! Hooking up phones and taking care of my honey! Yes, things would be fine in this new life!

When I got back to the house, Nancy informed me that Kwan had been there while I was gone, doing a little yard work. "God," I said, "is he going to be here every fuckin' day?" Nancy went on to say that he had asked where I was, and she had told him that I had gone downtown to get the telephone hooked up. He wondered why I was doing that, since we were only going to stay in the house for a week or two. At least that is what Debbi had told him. Things would be fine in this new life?

We were forced to set up a summit. Standing in the garden talking to him while he incessantly dug into the soil, I confronted Kwan about this apparent bit of miscommunication. "When I spoke to Ray, he said we could stay here for at least six months, until they got back from Kentucky!" "Ray don't own house." "Yes, I know that—but, he said that he had checked with Debbi, who said she had checked with you, and

115

he said that she said that you had said it was all right for us to stay for six months." "I never know what Debbi say. She say all kind of things. She say she going to come visit. She don't come visit. I don't know what she say. She crazy." "Yes, I know what you mean." "Crazy she is." "Yes. Anyway, is there a problem with us staying in the house, considering that it is empty?" "I no know what Debbi say. She say all kind of thing. One time she tell me she going to pick up kid and she no come for two week. I don't know what she say she say all kind of thing." "Yes, I know, I've dealt with her myself, she can drive you crazy sometimes. But, what about the house? Do you want us to leave?" "Debbi say all kind of thing and Ray no own house. I own house." "Yes, I know you own house." "I your friend. Ask anyone. Ask Debbi. I give her money to buy thing for kid never ask for it back. I don't care I her friend. Ask her. I help her and no ask for anything for myself. My wife and I help all the time. Never know if she is going to come but I no care. I her friend." "Yes, it sounds as if you are very good to her." "Even though I know never if she come. One time she say she going to come get kid. She no come for two week but I don't care. I her friend." "Would you like us to leave the house?" "I your friend. You need money? I give you money." "No, we

116

don't need money—we just need to know about the house!" "I can give you money. I don't care. I your friend. Ask anyone. They say that Kwan is friend. I give money to Debbi and she no come for two week. I don't care..."

This went on for some time, until we finally agreed that Kwan was our friend, that no one needed any money, that we could stay in the house as long as we paid rent, and that Kwan was a fuckin' lunatic in several poorly spoken languages. This final solution was fine with Nancy and me. The rent Kwan wanted was quite reasonable, and he told us that we could pay when we had money and jobs, that we shouldn't worry, that he didn't care. He was our friend. We could ask anyone! Besides, as much as we were looking forward to the free house, we weren't surprised that it worked out this way, as we knew that any dealings with Debbi had the potential to explode in our face. So we would pay rent to live in Kwan's house.

However, we figured that if we were going to pay rent, we might as well live somewhere else, closer to the action, on the other side of the river, away from Kwan, the fortune cookie lunatic, and the evil whims of Debbilry. We decided we would stay in the house for a couple of months and then move on, to start anew yet again in our new life of new hopes, in another new place in New Mauleens, with our new existence again re-newed, again, yet again.

~

Now that Nancy and I had "settled" the situation with Kwan, it was time for the two of us to start earning some money. Since Ralph from Rochester had informed us that there was much work in this part of the country, we were, of course, optimistic. This being the city of tourists, tits, and tequila, the restaurant industry—a most powerful institution in New Orleans (along with stripping and gaming), and one so befitting my university studies of Joyce and Pound—would be our chosen line of work. The day after we got the phone put in, Nancy and I hit the pavement, walking the streets of the Fucked Daughter with the intention of filling out as many applications as we could in as many restaurants as we could.

After wandering for some time, and avoiding going into certain places because they didn't look "right" to me, I finally saw a sign that did look "right" to me, on Bourbon Street. I went down a long, narrow courtyard. At the end of this courtyard was an open outdoor area, filled with nicely table clothed tables. This place seemed "right" so far. I then went through a single glass door and entered a dark brown room with no natural light. The ceiling was quite low, and I felt as if I was in a submarine miles below the earth's surface. There was a bar immediately on my left, and about a dozen tables to my right. The place felt homey in a way, with a touch of understated underground bunker ambience. This was Huang's Creole Kitchen.

The bartender was Oriental, neatly dressed, slender, and spoke English good, I mean well. I asked him if they were hiring waiters. He said he doubted it, but that I could fill out an application if I wished. I went into a small room, and filled out the application, lying about my waiting experience since I had never worked in a restaurant in my life. This being a standard application form, it also asked for educational background, so I dutifully listed my college and graduate school education, as if they were skills pertinent to serving gumbo and shots of Everclear. That was that and I left. I continued on my trek through the Quarter without filling out any more applications, as it had taken all my courage just to fill out the one in Huang's Creole Kitchen.

The next night I was shocked to receive a call from Lu, the bartender at Huang's. He asked me to come down the next night to start, five shifts a week! I was in! I found out later that the reason Lu hired me was because he had taught

English Literature when he lived in China and wanted someone intelligent to talk with during work hours. My two semesters of graduate school had finally paid off!

Later I met Huang, the billionaire from Hong Kong who owned the restaurant, and found out why a smart guy with an education like Lu worked at Huang's in the first place. It seemed that in exchange for using his influence to expedite the whole citizenship thing from China to the U.S., Huang forced Lu to work for him in his restaurant cheaply for a period of seven years. Ah, indentured servitude, just like I had read about it in the history books when I was a kid. I was now a part of living history. America, New Orleans, the Bill of Rights, ALP's slaves, Huang, Lu and me. "Oh beautiful for spacious skies..."

Nancy obtained work as well during her initial night's jaunt, at a bar called Bourbon After Dark, which actually closed early for New Orleans, at about two in the morning. It was an interesting place, as long as you didn't have to work there, Nancy would tell me. The owner was this big ten-gallon hat guy named Jim, you hear, (he would end most sentences with those two words) who was running for mayor or city council or some kind of political office. He had a "wife" who worked with him at the bar, as well as a teenage girlfriend on the side who called herself his "daughter," you hear. Nancy told me that the "wife" and "daughter" would often get into fights at the bar over Jim, you hear. Standard New Orleans fare.

Nancy only worked at the bar when it was busy, so she might work every day for a week or more, ten to twelve hours a day, and then have a week or more off. This schedule really depressed her. She was either too tired or too bored. In addition, she was having serious problems living with me, as all of our old difficulties from New York—the lack of passion, lack of commitment, etc.—were again bothering her Rob-phobic brain.

I, on the other hand, was doing fine. Even though she often threatened to, I knew Nancy couldn't leave me because she didn't have enough money to get her own place, and this, which made her feel trapped, helped to ease my usual terror-filled anxiety, since I knew she was trapped, and couldn't leave me. Also, I liked my job, and was working a consistent five-night-a-week schedule, so I had what my friend Nick said was all a man needed: steady work and his woman at home. All was fine and dandy for the men of the world, especially in the deep Southern tradition of New Awlins, you hear!

~

Meanwhile, back at the ranch, Kwan was gone! After we reached our rent treaty with him, he completely disappeared from our lives. One week went by, no Kwan. Two weeks went by, still no Kwan. We were so happy! We had never actually paid him any money, but we figured that he would come around and ask for it when he wanted it, because he had told us he was our friend. After seeing him everyday for the first few weeks, it was now a pleasure to see him no days for the next few weeks.

One morning the bell rang around ten. I rolled out of bed, and, figuring Kwan was back, shouted to a sleeping Nancy, "what the hell does he want now?" Sometimes we would hide when Kwan rang the bell, hoping he would go away. This morning, however, the ringing was constant, so I stumbled out of bed, cursing under and over my breath, and made my way to the front door. When I opened it, I was shocked to see Ray standing before my sleep-soaked eyes! "Surprise," he said! "Oh!" I said. "Came for a visit," he said. "Oh!" I said. "I've come to stay with you guys for a few days." I was fine with his visit, as it was always great to see him, but I wasn't too happy about his assumption that he could stay with us without even asking. I mean, we were on the verge of paying rent, if only Kwan would ask for it, so I naturally felt that Nancy and I should control who stayed in our house, or in what would be our house once we started paying rent, once Kwan asked us for money. However, since Ray was my friend, I didn't make a stink about it. But the next time!

In addition to bringing his bright smile and pleasant wit, Ray came bearing an interesting bit of news. It seemed that Debbi didn't like Kentucky because it was too cold, so they were coming back to New Orleans. To their house! In a month! "Oh, I see hmm, yes, that is, yes, very interesting Ray. And, umm, where are Nancy and I supposed to stay, since, well, you kinda told us we could stay here for like six months?" "Well, it shouldn't be a problem for you guys to find a place, you do have a month, and it could be a little longer, like maybe six weeks. I wouldn't worry." I'm sure he didn't. Poor Ray, his mind destroyed by that woman, the worst person ever to walk the earth, worse than Hitler, worse than Stalin, worse than Satan. My innocent friend, my companion once in love, music and life, now little more than a portion of his former self, a genius diminished by the foul loins of the foulest bitch ever to walk the planet. If only she would die, I thought at that moment (and many subsequent moments), it would be better for everyone, better for us, better for Ray, better for her children.

Nancy and I decided that it was time, now, to get the fuck out of there. Ray's news put a bit of a rush on our already theorized moving plans. It was a month before Christmas, so we decided we would get out by the first of the year, and we wouldn't pay Kwan a damn cent, fuck him, fuck this whole fuckin' situation.

For a short time, relative calm descended upon our lives. Once we had made the final decision to get out, we felt liberated. We had taken control of the situation, at least in our own minds, and were able to live an existence of moderate normality, at least as normal as Nancy and I could be in our constant state of uncertainty and doubt. Life was good, or at least it wasn't that bad. We'd rent movies, drink red wine, and only about once a week would Nancy feel the need to go by herself to the neighborhood bar down the road, where there was little chance of anything happening, since the place was filled with rednecks and yokels. I still wasn't too happy on the nights that she went out without me, especially one night when I got home from work and she had left me a note saying she was at the bar and I was *not* to come by and "surprise" her. Though I would get upset when she did things like that, I still maintained the hope that maybe, just maybe, when the two of us had a new home of our own across the river, we would find the love that I knew was just barely eluding us.

~

About two weeks after Ray's visit, Debbi came to see us. "Hey, it's been awhile, guys," she said as she walked through the front door. I stood and stared at her, the sweat dripping fast from my brow. Nancy was paralyzed and wordless, her eyes ablaze in terror. "I'm going to stay here for a few days. You don't mind." I must have passed out for a moment, because the next thing I remember, Debbi was in our house, in her bedroom. "Guys, what have you done to my house?" she said with a laugh. "Just for a few days. It's great to see my house again. I'm going to stay until Sunday. You don't mind." Debbi left and went over to Kwan's for some lunch. I went with her to find out what she wanted from us.

I sat across from her in Kwan's ramshackle Polynesian palace, while she sucked her food down, never looking straight at me, only at her plate. I ate nothing. Debbi seemed almost normal, for her, maybe too normal, saying nothing much, engaging me in the smallest of talk. I noticed her hair seemed redder than when I had last seen her, but I didn't remember when I had last seen her. I asked her about Ray, and her new baby, but I don't remember the answers she gave me. I was trying to ascertain her true intentions, because there were always true intentions behind the falseness of her concern for anyone. She just talked, chewed, and stared at her plate. "Just for a few days. You guys don't mind. By the way, I won't be staying with you guys tonight or tomorrow. I'm staying with my friend in Kenner and I'll be back Saturday night." And leaving Sunday! Ah, this won't be as bad as I had originally anticipated. Only a day or so with her, and I was sure Nancy and I could arrange something to do Sunday: work, visit a leper colony, anything so we could stay out of Debbi's newly-colored hair.

I left Debbi and went back to her house, where I told Nancy the good news. Two faces on a Thursday afternoon, two big smiles. Spared the agony of the black uterus of negation one more time, no tunes, no tits, no her in our. Nancy and I resumed our normal queasy business, thinking everything was now all right again in the burning Southern cunt of eternity.

~

Two days later, on Saturday afternoon, I was on the bowl in my blue bathrobe taking a shit. It was the end of the second week in December. All my life, the only place I had ever been able to truly relax, even during the worst of times, was atop the bowl. The singular ability to contemplate seems biologically connected to the singular need to excrete one's self. I have had this conversation with other men, the types who were not too squeamish about such matters, and we were all in agreement on this point. And, the consensus also concludes that the harder the stool, the better the mental acuity. Diarrhea, for whatever reason, doesn't lead into the hallowed inner workings of the soul the way a good one-piece rock-hard shit does. People wonder why I always stay in the bathroom so long. Well, its not because the process is time-consuming, but because I enjoy it.

I was thus sitting atop the bowl, enjoying my pleasant little time away from the world. Nancy was in the living room. All in all, it was a quiet and, for us, tranquil Saturday afternoon in the Big Squeezy. I don't remember if I heard the doorbell ring or not. Nancy answered it, as I was indisposed. They asked to see her "husband." There was a knock on the bathroom door. "Yes, Nancy?" "There are some people here to see you." "Well, I'm kind of busy." "Rob, I think you better come out here NOW!" I pushed one last time, wiped as best I could, closed the front of my robe, flushed, and stepped back out into the world.

As I walked into the living room, I saw two

policemen standing next to Kwan. "Can I help you gentlemen?" I said to the cops. "Are you her old man?" "Yes." "Have you been staying in this house for the last month?" "Yes." "Well, this man owns the house, and you are trespassing on his property, and you have to get out NOW!" "What are you talking about?—Kwan!" One of the officers immediately cut me off. "This man let you stay in his house out of the goodness of his heart, and you don't pay him any rent, and you stay here like a bunch of hippies. You should thank this man for letting you stay here this long." "Kwan, I don't understand, we agreed to pay rent, but you never came by to collect it. Officer, we made an agreement with him, but we haven't seen him in weeks."

Kwan English very badly now. "I not know. They stay in my house. They must leave." "Kwan!" "I not know." "You are going to have to vacate the premises right now. If you don't, we will arrest you for trespassing and throw your stuff into the street." We pleaded for some time, a week maybe. The cops, after talking to Kwan, gave us twenty-four hours. "We will be back this time tomorrow. If you two are still here, you will be arrested for trespassing, and your stuff will be thrown into the street. You should thank this man for letting us give you even that much time."

We didn't thank Kwan. "And don't even think of causing any damage to the house over the next twenty-four hours." Not that we were considering it, but considering it, not a bad idea.

The door slammed closed. The sky caught fire, and the ground sucked up our innards. Nancy fell unto the couch, sobbing into her hands. I started to pace, my thoughts careening all over the place, wildly, like a psychopath looking for a solution. We needed a solution! Nancy could cry all she wanted, but the truth of the matter was that we had twenty-four hours to get us and all our stuff out of there. Us was the easy part. Our stuff was not. Since Nancy's brother worked for that shipping company, we had gotten much more stuff sent down here than we should have. Just last week, we had had seventeen large boxes of items delivered to the front door. That was not going to fit on the bus, or in a cab, and even if it did, where the hell were we going to bring it to anyway?

As Nancy cried, I thought, who do we know in New Orleans? Answer: No one. Next question to myself: Who do we know in the general vicinity of New Orleans, i.e., in the southern portion of the United States? Yes, ding, ding, ding. Stephen and Mona lived in St. Louis, only about twelve hours away. If they left now, they could make it by tomorrow at this time. Questions asked, answers provided. A phone call was placed. An answering machine picked up. Damn, fuck, an urgent message was dispatched.

Now we waited. We must do something. I must do something. We needed back-up plans for our back-up plans. The more possibilities considered, I thought, the more possibilities for success. I thought about New Orleans again. Who did I know? Wait, that girl! The one at my restaurant! Celia! I had known her for a month. She liked me, we had hung out a few times. She had a car. I assumed she lived some place, though who knew in New Homelesseans. She could help, maybe. She was the only local answer. I had to head downtown, to the restaurant, to find her, to ask her.

I called the restaurant and said I couldn't work that evening. Fortunately, in New Orleans it is considered acceptable to miss work because of excessive drinking and drugging without having to offer an excuse, so I didn't have to say much more than "something came up" in order to miss a night on the job. Besides, the weeks before Christmas are the slow season in New Tourleans, so they could easily live without my waitering skills for an evening, even if it was a Saturday night. Whilst Nancy waited at home by the phone, in case our desperate plea to Stephen was answered, I headed downtown to find Celia.

I got to the restaurant that I wasn't working at that night because "something came up" and found her. Yes, she would help us. We could stay at her house in the Marigny, and better yet, she had a big shed in her yard where we could store our stuff. Beautiful child, beautiful girl, I was so in love with her at that moment. The only catch was that she would be working her second job, at a strip joint, until five in the morning. After that she could and would help us.

I returned to the house. Nancy told me that Stephen and Mona had called from St. Louis, saying that they were available to assist us if Celia didn't come through. Of course, we would have to leave New Orleans and go back with them to St. Louis, but it was better than getting arrested, Stephen had figured. I called him back and told him that his services were not needed, but that I forever loved him more than ever.

Nancy and I didn't have much packing to do, as we had never done much unpacking. At about four-thirty, we took a cab down to the Quarter, where we met Celia. Everything went off without a hitch. Because Celia had a small car, we had to make seven trips back and fourth across the Mississippi River Bridge, the car stuffed with boxes and our three exhausted bodies. We were done at about nine in the morning. Giddy with relief and exhaustion we smoked some pot, and Celia allowed Nancy and I to sleep in her bed. What a comfortable bed it was, much better than the bed at Kwan's house, or the bed at Jefferson Parish Prison, I imagined.

I never found out what happened to Kwan or Debbi, nor do I care. I just hope they are dead, or if they aren't, that they are suffering greatly somewhere. That is all I will say about them. As for Ray, all I will say is that I saw his face one more time, one night while I was working at Huang's Creole Kitchen. He came by to see me on a slow night just before Mardi Gras, while I was standing bored and I think a little drunk in front of the restaurant. I asked him if he was still with Debbi. He said yes, I cursed him out, and he left. I never saw Ray again.

~

We remained at Celia's for the next few days, desperately searching for an apartment. While Celia, bless the child, was as sweet as lemonade toward us, her roommate was another story. He was some fuckin' kid who obviously had just left mommy and daddy and wasn't used to the intricacies of living on his own, and thus couldn't stand or understand us staying in his house. While he was nice to our face, he would constantly complain to Celia real loud in the next room so we could hear how much we were ruining his life or something like that. I didn't care at all—I was in survival mode, and the rantings of some spoiled child meant absolutely nothing to me. On some level I actually enjoyed making this fool's life unpleasant—I thought it was pretty funny, a little laugh at someone else's expense in the middle of the hell we were currently residing in. And since Celia didn't seem to mind, I thought, fuck it and fuck him.

Nancy however, was sensitive to such things from strangers, and after a few days she could no longer take it, so we had to leave. When I gently pointed out to her that we had no place to go, and very little money to spend, she pointed out to me that we could stay in a hotel, and that my parents could wire us some money. Her parents were too poor to help or something like that, and besides, she had always said that she could not rely on me in a crisis, like she could rely on *him*, so here was my big chance to outdo *him*.

Since it was too expensive to obtain a room in the Quarter, we wound up staying at the same hotel that I had stayed at on my ALP visit to New Orleans, outside the city in that memorable slum section part of town. Talk about seeing the flip side of life flipped! Mardi Gras wasn't yet in session, so the $150 a night room tax was lowered to its regular rate of twenty-five dollars a night, which we could afford, at least for a few days.

Life was grand in our ungrand hotel. Since she wasn't working that particular week, and we had no cash to spare, Nancy stayed in the hotel room each night while I took the bus to work in the Quarter, the same bus I had taken a few years previous to see Annabel Lee. As it was the holiday season, things were real slow at the restaurant. I would make between ten and twenty dollars on my shift, use it to buy some food and alcohol for Nancy, and then get back on the bus to go "home," living in the hotel like a washed-up rock star. Back and forth to the restaurant, forth and back to the hotel, with nowhere else to go except back and forth, forth and back.

Nancy and I began to fight terribly, the type of openly hostile arguments that we had managed to avoid during even the worst moments of our relationship. As feelings of homelessness gripped at my thoughts more and more, I became increasingly violent and intolerant toward her. I blamed her for the further deterioration of our already deteriorating situation, since she was the one who forced us to leave Celia's. I felt that she was useless, more concerned with drinking to forget than dealing with our situation head on. What was she doing? What the fuck had happened to us? We had come down to New Orleans at the generous beckoning of an old and dear friend of mine, to start a new life, and what had we been shown by the beautiful Crescent City in six weeks time? Homelessness up close! I left New York for this? We were now one step ahead of the street, our money running out, our patience with one another already run out.

Each night that I slept beside Nancy in that hotel, the same hotel I had stayed at when the world was old and I was younger, I would have this recurring nightmare. In it I would see an empty street, covered in garbage and dog shit. In the middle of the street, in the gutter between the sidewalks, there would be a man facing toward me, a man who looked like Mao Zedong. He had only one arm, and on this arm one long finger that looked like a gigantic penis. At the end of this "finger," where the tip should be, was instead the head of Debbi. The head would address me. "Give me your ass and your feet and your mouth and your stomach," it would say through its hole, "and come lie in my shit and my piss and my vomit and my beer and my nails and my shards of glass. Come home to the blacktop, lay your back gently upon thy sidewalk, use thy dog shit as your pillow, and rest your weary soul in the concrete night. Come, come, my comrade, take a great step forward and sleep in the rain and get to know your fellow man, and maybe if you're lucky you won't get stabbed in the heart at four in the morning, and maybe if you're real lucky you'll get to live in a nice new perfect cardboard box that you can take home with you right out of the abandoned lot of human street existence!" Night after night, I would hear the same utterance from this horrible, distorted image of tar and roadway (plus some stuff about steel furnaces). And it was not only in dreams that I heard this voice. In my waking reality, at the restaurant, on the bus, in the hotel room, taking a shit, I felt that it was only a matter of time before the sidewalks would be our home, and we would be discarded like human trash. "Trash, don't try to take my life away!"

~

It didn't come to that. We finally found a home, with a roof, walls, and floors. Everything! No bathroom door. Well, almost everything, but hey, there are no secrets between lovers. After searching for a week, we saw a sign on Burgundy Street in the Quarter advertising an apartment for rent. We called the number, and the gentleman on the other end said that the apartment advertised had been rented, but that he had another apartment, which, while in need of major repair, was inhabitable, sort of. We could have that one if we wanted, no deposit, no lease, just the rest of the month's rent. We immediately said yes, sight unseen.

The first thing Nancy and I saw the next day upon the opening of the apartment door was a fireplace in the center of a beautiful all-brick wall. Hey, maybe this was going to turn out all right after all! Then we turned to the left and saw the rest of the place. In the back of the apartment was a loft, cutting in half two windows which were at least twelve feet in height. The ceiling was at least fifteen feet high. Under the loft, which stretched across the entire back of the apartment, was, on the left side, a stove, a sink, and a fridge, in the center, a little gas radiator, and on the right side, in a small room with no door, a sink, a toilet, and a tub. In addition to there being no bathroom door, there was also no ladder to the loft. There was a second fireplace, in the back room of the apartment, on the right side, near the bathroom. We were told that the building had been constructed in the early part of the nineteenth century, and had once been an estate of some sort, hence all the fireplaces. At some point between then and now, the loft had been built across the back of the apartment, and a "kitchen" and a "bathroom" had been stuck beneath it.

The place had potential. The front room, with the brick wall surrounding the fireplace, certainly was pleasing to the eye upon entry. The twelve-foot windows in the front room were imposing in their sheer size and grandeur, like the windows King Kong would use for his apartment if he were renting. They were so large that a person could easily climb through them, especially since we were on the first floor. On several occasions, I did so instead of using the front door, just to scare Nancy. The apartment was one big open space, from the front windows to the loft, with only a high arch to delineate separation from one room to the next, so you actually could have held full court basketball games inside. I wanted to put up nets, but Nancy would have none of it. The loft was made of solid wood, and was in tip-top shape, with nice-looking stained pillars supporting it. Overhaul, the apartment was certainly an unusual space, open and free, and while maybe not the best use of space, was nevertheless quite interesting in a pure *Architectural Digest* sort of way.

The place was a mess. The beautiful, majestic, grandiose, breathtaking to the heavens twelve-foot windows in the front were missing

several panes of glass each, giving us the pleasure of natural air-conditioning. In the kitchen,
the stove looked like Civil War surplus, and nothing worked on it except for one front burner.
Sometimes, when Nancy and I would playfully
wrestle, in our first happy days in our new home,
I would try to overpower her and force her to lick
the stove. On the wall beside the stove, there was
a big hole, which someone had plugged up with a
cloth rag, conceivably to block out the elements.
Imagine my surprise in pulling said rag out of the
hole one day, feeling a pleasant gust of wind on
my face, and seeing the courtyard behind the
house staring back at me. The bathroom, in addition to lacking a door, had no tiles on the floor,
leaving filthy exposed concrete to chill and dirty
our feet summer, winter, spring, or fall. The walls
in the back room of the apartment, in addition
to needing a paint job, were also in the process
of completely decaying. The apartment had no
closets whatsoever, so Nancy and I literally did
live out of our suitcases while we resided here.
There were no working lights, only wires hanging out of the ceiling. There were no working ceiling fans, just more wires hanging out of the ceiling. All in all, the place was a handyman's dream,
but our nightmare. But at least we now had a
home, after wandering through the streets and

swamps of New Horrorleans for the past week. Like Moses, I had led my people home, to an unfurnished two-room loft apartment in the spread-leg city of New Hairleans.

We slept unadorned on the hard floor of the loft the first night in our new home, as all our stuff was still at Celia's. It was so uncomfortable; it was the greatest night of sleep I had ever not had. We had a home, we had an identity, and the streets would not be our final resting spot, and we would not be buried in unmarked graves! We could wash ourselves in a shower, eat in front of the television (if we had had one), and walk around naked if it was hot and not get arrested for indecent exposure. We were home, so damn the Kwans and full speed ahead into our cold, hard classroom-style floors, and look at the rain as it falls ever so gently tip tip on our empty window panes. We were home, so look at the exquisite outlines of black as the fleas come through the cracks in the wall. We were home, and this is where we shall remain, endless, in love, indifferent to one another, until the ceilings collapse, which may be soon, and we are crushed under the weight of decaying concrete and windowless windows that go crash in the night. We were home. In our hubble of rubble, under the broiling sun-blazed sky of bucolic and law deserted New

AwSchuckslin. Our home. Together. Never to be taken away by any fuckin' Chinaman or any friggin' whoreslut. Our home. Embellished by the simple act of love and commitment. Our home. Never to be taken away. Except by each other!

~

The apartment also came with one other feature, our new landlord Big John. BJ was a bull of a man, five foot ten in height, 300 pounds of blubber and belly in width, with a big white beard, a bald head, and a trach tube around his neck with corresponding hole in the throat. He had a halting and agreeable, if rambling, way of talkin' to you, which made Nancy and I initially believe everything he said. The day he showed us our new love nest, he told us without our asking that he would: paint the ceiling, paint the walls, redo the floors, build a ladder to the loft, replace our stove, build a bathroom door, and fix the many holes in the plaster. Furthermore, he explained to us that he was going to go to City Hall just as soon as he could to obtain the necessary permits to repair the windows, because in the historic French Quarter you needed the necessary permits to do any kind of window work. So, he told us in his agreeable and rambling way, that he would go down to City Hall tomorrow, or the next day at the latest, to obtain those permits.

Our initial confidence in BJ increased when he came by the apartment the next day as promised, bringing with him tools, a paint ladder, and Louie, his Cuban assistant who spoke no Inglés, and who we quickly discovered did all the work while BJ yelled instructions. "Louie, a little over to the left!" "Louie, you missed a spot!" "Louie, what the hell are you doing?" "Louie, watch out with that paint!"

BJ announced that the first project he would tackle, the obvious and most glaring problem as he saw it, was the living room ceiling. He said it needed to be painted. I looked up fifteen feet at the fifteen-foot ceiling. It looked fine to me—white in color, not in any real state of disrepair, certainly in better shape than the windows, stove, ladder, bathroom door, walls, and hole in the kitchen wall covered with a rag. But hey, he was the landlord, and he must have done this kind of thing a million times, so he undoubtedly knew best.

That afternoon, BJ painted the ceiling. Actually, Louie painted the ceiling, with BJ occasionally pulling the paint brush out of his hand to show him where he had missed a spot. When they were done, the ceiling didn't look any different than it had before. But the living room floor did. It was black. At least it used to be. Now it was black with streaks of white paint everywhere. You see, BJ hadn't put a drop cloth down! But hey, we didn't worry, because he said he was going to redo the floors, so who the hell cared about these old crummy floors because soon we would be getting brand spanking new paint-free floors!

BJ and Louie returned the following day. BJ informed us that *Louie* had made a mistake and forgotten to put a drop cloth down on the floor, but no problem, he would make everything all right again. He had brought with him an industrial-sized floor buffer, and he personally took it upon himself to buff all the paint off of our living room floor. What a beautiful sight he was, buffing that floor, barely controlling the buffer, his shirt riding up and exposing his belly, the flesh jiggling with each movement of the machine. Pure performance art. I could have sold tickets and called it Big John and his Industrial Buffer with Louie the Cuban Man Servant. When he finished, we had a shiny buffed black living room floor, covered with buffed dried streaks of white paint.

The next day it rained. No BJ. The following day was sunny. No BJ. The weekend came. No BJ. A partly cloudy Monday followed. Still no BJ. He had told us that he was going to come every day to work on the apartment, yet he had only been here twice, once to paint the ceiling, and once to clean the paint off the floor. We called him, inquiring when he would be paying us another visit. He told us that he would try to make it the next day, unless it rained. The next day it rained and he didn't show up. The day after was sunny and he didn't show up. We called him yet again, and he told us he would definitely come the next day, unless of course it rained. Since all of the work was to be done indoors, we didn't quite understand the rain excuse, but as time went on, and BJ stopped showing up, rain or shine, it became clear to us what BJ was good at doing: very little. Our faith that he was going to turn our Taj Garbagehaul into a Taj Mahal started to evaporate. It wasn't that BJ was a liar, because I think he believed everything he was telling us, and he really intended to do all the work he had promised. It was just that there was a gap, a chasm, a gulf, an open field the size of Montana, between *attempt* and *do* with him. He would say he would do one hundred percent of a task; he would attempt maybe forty, and he would actually complete about five. Not good odds for the reconstruction of our new apartment.

We thus realized that we would have to become more aggressive with BJ to get even the essentials done. The thing that we considered most essential at this time was the windows, or the lack thereof in the area of glass, which I had been raised to believe was a natural and necessary component of what is known as the window. On a cold January day I called BJ, angry and desperate sounding, telling him how cold it was going to get that night, and how we didn't have any fuckin' glass in our fuckin' windows, and how we thought it wasn't fair that we had to pay rent on an apartment that had no glass in half of its front windows. He told us he would be right over.

An hour later he showed up with Louie. Nancy and I congratulated ourselves because we had finally learned how to deal with BJ: the *threat*. However, while the *threat* may have succeeded in BJ getting his big ass over to our place, nothing in this great world of ours, nothing in these heavens and these earths, indeed nothing in the whole expansive and wondrous universe, could infuse BJ with the one morsel of human ability he lacked above all other things that mattered—common sense! He had indeed come to fix our windows, to put an end to the open air that we shared with the outside world, to place a barrier between the alcohol-infested shit-drenched oxygen that permeated New Soreleans like a vaginal infection, and our new home-sweet-home shanty. However, while we thought glass for our window, that see-through stuff that comes from sand, BJ was on a different level of abstract thought altogether. When we thought glass, he thought Styrofoam. Yes, beautiful, perfect, angelic, bright, pure, clean, brand spankin' new, cut-to-order for all your window needs Styrofoam.

Nancy and I watched in horror as Louie cut pieces of the white gold to fit into the missing panes. Measure, cut, plug, fin, perfecto! While others in the Quarter had windows with real glass, plus those decorative shutters, we had broken glass, we now had Styrofoam, and we always had BJ. And since the top half of one of the windows had many consecutive missing panes, Louie thought, hey, what the hell, why not cut one huge piece of Styrofoam, and seal the whole window. Nancy, who was a fan of light, just stood there with her tongue hanging out. After BJ left, saying that this was only a temporary solution, that once those permits came through we would have our glass, Nancy ripped down some of the Styrofoam so there would be light shining on the garden of our life. From that day forth we quit asking BJ to do things for us. Eventually we just did some work ourselves and made him take it off the rent, which he seemed quite glad to do.

~

Despite all that we had been through with BJ, I was confident that with a little plaster, a few pieces of glass, and a few gallons of paint, we could transform this discombobulated structure of disrepair into a real home, our home. And, despite all that Nancy and I had been through, I was confident that with a little love, a little luck, and a lot more loyalty, we could transform the discombobulated disrepair of our lives into a real life, our life. But from the very first night we spent there, to the very last night I would spend there, things would be the same in this home as they had been in each of our "homes" before. The walls would continue to decay, the glass, no matter how many times it was replaced, would break again, and despite what I did, or didn't do, Nancy and I would continue to exist together in a world apart. Fear, terror, anxiety—all the constant companions of my life with her—would blanket my existence more completely than ever, now that we shared a place and there was nowhere for her, for me, to go. There was now no escape for my body, no rest for my enfeebled psyche. We were trapped in our home, together, where I was always to be alone.

To add to my already regular schedule of dread, Nancy started to go out to the bars and backrooms of New Fornileans, without me, in search of booze, fun, and what the fuck else I didn't want to think about. Day after day I feared, from my first waking moment, her deciding night after night to go out without me. What had started as "the break" back in New York had now escalated into twenty-four/seven terror for me. Since the sharing of a home made Nancy feel less and less at home with me, she was now looking for ways to get away from me, so she could free herself.

To rub some salt into my already pepper- and paprika-stained wounds, each night before she went out, she would bluntly inform me that, while not actively searching, she was not averse to a tryst or two with a member of the opposite, or same, sex, should the situation happen to arise in four in the morning barstool land. These constant declarations shattered any illusions I had about our relationship and our future. Had I had more faith in myself, or less fear of life without her, I might have gotten up and left her, left this stinkhole of a town, this stinkhole of a life. But by this time it was too late. I was too deeply attached to her, like cancer to a cell, to do anything other than suffer at her whim. So I stayed when I should have gone, and that choice, or lack of choice, condemned my life to a whirlwind of pain.

The funny thing was that, in truth, despite my full-time misery, she probably only went out twice a week on average. And, in truth, she never actually cheated on me, at least in a fucking sense. However, in truth, the truth didn't matter to me. Her threats made it feel as if she were unfaithful to me night after night, even if she wasn't unfaithful to me night after night. So I suffered, night after night, regardless of the truth.

She generally made up her mind in the late afternoon, before she went to work. If she decided yes, as in "yes, I'm going to come home to you," then I felt instantaneous relief, as I knew she would be at my side all through the coming night. However, if her answer was no, as in "no, I'm going to go out, without you," then I would suck in my emotional gut and wait for it to burst later, when my night alone began.

Sometimes I would try to bribe her to stay home with me, under the guise of doing something special for her. I learned to cook all her favorite vegetarian dishes, so when she would say to me, "I think I am going to go out tonight," I could respond, "Gee, shucks, that's a shame, 'cause I was going to make your favorite, zucchini and tomato gratin, or vegetable and pasta stew," or a zillion other things that I would whip up from the many cookbooks I had purchased, all for her!

On occasion, it worked. Most of the time, how-ever, it was just another expression of the use-lessness of us.

~

Once she had put her makeup and mini-skirt on, and closed the door behind her, my night alone would begin. What a thing of beauty these nights were, a work of art if I don't say so, my Duchamp in despair, my Picasso in pain, my Monet in madness. The evening would begin with me staring upon the blank canvas of my isolation, dumbfounded and lost as she left the apartment.

After a few minutes of contemplation (usually me cursing her out loud to the empty room), I would gently cover the background of the white canvas in the light and vague color of the fool. Some beautifully lame color, such as aqua or teal. Then, in order to give this first coat of the night a chance to dry, I would leave the canvas, and pace around the apartment for about an hour or so, talking to myself out loud in ram-bling streams of unconsciousness about Nancy, about me, about life, about why.

When the hour was up and my feet were tired, I would return to my portrait of despair and paint in the left hand corner a little goblin-like caricature of a she-male, which represented the lucky fuck Nancy might or might not sleep with that night. This was always an extremely abstract figure, as I never knew in reality what it would look like, nor did I really care. It was just someone, something, that needed to be represented, even if it was to forever remain a figment of my imagination.

Upon completing this section of my painting, I usually felt a surge of unexplainable euphoria. I would put the radio on as loud as possible and dance around the apartment like a ballerina on acid, flowing through the air as if my bones were kept together by an invisible skin. Dancing, singing, and dreaming—I didn't care if Nancy was fucking the whole wide world! For a few moments, I had managed to release all my fears into the realm of unrealistic, unlimited, and uncontrollable joy. I had temporarily given up living, and had been swept up into the amorphous dust of pure desire. What a wonderful time it was, however brief it was.

However brief it was! Over the next two hours or so, feelings of anger and hatred would well up in me, crushing my dance of desire. By two in the morning I hated Nancy, hated the bitch, hated what she was doing to me night after night, hated what I was letting her do to me, night after night. To demonstrate my swelling anger, I would splash some red all over my canvas, deep bloody red applied freely and without restraint. Here a dash, there a dash, everywhere awash in red! The whole room was now flammable, while I walked on the ceiling shouting in full-throated passion.

By three o'clock, I had started taking sips of the Jack Daniel's that I kept by the stove, and after a half dozen or so swigs from the bottle, my unrestrained anger would metamorphose into a controlled drunken rage. It was now time to add some black to the picture. Black for a structured, focused psychopathic fury toward Nancy. A black that said, "kill the bitch, rip her heart out through her mouth, fill her pussy with concrete, stick sharp fingernails in her eyes, and while you're at it, how about some psychological torture for her to remember in her dreams." A black that, however irrationally expressed, was always painted rationally in the JD-induced palette of my brain.

Occasionally these black thoughts were accompanied by violent actions. Mostly it was just small acts of vandalism against the innocent inanimate objects of our home, such as breaking a glass into pieces by smashing it on the floor and later telling Nancy that it had fallen, somehow, or kicking over some small bookcase or stereo speaker. Nothing more than that, usually.

One night, however, when I was in a particularly whiskey-dark mood, I performed my greatest physical feat of hatred, the sword-fling. Nancy owned an authentic broadsword, heavy and dull, which hung in the living room. One night, feeling dissatisfied at the shards of glass lying around me, I removed the sword from its holder on the wall and flung it, full force, into the opposite wall, where it chopped out a huge gash. When Nancy came home and asked me what had happened, I told her that I was playing with her sword while I was eating potato chips, and it had slipped because my hands were greasy. I added that it was very dangerous for her to have a weapon like that around the house because someone could really get hurt!

After violence came acceptance, which began around dawn, during what I liked to call my white period. I would sit at the foot of the fireplace, holding the bottle of JD in my arms in a state of total calm. In my mind, it had happened. It was light out, night had turned to day, Nancy had gone away, and all my fears had been realized, thus there was nothing more to fear. I would plot the rest of my life at these moments, the things I was going to do, the places I was going to visit, now that I was without her. It was often a beautiful dawn for me in the Crescent City. I would watch the sun come up, and see the black turn to blue-black and then to blue and finally to yellow and red, the colors of fire which always lit the early morning New Orleans sky. It was as if the random words of the night, the shapes of debauchery and destruction which I had articulately unexpressed, had burnt off with the first violent rays of the new morning sun, to be reformed within the fiery gasses that framed the newborn sky in shattered pieces of desire and forgetfulness. I would forget what I remembered, forget what I had been through, and could, now that my mind was at peace, allow the day to breathe, the sun to alight, and the people of the earth to walk again, saintly and god-fearing past my soul.

As the first piece of red smoke passed the sun, I would be prepared to sign my portrait of the evening and hang myself away when the telephone would inevitably ring. I knew it was her. It was always her. She missed me, and wanted me to come out and meet her for a drink at some god-awful twenty-four-hour hole in the whore New Pourleans shithouse. Elation and regret would well up inside of me as I put down the phone, elation at the reality of her phone call and the temporary release that it allowed me from my own private purgatory, regret at what could have been, if only the phone had not rung for once. Maybe the fire of the new day would have engulfed my torment, and carried me somewhere else under the sun-burnt sky, somewhere away from her. Maybe to some other reality, a respite for my battered consciousness, a real place to stand and smile on my own, happy and alone. However, I thought as I put my shoes on to go out, not this morning, again.

I would meet her at whatever bar she was at wherever, and we would have no more than a drink or two together, since we were both wasted, her from her nocturnal wanderings, me from my nocturnal wonderings. We would stumble home, her feet unstable from drink, my feet unstable from frayed nerves, and fall into bed together under the light of the morning, the perfect scene of two bodies merged together in their absent and separate desire, awaiting the start of things again. We would sleep through the new morning, through the new afternoon, and awake at the cusp of a new evening, waiting for my fear to be re-born, for my picture to be repainted as the cycle of things reemerged in hues of uniformity and limitation. Again and again, it would be the same night again, and I would be sitting by the fire-place, with sword in hand, waiting for her not to come home, hoping for the phone to ring, won-dering what would happen if, for once, it didn't.

~

This was the way things were, night after night, until one night when Nancy came home about two, quite early for her. I initially felt relaxed and calm, figuring that home early meant no fucky sucky for her that night in the land of the chilled genitalia. But, I could never relax when it came to her, not for a moment, not even when time for once seemed in my favor. She bluntly informed me, without my asking, that she had been with someone that evening. Immediately from my mouth, "Did you go all the way?" She didn't want to say. "Did you go all the way?" She didn't want to say. "Did you go all the fuckin' way?" "No, we just made out." "Was it a man or a woman?" "I really don't want to talk about it." "Was it a man or a woman?" "I told you I don't want to talk about it." "What the fuck was it?" "A man."

I refused to sleep in the same bed with her that night. "If you think you're going from his arms to mine, you're nuts. I'm sleeping on the couch." "Please don't," she replied. What did she expect me to do? I guess roll over to her will like I always did. Not this night, though, not with this. Some things pushed me over the edge and gave me some backbone. This was one of them. I was strongest when I actually had to face the reality, rather than having to face the fear of the reality.

She woke me several times during the course of the night, asking me to come up into the loft to bed. Each time I refused. In the morning she cried. Then we went to a park and had a fight by a fountain. Then I went to work. Then she went to work. That night I slept in the same bed with her. Nothing changed. Well one thing did: deception. She kept seeing the guy, she later told me. She just didn't tell me about it. Nothing ever came of it, she said; they never actually slept together.

Even though nothing had happened (and nothing would ever happen—as I said, Nancy would never cheat on me), it didn't matter. There was now no safe time for me anymore, no time for my frazzled mind to rest, to renew, to revel in the temporary hope of no hope I would feel when she was home with me. I had lost it all! She would do what she wanted when she wanted, come home, not come home, whatever, and I wouldn't know when it was happening, or when it was not happening, when to rest, when to cry, when to smash a glass, when to face the dawn. It would never be late again, never be early again. She had blotted out the last shredded fragments of time for me, and left me with no time to know, no time to smile, no time to be unafraid. One hour was the same as the next, and I was trapped, without even the gradual pacing of the clock toward death to reassure me that things could change. I had nothing more to put my arms around except for an empty body, empty for me, a soul beside me in the night, in the dream embrace of strangers, anyone, anytime, not me. I was a hollow shadow looking down a hill, afraid and barefoot in the snow, with no one around to save me, no one to push me. I was alone, my face facing the winter wind as it churned in remembrance, whispering ugly childhood.

It was now time for me to go home, again, as I did over and over again. Home to the snow and heart attacks, and the cool crisp stagnation wafting through the Hanukkah air. Time for me to return as I did eternal to the living room of rotting dialects and frugal corpses celebrating life with a barbecue like so many crushed ants on the backyard patio. Death, birth, breathing, choking, what's the difference in deep Queens, in my life? None, anon, rerun. Life is your bankbook hidden in the underwear drawer. Return, retell, regress, rebirth, ruin! I would go back again in shapes of misery, to embrace the unremarkable and try to call it fortune. I'm coming home mother, have some bagels on the table for me. I'm coming home father, let's get on the ground under the car and see if we can figure where that sound is coming

from. I'm coming home, old neighbors who remember me as a boy; don't be afraid to stare and
whisper at my returnal presence. I'm coming
home, to assume my rightful place at the corner
of nowhere and nuts-up-my-ass. I'll leave my
cock behind, Nancy—I won't be needing it any
longer. I am going home to the land of borscht,
baseball, angioplasties, and angel asses playing
Mah Jongg. Home, home, home, here I come.
Prepare my childhood bed, draw down the covers, wash the sheets, wipe my ass for me, and I,
having left as a man, return as a child,
sphincterless, filthy with isolation, horny without a dick, to be held by no one, nowhere, atop a
hill, covered by snow, surrounded by the Jews of
Fuckdom, trying to become a man again. "Welcome home, our dear child," they will say, "alone
as we like you to be, without your shlong as we
like you to be, defeated as we like you to be."

    I made plans to leave New Orleans and
return to my parents' house in Queens. I had
some vague idea about going back to graduate
school and getting an apartment in Manhattan
once I had saved up some money doing god knows
what. I made my decision in April, but trying to
live on in indecisiveness and false hope, I kept
putting off my departure until finally I bought a
plane ticket (after my parents sent me the

money), and set my departure date for the first of June. I was to leave the life I knew, hated, and was running away from, to return to the life I had known, hated, and had run away from just a few months before. All comes full circle, I thought, especially pain.

~

On my last night in New Orleans, Nancy and I decided to have a final meal together. I went to the store to buy a bottle of wine for the occasion, and decided that before returning home I wanted to see the Mississippi one last time, alone. As I walked along the river, gazing out at the West Bank straight ahead, the lights of the bridge to my right, the endlessness of the water to my left, a sensation of tranquility swept over me. Thoughts passed through my head quickly and peacefully, thoughts of ALP, of Nancy, of where I was going, and how I had gotten here. The night was quiet and dark, and the city, for maybe the first time, felt like it was mine, like it finally understood me. In the distance, somewhere, a man sat and played guitar, singing "A Change Is Gonna Come." Was this a sign to leave, or a sign to stay? Or just a meaningless song?

After a few more minutes of contemplation, I left the river. As I walked through Jackson Square, a man approached me and asked if I knew where I was going. I said yes without looking at him and walked on ahead through the winding streets of the French Quarter, a strange place in a strange city that I had visited once, in the light of my life, and was departing from in what felt like the twilight of my life. Still I had to walk, to go home one more night, so I could leave home tomorrow to go home and try to find another home, *my* home this time.

I roamed, I thought, I whispered to myself so I couldn't hear, past strange wood-frame houses attached to empty balconies that meant everything to me, and past unknown girls with closed eyes who didn't smile at me. When I got back to our street, Nancy was sitting outside on the sill of one of our huge windows, crying. She said I had been gone for a long time. She had been worried.

We spent the rest of the night eating, drinking, and watching television. Nancy got mad because I called Stephen and spoke to him on the phone for awhile, but I eventually convinced her not to be angry because this was to be our last night together. She agreed with me for a change. Later, we didn't have sex. Nothing changes.

I didn't sleep well that night, tossing and turning endlessly, before waking for good soon after the birth of the Cajun dawn. As I saw the

161

first rays of the almost summer-sun through the cracks in our broken windows, I left Nancy asleep in our bed in the loft, and went down to the couch. There I sat alone, staring at the apartment around me, the ramshackle shack I would soon be leaving, our home that from now on would be her home. Had it ever been my home? There were marks of me everywhere, from gashes in the wall to invisible footprints upon the floor. I had paced a lifetime and back in this place, and had felt all the pain that I cared to know in this lifetime.

I looked up at Nancy sleeping in the loft. Did I really love her? Had I ever really loved her? Did it matter? Had it ever mattered? Suddenly, I was seized with panic at the thought of the next day's plane ride. I didn't want to go! But, I couldn't stay—she had seen to that. I tried to convince myself that everything would be okay, that once home, again, I would find my way, again, and would never again feel so alone as I did that morning, on an empty Southern couch at the break of day, in a New Orleans apartment with a woman who always said she didn't love me. I decided to smile, if only for a moment, if only because I didn't know who loved me.

~

My plane left at noon. Nancy had to go to work at the same time I had to go to the airport.

She cried and told me she couldn't believe it was over. We hugged more than kissed as I hailed a cab. I watched her disappear around the corner, as she headed toward her job, toward her life without me. She was gone. Then I got into the back of the taxi, and headed toward my life without her. I was gone.

As the cab sped away from the French Quarter, I felt a brief surge of raw determination and correctness in my being. I knew I had made the right decision to get away from her, from this place, and to restart my life in the rightness of my birthplace. This feeling lasted seconds, maybe a minute. Then it all unraveled as if I had been shot. Fear—no, not fear, but total and complete and utter and all-encompassing and never-abating and long-acting and heart-seizing and vomit-inducing terror—gripped me. The cab arrived at the airport. I paid the cabdriver. I could hardly talk. I got out of the cab. I could hardly walk. I found my airline. I could hardly act. I managed to find my gate. I managed to check my bag. I limped onto the plane. The plane took off. I sat in my seat and stared straight ahead. I thought about asking the pilot to turn back. The stewardess asked if I was okay. I told her I was okay. I refused to eat the in-flight meal. I tried to fall asleep. I couldn't sleep. The plane landed. I got

off the plane. My mother met me at the airport. I
lifted her off the ground in a show of mock en-
thusiasm, hoping I could fool myself into believ-
ing something. We drove back to my parents'
house. I walked in the door. I noticed how low
their ceilings were compared to ours in New Orleans. My father told me to get a good night's
sleep so tomorrow I could start looking for a job.
I woke up the next day and made plane reservations to go back to New Orleans. I called Nancy
and told her. Nancy told me not to come back
because she would lose all respect for me. I canceled my reservations. I moved back into my
childhood room. I stopped showering and eating
regularly. I had frequent panic attacks. I made
more than $1,000 worth of long-distance calls to
Nancy and to Stephen and Mona in St. Louis. My
father refused to talk to me after the phone bill
came. My mother was redecorating the house and
was more interested in wallpaper than me. I got
a job as a waiter across the street from my old
junior high school and quit after two hours when
my mother came in to see how I was doing. I got
a job driving a taxi but quit after one day. I
stopped looking for a job. I decided to move back
to Philadelphia where I had been happy in the
past. I started to see a shrink. I had to walk three
miles to my shrink appointments because no one

in my family would drive me. He smiled a lot and didn't help me. I wrote long impassioned love letters to Nancy, who never answered them. I slept on my friend Paul's floor for a few weeks because I couldn't stand being in my parents' house any longer. Paul left town on vacation. I went back to my parents' house. I lost my mind. I went to the bank. I stole some money that had been entrusted to me by my grandmother many years before. I got up at dawn one Saturday morning. I think it was VJ Day. I showered. I shaved. I packed a small bag. I took a bus to the subway to Amtrak to Philadelphia to another train to a plane to New Orleans to a taxi to the French Quarter to Nancy's bar where I sat down, and, as her face turned red as a bleeding devil, I said "surprise," and she said to some girl she was talking to, "this is my ex-boyfriend Rob who has come to surprise me NOW," and I, gaunt and thin after a summer full of misery, simply said, "I would like a beer, Nancy!"

~

After my summer-wrong emotional confinement in Queens, I went on a binge of booze and sex when I got back to New Orleans. I slept until it was too dark to see, drank until I couldn't see, and fucked Nancy until she couldn't see. She had missed fucking me, she said, though I think she really just missed fucking someone (she had never hooked up during my time away), so when I returned to the city of the lemonade Jesus a young, able-bodied whore of a man, we fucked a lot, at least for a week or so, until Nancy had had a satisfactory number of orgasms. Then, things returned to their normal state of conjugal indifference between us.

To add to my already prick-kicking summer, during my time incarcerated away Nancy had, real ironically, gotten a bartending gig at that house of lesbos licking and Arkansas alienation, The Cage. While this was indeed a strange turn of events if you think about it, I was having too much fun drinking and fucking to think about it—to think of implications and echoes and shades of meaning and things such as that. Therefore, I didn't think about what Nancy working at The Cage meant to me at all. I now considered it just another bar.

Since The Cage didn't open until midnight, Nancy and I started living the life of the alcoholic vampire. We didn't get up until nine, post morning. Upon waking, we would flip on the television and watch *Star Trek: The Next Generation*, while Nancy ate "breakfast" and got ready to go to work. After she left, I would eat a leisurely "breakfast" myself, listen to some music, take a shower, have a few swigs of whatever was lying around the house, and go out at about two in the morning to begin my day in the dark.

I would spend the hours between two and six bouncing heartily and happily around the holes of the Quarter, drinking in joyful isolation. Around dawn I would head to The Cage for a nightcap and a glimpse of my Nancy. Then, after last call was called, I would go to the twenty-four-hour bar next door and wait for her to get off work. Most mornings Ivor, a pleasant fellow who drove a tour bus through the historic Quarter and liked to get properly liquored up before he began the day's sightseeing, would wait with me. After I had had a few shots with him, Nancy would usually show up around seven, and after we drank a final shot with Ivor the bus driver, we would be alone, to face the Bloody Mary morning.

We would spend the next few hours talking a little, laughing a little, and drinking a lot. Then, as the morning sun shone in the ten to twelve slot, and evening could no longer hide us, Nancy and I would stumble home, watch another episode of *Star Trek* (the original series), eat another "breakfast," and fall into blissful four-Advil slumber.

This went on for a month. I had as much fun as fuck! I had gone in one wild summer from the depths of misery, anxiety and terror, to the heights of drifting, drunken, and debauched existence. Drink, sleep, eat, Trek. Endless meaninglessness going nowhere down the alcohol-soaked gullet of remarkable indifference. I didn't want any "direction" in my life, didn't want to go anywhere but nowhere—every attempt I had made in my life to go "somewhere" had led nowhere, so I figured that if I tried to go "nowhere," maybe I would end up somewhere. Or something like that.

However, all things must pass. After about three weeks, Nancy grew impatient with my presence, as she felt we were slowly falling into our same old routine. So, even though we had had fun for awhile, and a little sex to boot, she now wished me gone. I left and went back to my parents' house, where I stayed for one day. The next morning, I got on a train and headed to Philadelphia, where I was going to live again. I was returning to the locale of my happiest times, to try and be happy once again, and I was happy at the thought of returning unhappily to a place where I had once been happy, in order to try to be happy again.

Well, you might wonder, why wasn't I upset at the prospect of leaving Nancy behind in New Orleans forever? No tears, no breathing difficulties, no terror-stricken panic? Prozac? Well, I wasn't exactly going to Philadelphia empty-handed. I had convinced Nancy to join me in the city of brotherly humping! While I was away over the first part of the summer, she had decided to straighten out her life and get a "normal" job. She professed to being sick of the life she was leading in New Orleans, and the life she had led before that in New York, and before that in Boston, and before that in Florida, and before that, etc. She was tired of the drinking, the nameless fucking, the late hours, and the lousy pay. Well, mostly the lousy pay. She had a friend in New York who was a nurse and made lots of money and did lots of drugs and worked whenever she wanted. So, Nancy decided she would become a nurse, even if she was a bit squeamish around blood and shit.

Her first step in this new life was to decide where to attend nursing school. Initially, she was going to remain in New Orleans and do her schooling there. One night, however, during my month of Caligulafication, while I was chatting half-drunk with her about god knows what, I started to reminisce about my previous life in Philadelphia, the city of the utterly bored. I had been happy back then back there, I told her, when I had been innocent and young, and life seemed

opened to nothing but possibility, before I had
met ALP (and before I had met her). I told her
about the simple splendor and peace of the city
of Philadelphia, where everyone knew everyone,
the rents were cheap, and the bars closed at two.
Upon hearing the words "bars closed at two,"
Nancy's face went from adrift to awake. She had
never liked New Orleans, for some reason hating
the stupidity, open racism, and all-night alcohol-
ism. She asked me if Philadelphia wasn't very far
from New York City, which for her was the center of the universe. About one hundred miles, I
told her. "Hmm," she replied, "only one hundred
miles!"

Two weeks after I moved back to Philadelphia, I stole more money from my grandmother, wired it to Nancy in New Orleans, and
she came on the next train (or a few days later)
to Philadelphia. I had brought my baby home,
and now we were going to bring our disintegrating relationship to new lows, beginning our dysfunction in a third metropolis of these United
States! Three homes (for those counting), two
souls (for those praying), and one love (two so
far for those reading).

~

I moved into a small one-bedroom apartment, while Nancy got a place of her own a few

blocks away. For the first few months, we continued to hang out together all the time, never fucking, always drinking. It was just like New Orleans, only worse. My panic and fear had grown stronger and deeper, and even the hope, the false hope, that I had in New Orleans that we would somehow work things out, was gone. There was no future, no present, no past. We spent day after day, night after night, at my place, at her place, eating, watching television, and drinking until we passed out alone in each other's arms. We didn't ever have sex, not even by accident. She wasn't going to start nursing school for a year, and I was earning a barely sustainable living working as a nude model throughout the art schools of the city of the brotherly unclothed. Our lives apart were as sad as our life together. I was nowhere, she was nowhere, we were nowhere.

(Now, while some of you may chuckle in purient excitement, the nude-modeling world is not all it is all cracked up to be. It was usually cold in the studios, so I was not hard [you could get fired, supposedly, if you got a hard-on while modeling. Reason for leaving previous job?] up on the stage, where I posed until my limbs went to sleep and atrophied, twenty minutes at a time, with a five-minute break [union rules]. Sometimes, I modeled with others—mostly strippers and homeless men. One time it was Caesar, a middle-aged African-American gentleman whose balls gave off the mustiest stench one could imagine and allow me to remember to this day what a man's unwashed cock smells like. On another occasion, I posed with a stripper who had a shaved cunt. For our pose, she laid on the stage, while I sat in a chair, staring down at her. My direct line of sight was her snatch, the line that divided her body from here to in there. How I got to know that shaved piece of flesh, that crack in my eye, desire unmasked and unfurled for my general perusal, six hours a day, three days a week, for two weeks. After lunch she used to fart into my face. This job paid ten dollars an hour, no taxes taken out.)

~

Then, after the first few months passed, Nancy started to go out more and more upon the unquenched night, in search of something to satisfy the desires in her that I could not satisfy. And, as it had been in New Orleans, I went crazy the nights I was alone without her. I was afraid to leave my apartment, afraid to get even a simple beer in a simple bar, as I was afraid that I would see her, and would find out what I had always been afraid I would find out. So I stayed home night after night, carousing the inner trap of my endangered mind, fretting about where the hell she was, and why the hell she was, and where the hell I was, and what the hell I was. Every night I was alone while no one with her was alone, and she was every place except my place, and I could be no place, because she would be there, and near her I was starting to feel more and more that I had no place.

Eventually, she started to see other people, though it was nothing serious, she said. But to me, everything was serious. There was now no one for me to turn to, again, nothing to save me, again, nowhere for me to go, again. Why had I thought it would be different when we moved here? It was the same, it was always the same, it was worse than the same—it was insane!

A day, any day, all days, any days, every-day, became the same day. I couldn't eat, I couldn't sleep, I couldn't relax, I couldn't breathe. I would sleep fitfully at night, if I slept at all, tossing and turning, getting up and pacing, cursing, stomping, wondering where she was, wondering where I was. I would usually relax around dawn, much like I had in New Orleans, maybe even sleeping for a few hours. Around noon, however, I would spring up, agitated and angry, full of the tremors of nausea, and run to the toilet. This would happen Monday, Tuesday, Wednesday,

Thursday...etc.! The same feelings, the same dread, the same changing unchanging until the next day, when it would all begin again, unchanged.

To describe one day is to describe all the days, though I remember it as if it were one never-ending day. Waking up sweaty and alone, my head pounding after a night of fear and loathing. Entering the narrow, paint-chipped bathroom with the imitation wood floor linoleum. Getting down on my hands and knees to kneel beside the bowl, peering down into the bluish water. Sticking my fingers down my throat—once, twice, thrice—until I could feel the first hints of reverse peristalsis. Gagging, and spitting, until it would all come up, and then go down, splat into the open water. Then, wiping my mouth and looking into the bowl, to see what I had left. (Usually, since I hadn't eaten, it would be yellow. "Yellow," I would think, "what a weird color to come out of my body.")

Then the pacing and spewing would begin again, as I screamed out loud to myself in the empty apartment. "When the fuck is she gonna call? Every fuckin' night the same thing! Drunk, fuckin' drunk, sleeps with any fuckin' person that looks at her. With that stupid drunken smile of hers. She looks like a feeble-minded infant. I know she's not home. She could be—but what if she is with someone? I don't want to look stupid by leaving a thousand messages on her machine. Though if I did I bet you then she would know how I feel but I don't want to look stupid. I have self-control. Sure this shit sucks but she doesn't know it, no one knows it because I keep it under control. Sure it's all fucked up, but no one else knows about it so it's all right. Fuck, fuck why doesn't she call?"

This would go on for awhile, half an hour, an hour, these eternal monologues to my madness. Then, as my feet became increasingly sore from pacing, and my throat dry and scratchy from vomiting and yelling, I would find my way to my bed, where I would fall flat on my back and stare at the ceiling, observing the cracks in the plaster, seeing if their pattern had altered since the last time, an hour before, I had laid there.

At some point, I would develop an intense hard-on. Lying on the bed, I would take it in my hand, and start thinking of her, of her fucking someone else. I would imagine her long ivory legs covered with sweat, her moist and supple vagina rubbing, to the point of ecstasy, the upper leg of some faceless person, some faceless woman. Probably some black chick. She always told me how much she liked black women, how the only woman that had ever made her cum was black. I knew that if she had gotten her way last night, she was in bed beside a beautiful black woman, the two asleep and intertwined in a post-fuck sweat upon her mulatto mattress.

I would start to rub my palm up and down over my smooth dick, thinking of the two girls bumping and grinding, the shared moisture of their organs driving them to moans of delight. In my balls I could feel the cum forming, the hot jism getting ready to shoot, to explode all over my chest, the sheets, the floor, the whole fuckin' world. "Yeah, Nancy, fuck that pussy, put your tongue on those fuckin' ebony nipples, stick your tongue down her scream-muffled throat. Fuck her fuck her fuck her tits fuck her. Nancy fuck her rub your wet pussy against hers oh yeah fuck Nancy pound her fucking yes fuckin' a pounding oh Nancy oh Nancy oh Nancy fuck me fuck her fuck her fuck me fuck me yes yeah fuckin' a fuck me fuck me fuck me fuck...YES!"

I would fall asleep, dead to my world, for maybe an hour if I were lucky. Then I would awaken and, since she still hadn't called, the need to run, to escape, would suddenly surge through me. "Fuck it," I would say to myself, "I've got to get the hell out of here. I can't wait for the damn phone anymore!" I would throw on what ever clothes were lying on the floor, and bound down the stairs out into the open air, out into the world.

~

My usual path took me down Eighteenth Street, through narrow side streets that housed pretty red Philly row houses. Then, after about five blocks of walking uncomfortably, trying to avoid the gaze of anyone who happened to look at me, I would reach Rittenhouse Square, the center of town. At the entrance, I would pause for a few moments and stare at the people who were in the park. People sitting on benches talking to one another. People lying on the grass sunning themselves. Girls whizzing by on roller skates. Old men sitting in the shade under the tall tress, staring into space, feeding the birds. Human sites, human interaction, people together, people alone, people living, people dying, people not quite sure, people certain. I was completely removed from all of it, from all of them, from everything except my own internal horror show. I would think for a moment of sitting on a bench like anyone else, or lying on the grass in the sun like anyone else. But, I wouldn't stop, couldn't stop, couldn't sit, couldn't be with them. They would see me, see my fears, see my tears, see all the years I had spent with her. I had to keep going to where I belonged, further along, where there was no one, where there was nothing.

I would leave the Square and walk up Walnut Street to where she lived. This was where I always wound up, in front of the pizza place directly across from her apartment building. I would stand on the corner and stare up at her two tiny fourth-floor windows, trying to answer my unanswerable questions. Had she come home last night and passed out drunk in her bed with the make-up still stuck to her face? Was she alone? I would try to answer all of this and more by staring at her windows, as if I could figure something out from the movement of the curtains, or the way the light hit the glass, or how much the window was raised. Something, anything, that would calm the somersault of nerves that shook my belly in continuous turmoil. I would stare at the curtains, and watch the wind blow them away from the glass. Then the wind would recede, and the curtains would fall back into place.

All of a sudden, I would rush towards the pay phone on the corner. Maybe she had called and left a message on my machine while I was standing there staring at her windows! A surge of certainty would shoot through me. My life had purpose for the moment. I would whip out my phone card, and pay two dollars a minute for the privilege of calling home on the chance that her voice would be on the answering machine. I would dial nine numbers, wait for the tone, dial nine more, wait for another tone, then dial my own number. My voice, I'm not home now, leave a message after the tone, thank you. I would then type in the three-digit code to check my messages, and, after a brief pause, hear nothing back except a recording of me typing in the three-digit code.

My stomach would immediately drop onto the sidewalk, and the fear would shoot even more strongly through my body. I might even cry for a second. Then I would straighten myself up, arch my back proudly, and walk away from the phone, away from her building, to head to where I belonged, where I always ended up—the river!

Two blocks away was a bridge that ran over the Schuylkill River. Halfway across this bridge was a stairway that went beneath the highway, down to the side of the river. I would disappear down this stairway, and quickly find myself surrounded by a strange vacuous silence, the sound of 3000-pound cars pounding the roadway overhead being the only thing to disturb this sudden and bizarre peace. I would walk about fifty feet, though a field of dead grass and discarded garbage, until I came to the edge of the river. I would stop at the point where land met water and stare into the murky dark, thinking of home and childhood. For some reason, this place under the Schuylkill River, beneath the highway, always reminded me of Queens, and of my youth. Happier times would waft into my head, memories of summers when I was a kid. No school for two months! Staying up all night calling Sports Phone to get the latest score on the West Coast ballgames, to find out how my Dodgers were doing. Not another soul was awake, and I controlled the night. How great that late night world was! The best of times!

For a moment I was gone. Then, as I stared further into the river, further into Philadelphia, further into my present condition, I would wonder how I could ever have been happy without her.

I would continue along the river, under the highway for a little while, until I came out under the open sky into an unkempt field of grass, broken bottles, and assorted tires. For a second, I would feel free. A second later, it would all come back, and I would stick my fingers down my throat and cough up more yellow shit. Why do I love her so, I would wonder, why do I need her so?

As I moved further along the grassy ruins

of this field alongside the river, I would start to notice the people around me. Yes, there were people here, but I had no fear of showing myself to them, since I knew they felt as I did. I was among the underside of society. This was home for them, this was where they came to sleep each night, to rest up for the following day's useless wandering. All their belongings, so much shit in a bag, slung over their shoulders, or just weakly hanging by their sides, dragged a few feet, or a few miles, and then stop for a rest and a stare into their own remembrances, into their own despair and nothingness, into their own street hardened-delusions. Here under the street they resided, I resided, beside the deserted banks of the polluted river, beneath the automobiles of Ivy League kids going back and forth between Center City and the University of Pennsylvania. Beneath the asphalt gateway to a better life, a first class education, a fine job, a dutiful spouse, a huge house in the suburbs, and winters in Aspen. Beneath the rain and snow and sun and dog shit they walked, I walked, untouched and undisturbed, past nothing, from nothing, toward nothing. Step, sit, shit, wander. Tomorrow, today, yesterday, lice. At night they avoided the lights and hid beneath the street, sleeping by the banks of the American river, undisturbed except by the sounds of cars going somewhere overhead, undisturbed except for the frozen rain in fall and the river bugs in summer and the fresh air all the time. Plenty of time for them, for me, to rest, to think of nothing, to go nowhere, to be silent and alone. They could jerk off in the open air, thinking of the tight twats of unmade Ivy League bimbos driving BMWs overhead. To sleep, perchance to cream. To cum all over the street, to lie in their own lifeblood, to have the dogs sniff it before being pulled away by their masters. The smells of the street, so fantastic, so full of existence, so bright and clear under the wordless sky. Stare, think, cum, run. Love a million unknown girls, maybe they'll take you home to mother one day. I loved one girl, who would never take me home. We all lived in the land of miracles and dreams, of anyone getting everything anytime.

I would pass through the people-strewn field, toward the train tracks in the distance, skipping past crushed glass and random pieces of automobile and person. I would think of Neil Young, of journey (not the band), of ALP. "Better down the road without that load," I would sing as I approached the tracks. The tracks! God, they were so beautiful! Just like tracks should be, overgrown with grass, covered in rubbish, coming from who knows where, stretching out beyond where the eye can see. I was the poet of the tracks, walking in perfect trochaic hexameter towards her heart, following the twisting and turning steel, forging my own path along what had been forged by the history of my people. In the old days, before WWII, the coal, the metals, the millions of goods that must have traveled along these tracks, everyday, everywhere, when there was no grass, no glass, but clean perfect steel to lead and love the earth. Oh, if she could feel me now, feel the blood in my veins pumping, the blood in my dick flowing. If only I could take this feeling, past these tracks, past the river, over the bridge, down Walnut Street, through her front door, and up the four flights of stairs into her worthiness. I would ram my cock into her indifference, bleed her dry, and then refill her with my reverent cum. I would devour her as she dreamed of me and creamed of me. She would never be able to forget me!

~

Eventually I would grow tired, tired of all of it, and begin to retrace my steps back to civilization. Through the grassy field, along the riverrun reversed, up the stairs, and back unto Walnut Street I would go, heading toward Nancy's apartment, toward those two life-altering windows. As I looked up, I would see the curtains, and the glass, and realize that nothing had changed. I would go to the pay phone, type in eighteen numbers, hear nothing and hang up. It was now time for me to head back home. I would avoid Rittenhouse Square on the way back, and head up another quiet side street, past nothing particular, towards nothing special. Just another path to mutter to myself alone along.

A feeling of intense terror would well up in me as I got closer to my apartment, usually developing concurrently with an intense hard-on. If there was no one on the street, I would put my hands down my shorts, just to feel it, the smoothness, the rigidity, the essence of my manhood. This was my life. Train tracks, jerking off, and phone calls to myself to hear no one. My whole existence was a waste, a sham, a joke on myself. Why couldn't I have just died as a boy, I would think to myself, or even better, just like George Bailey, never been born. Whatever. Hollywood. My life as a film, an unending rerun unchanging.

I would arrive at my block, arrive at my building, turn the key in the security door, open the door, enter my apartment, be greeted happily by my cat, pet the cat, turn left into the bedroom, and look down at the answering machine on the floor. It would be flashing, one time, over and over again. I would bend down and press the flashing red message button:

"Hi cutie. It's me. What are you up to? Sorry I didn't call you earlier, but I had to get up early this morning to mail something, and then I went shopping at the health food store, and then I sat in Rittenhouse Square for a little while. I went out last night, but had a lousy time—got in at about two-thirty. Call me when you get in, I'd like to see you tonight, maybe we could have some dinner, get a movie, and some wine. Talk to you later." Beep.

The smile would return to my soul. My whole body would be enraptured and electrified. "She loves me, she loves me, she loves me," I would shout! The world was now perfect, absolutely perfect! I would immediately forget the previous hours, the yellow bile, my aching feet, the river, the tracks, the homeless! None of it mattered anymore. She loved me! Well, maybe she didn't actually love me, but close enough. She wanted to see me, to eat with me, to drink with me. She wanted to be with me! The past would fade away. Emotions from a few minutes back seemed of another time, long past, centuries before my rebirth, a story I had once heard and had remained in my memory, but which I had never actually experienced.

I would call her and tell her I would be right over. Then it was back down Eighteenth

Street, through narrow side streets that housed pretty red Philly row houses. After about five blocks of walking confidently, happily returning the gaze of anyone who happened to look my way, I would reach Rittenhouse Square, the center of town. At the entrance, I would pause for a few moments and stare at the people who were in the park. People sitting on benches talking, people folding up their blankets as the sun moved into the evening, girls whizzing by on roller skates. Old men sitting and staring into space under the tall trees and feeding the birds, men in suits walking home, another day's useful energy spent! Human sites, human interaction, people together, people alone, people living, people dying, people not quite sure, people certain. I felt so connected to all of them! They were part of me, and I was part of them, eternal, endless, through day and night, and life and death!

I would skip out of the park and head up Walnut Street, passing a crowded pizza parlor and an unoccupied pay phone. I wouldn't even look up at the windows as I leapt into Nancy's building, ran up four flights of stairs, four flights of light, four flights and a knock on her door. I would hear the floors creak, hear her approach the door to let me in, and I was there.

III

When I was in seventh grade, my three main interests were baseball, the Beatles, and not showering. As far as baseball was concerned, I was a fanatic, following each game that my beloved Dodgers played out in Los Angeles, three thousand miles away with a three-hour time difference, as if it was a religious experience. If the Dodgers won, god was good. If the Dodgers lost, god was a bitch. Good god, bitch god, all determined by the final score of a ballgame at two o'clock in the morning, when the West Coast games generally ended in my Queens childhood.

As far as the Beatles were concerned, they were god themselves. We used to argue amongst ourselves, the debates of twelve-year olds, about who was the best rock group of all time. It was of course the Beatles, except when I would throw Jan and Dean into the mix (don't ask!).

As far as showering was concerned, it was once a week, Sunday night, unless my father wondered aloud by Wednesday who was smelling up the damn house.

Stephen and I became friends when we were twelve years old because of our shared love of baseball, the Beatles and not showering. Like me, he was a religious sort around baseball and the Beatles, and like me, a regular non-showerer. Thus we bonded because we were one in mind, spirit, and body odor. We stayed friends through the many ups and downs of childhood, high school pimples, the death of John Lennon, and the increased frequency of showering that adolescence generally awakens in the male body.

After high school, Stephen went away to college, while I remained in New York to go to school. Rather than separating us, the distance brought us closer together, and by the time Stephen and I graduated college, we were the best of friends. After college, he decided to attend graduate school in Philadelphia, and about a year after he moved there (and after I had finished about a year of grad school myself), I joined him in the city of brotherly blood. I thought it would be great for us to live in the same city again, so we could do all the things together that we had always talked about, and dreamed about, during three-hour late-night long distance phone calls.

~

At the time I moved to Philly, Stephen was involved with a woman named Mona. She was from somewhere in the upper Midwest, and worked as a photojournalist. The two of them had initially hooked up at some political convention, enjoying a weekend of intense licking, sucking, fucking, and I presume cumming. Despite the fact that they lived in different parts of the country, they had stayed in touch after their initial fuckfest, and after about a year of the long-distance thing, they fell in deep and everlasting love.

About two months after my arrival in the city of the motherly thumb, Mona came to visit Stephen. I hadn't met her yet, but had heard many wonderful things about her from Stephen. He was excited that the two of us meet, his best friend and his best girl. I was excited to meet Mona as well, to meet the woman who made my best friend's head spin, his voice race, and his dick hard.

On a cold street corner on a cold winter night, I met Mona for the first time. Stephen had arranged for the three of us to meet over dinner, but I was, as usual, late. As I was rushing toward the restaurant where we were supposed to meet, I noticed, from about a block away, a shapeless figure standing on the corner, looking nowhere particular, waiting for someone particular. As I moved closer, this shapeless outline gained a shape, a nice feminine shape, with large breasts in a tight black turtleneck beneath an unbuttoned black leather coat, a muscular ass framed by skin-tight black denim, and shoulder length red hair blowing freely in the light winter breeze.

I walked toward her, and my eyes met her eyes. Her eyes met mine back. Eyes met, a moment, two. We didn't stop. Three. I felt something. "Mona?" "Robert?" We said each other's names as we looked into each other's souls. Just then Stephen, who had been down the street on a pay phone calling my house, came by. "Hey, there you are!" Mona and I unlocked our eyes, moment over. But remembered.

Over dinner, I told Mona embarrassing stories about Stephen, such as the time when we were teenagers and the toilet didn't work in his house, so he scooped the leftover remains of another day's useless energy spent (shit) out of the bowl with his bare hands. We all laughed, hardy har har. (During those times, shit on the hands was considered a Derridean transgression, or a sign, or signifier really, of the hole of the Other.) Mona then started telling stories herself, tales about the Midwestern stoic farm life that she had grown up in, a world where men would bobsled across frozen lakes with chainsaws, cutting off dead cow heads that stuck out of the ice because the stupid cows didn't move during the ice storm when the lake started to freeze around them. "Interesting," I replied. "Dialectical," Stephen replied. "My life," Mona replied. Over the next few hours, I drank more, Mona drank a lot more, Mona talked even more, and all three of us laughed until we could no more, as we all hardy-har-harred-to one fucked up story of Mona's after another.

At some point, Stephen and I excused ourselves and went into the little man's room to relieve ourselves. Standing beside each other stall to stall, Stephen asked me what I thought of Mona. "She's great!" I responded as I zipped my pants up. With nice eyes, I thought.

Eventually we closed the restaurant, and decided to go to some legal after-hours dance club downtown. In Philadelphia you could operate a legal after-hours place as long as you had the proper permits and paid off the cops, whereas in New York you just paid off the cops.

Drunk off our asses. Especially Mona and I. Stephen wanted to go home almost immediately, as he had to work this lame security guard job the next day where he slept and read Foucault while guarding a house built on a radon site. Or something like that. Ha, ha, I thought to myself, you're not going anywhere! I am drunk, Mona is drunk, and we all need to dance the night away! "Be a good boy, Stephen, and fetch us some more beers, will ya!"

Dancing in the glare of darkness. The pounding of the drums and the thump of the bass twisted together in a transmogrified orgasm of smoke and water, bodies oozing sweat, my mind oozing dreams as I imagined myself somewhere, nowhere, everywhere. Dancing until my cock was wet and the night a spinning fantasy.

Mona started to dance with me. Or maybe I started to dance with her. She was behind me, that much I am certain of, even in the sketchy corridors of dance hall memory. After this, the story diverges, the tale takes shape, and it is a distinct shape depending on whom you talk to. In the interest of fairness, here are both sides presented for your impartial judgment:

Robert: While we were dancing together, Mona grabbed my genitalia from behind because she claimed I was messing with her, and therefore, to teach me a lesson, she grabbed said balls. In order to repel this violation of my most prized manhood, I fell back upon Mona, and in the innocent confusion that followed, Mona and I ended up on the dance floor in the sixty-nine position, biting on each other's privates. Teeth on the mouth with no teeth. End of testimony.

Mona: (Testifying in absentia, by memory of

Robert) Maybe I grabbed his balls, maybe I didn't! I just know that all of a sudden, this guy who I hardly know, and who has been messing with me all night (not that I minded—he had nice eyes), flipped me on my back, and started nibbling on my crotch. Teeth on the mouth with no teeth. End of testimony.

Robert (cross-examining his own memory): Yes, my dear Mona, that is all well and good, but didn't you later testify in an intimate moment with Robert that you in fact enjoyed feeling his teeth on your crotch through your nice tight jeans, that you in fact were infatuated with Robert the moment your eyes met on the street corner?

Mona: What? Yes. I don't know. Maybe. (Sparse stoic statement from a Midwesterner.)

Robert: I thus offer to the court of Robert's imagination Robert's opinion that Mona in fact wanted to get Robert's teeth on her crotch all that night, and that she in fact pulled him down onto the dance floor to get said teeth on said crotch!

Mona: I object!

Robert: Your honor, I present into evidence Mona's crotch, with said teeth marks on the pubic hair, which my expert witness myself has in fact certified, through dental records and the fact that I am writing this book, as being the aforementioned molars of one R.E. Lasner of Queens, New York, and other places sometimes.

Audible gasps from the assembled masses in Robert's courtroom-infected brain.

Judge: Order, order!

Mona: I object! This is a travesty of justice!

Robert: No further questions.

Judge: May the testimony of the accused, and his memory, be stricken from the record.

Verdict: We have a hung jury. Very well hung. All's fair in love and after-hours dance clubs.

Mona and I agreed to disagree about the dance hall incident, and over the next few months we became good friends, as she and Stephen continued their long distance relationship, with corresponding expensive long distance phone bills, accumulation of frequent flier miles, and cum on lonely late night sheets. Finally, after about a year of playing weekend spouse, the two of them decided to take the next step and move in together. They chose St. Louis as the place to start their new life, as Stephen had finished his master's and had been admitted to a Ph.D. program in the city of the silent arch, while Mona had gotten herself a fine job at a prestigious magazine.

According to the phone calls and letters I received from him over the next several months, Stephen was happy in old St. Loo, the home of Chuck Berry and Stan Musial, who my grandfather used to say was the greatest ballplayer ever to play the game. He told me he was enjoying school, and that Mona was enjoying her new job. And, he said, they were enjoying each other! Their life seemed to me to be trouble-free, unlike what mine was in these post-ALP, pre-Nancy hangover days of confusion and delusion. However, while things seemed perfect for them on the surface, there was a slight problem below the surface, one that would grow into a larger problem above the surface over the next nine months or so, a little eight-pound, four-ounce problem named Leopold. "So, she's pregnant," Stephen tells me one night on the phone. "That is, ah, um, great, right?" I respond. "Well, yes of course, it's a wonderful thing. I'm looking forward to being a father. I mean, you know what Lacan always said about fatherhood, and I love that Cat Stevens song." Yes, Lacan and Cat Stevens. Stephen was definitely ready for fatherhood.

Despite this unplanned change in plans, and corresponding size in Mona's belly, I thought life was still grand for the two of them. Stephen had a keen mind and an inquiring intellect, and I easily imagined him as a college professor one day, a disheveled genius shaking up the world of ideas. Though I didn't know her as well, I also imagined a bright future for Mona. I had seen some of her work, and she was quite talented. Her specialty was photographing abandoned buildings in the middle of the West, in the middle of nowhere, right before a storm would hit. Fascinating stuff, like a Norwegian nightmare in the middle of a washing machine, silence combined with complete upheaval as the echoes of destruction approached. Breathtaking! She would then write these little poems to go along with the picture, abstract dada-like haiku that just added to the mystery and wonder of it all. I was so very impressed with her in those early days—she seemed to me everything that ALP had turned out not to be. I used to think, "If only I could find a woman like Mona, I could be happy too!"

~

When Leopold was about three months old, Stephen and Mona came to New York to visit me. I was excited to see them, as it had been awhile. I was quite excited to see Leo, as it had been never. I was also excited for them to meet Nancy, my latest love. She was excited to meet them too, based on what I had told her about them being so wonderful and all. Everyone was excited then when Stephen and Mona arrived one night at my parents' house, with their newly minted child sleeping unawares in baby dreamland. At first, it was a beautiful meeting of friends and lovers. We talked a lot, drank tequila a lot, laughed a lot, and drank more tequila a lot. Since Mona hadn't had a drink in over a year because of the pregnancy, she started to get a little crazy, particularly with me. Somehow, we started rolling on the floor, like in our dancehall days. This was not new to any of us, except for Nancy, so no one paid too much attention at first, except for Nancy, who stared at me with a look of what-the-fuck on her face. In order to set her mind at ease, I told her that Mona and I did this kind of thing all the time, that it was just a joke, no big deal. Nancy was not amused. Stephen, on the other hand, was oblivious to what was going on, as the presence of the baby seemed to drive him to distraction. While his wife and I were roll-

198

ing around, he was running around for no reason I could discern, ignoring us, consumed by whatever he was not doing, acting more like an abstraction than a husband.

Mona, getting drunker and drunker by the minute, started growing more and more daring in her actions toward me. She started trying to put her hand down my shorts. "Oh, she's done this kind of thing before," I said nervously to Nancy, who was staring at us in disbelief. I kept hoping Mona would stop, stop before she went too far, stop before I would have to get physical with her.

She touched the tip of my penis. Oh, the violation! I told her to stop. In response, she put her hand around my entire dick, brushing against my balls for a moment. I now realized that she wasn't going to stop. So I ran away. She ran after me. I ran upstairs. She ran upstairs. I ran into my parents' bedroom. She cornered me in my parents' bedroom. She pushed me down on my parents' bed. I felt her breasts on my chest, her wet body pressed against mine, oozing desire and alcohol. She felt good against me. Oh, what I would have liked to do to her, lift that shirt, put those nipples in my mouth, then turn her around and enter her, pumping until I filled her loins with my forbidden jism. She wanted me at that moment. I wanted her at that moment. But it was wrong, even though my dick didn't want to know. Fortunately, the rest of me did know.

I finally pushed her off and ran into the bathroom. She ran after me, cornered me again, and shoved me into the wall. In the hope of getting away from her for good, I grabbed her tight to me, and gave her a deep, long kiss, a kiss that said, "here it is, you got what you wanted, now leave me alone!" My tongue met her tongue, her tongue met mine back, and after a few seconds, it was over. Then she looked at me, deeply, with eyes from a street corner of the past, with eyes of tequila of the present, and said my kiss was too wet. Then she stopped and let me go. I turned away and walked down the stairs in a complete daze, with a deep bloody cut on my arm from when she had shoved me into the wall. I was in shock. Nancy came over to me, saw my state of emotional and physical disrepair, and cleaned out my wound with peroxide. It didn't sting.

Later that night, Mona started sucking on my fingers while I was talking with Nancy and Stephen. They both did nothing. Even later, Mona almost dropped her baby on the floor, while screaming at all of us to get away from her.

The next day, I woke up with a hangover in my head and a cut on my arm that would develop over time into a scar. Nancy immediately blamed me for the previous night's activities, saying I didn't do enough to fend Mona off, and I, incredulous at her accusation, threw a glass picture across the room at her. I missed.

That night Stephen and Mona came over, sans infant. I was sans Nancy (it was "break" time). There was tension in the room, a strange emotion between we three good friends. Mona sat there silently, looking down at the floor, while Stephen offered an explanation for the previous night's madness. He told me it was postpartum depression combined with tequila that had caused Mona's extracurricular activities of insanity. She could have done it to anyone. Luckily it was me, a trusted friend who wouldn't take advantage of the situation.

Mona herself then offered a brief apology, reaffirming what Stephen had said. She told me she was sorry, and professed to being embarrassed by the whole incident. For some reason, I didn't think she really was, though I don't know why I felt that way. But I let it go, and the three of us agreed to put it behind us. I did feel weird about the whole thing, but was never angry with Mona. Nancy, however, hated Mona from then on, and when we lived together in New Orleans, she told me that Stephen could come visit us, but "that woman" was not allowed in our home. Because of Nancy's anger, things were chilly between Mona and I for awhile. While I didn't like it, I understood Nancy's feelings on this matter, and was loyal at the time to my girlfriend who craved disloyalty.

~

Life continued on, as Nancy and I relocated to New Orleans. A year passed. That part of the story you already know. However, what you don't know is that as the year passed, things changed for my friend Stephen. His letters and phone calls to me, once so happy and full of hope for the future, became morose and pessimistic. He told me that marriage and fatherhood had now become a burden of unending responsibility, a burden that he didn't think he could handle much longer. I told him to focus on school, something that had always given him intellectual and emotional sustenance. He told me that school had ceased to be fun anymore, and now felt like any old nine-to-five job. He told me he needed an answer, something, an answer, anything. I felt bad for my childhood friend, but trapped in my own private hell with Nancy, what could I do for him?

Eventually, he flunked out of school. As a result, Mona was now thrust into the role of sole breadwinner for the family, which meant she had to find a higher-paying job in order to support her one man and a baby. Because of her immense talent, she was quickly able to secure a superior position, but it required that they all move to the flattest state, ground-wise and people-wise, in the Union—Indiana!

They moved in the spring. For the first several months after their arrival, while Mona worked long hours, and the child was day-cared for, Stephen, though he was supposedly looking for a job, did nothing but sit on the couch playing guitar in his underwear. He and I spoke often on the phone since I, nude-modeling part-time, was also generally free at what for other people were the working hours of the day.

I remember one day particularly, when I was lying on my bed naked on a Friday afternoon at about three o'clock. Since it was a humid day, I had decided to lie around the apartment sans clothes. As I was contemplating what not to do, Stephen rang me up. He was alone at home himself on a Friday afternoon at three o'clock Eastern Standard time, two Central Time, playing guitar. We talked, as we usually did, for hours, about what we usually did, his life, my life, all of life, baseball, world hunger, and the rhizomes of Gilles Deleuze. A typical conversation in the middle of the day for those who had flunked out of graduate school and were yet to find their way.

At about the two-hour mark in our conversation, I told Stephen that I was naked, it was Friday afternoon, and that as I looked out my window, I saw all kinds of strange people wearing clothes, coming from work I assumed, going home I presumed. "Stephen, I'm naked! I have no job! I have no reason to put on clothes!" I laughed, he laughed. Then he picked up his guitar and starting playing "Nowhere Man." But, today, naked on a Friday afternoon, it was, "He's a real naked man, sitting in his naked land!" We sang, we laughed, I made strange gestations on my bed, all the while screaming "I'm naked, I'm naked!" Stephen then told me that he had taken his clothes off too, and was now wearing only his briefs. This was even better, I thought. I quickly picked up a pair of boxers lying on the floor and put them on. As I knew from the art world, nudity was a very natural and beautiful state, a state of absolute perfection, unless you were fat and hairy like my father, and most fathers. If the police rushed into my apartment at that moment and found me naked, they would most likely dismiss it as being part of my "artistic temperament." However, if they found me lying on my bed in my underpants, screaming "I'm naked, I'm

naked!" then they would quickly identify me as a
failure, and cart me away as nuts. "Yes Stephen,
underwear is much better!" So, we were on our
respective beds, thousands of miles apart, singing "Naked man, please listen, you don't know
what you're missing," shouting, laughing, and
rolling in our own bodily filth (I hadn't showered
that day, and neither had Stephen—we were still
young boys at heart). Suddenly, as we reached a
crescendo of giddiness and mirth, and were ecstatic to be young, naked, and underemployed, I
heard a door slam on Stephen's side of the phone,
followed by a "what the hell!" yelled in the background. Stephen informed me that Mona had
come home from work, and that they had to go
to day care to pick up the kid.

~

As the weather grew colder in the fall,
Stephen managed to get off the couch, put his
pants on, and get a regular nine-to-five, five-day-
a-week job, the kind of thing that we had always
shuddered at and thought beneath us (or were we
beneath it?). After stumbling through the next
few months trying to find the "right" job, Stephen
called one day and excitedly told me that his big
break had come, what he had been looking for
all his life, without realizing it, lost on the twisted
and Plato-holed highway of academia. He had

gotten a job selling life insurance door-to-door in the poorer areas of rural Indiana, where most of the folks couldn't afford a life, let alone life insurance. If he did well, the company would make him Executive Sales Director and Leader of the Midwest Regional Office. And, he went on to warn me, when this happened, there would be a job in it for me, and we would run the Midwest Office together, happily ever after! First, however, he needed to borrow $500 so he could purchase a second family car to go door-to-door in. Since I was still at times dipping into my grandmother's forbidden till, I told him it would be no problem.

Three months passed. On the first day of the fourth month, Stephen called and told me that the insurance business just wasn't working out the way he thought it would. For some reason, the poor black folks he tried to sell life insurance to desired to spend their scant monetary accumulations on such luxuries as food, clothing and shelter. Thus, since it didn't look like he would soon be heading the Midwest Regional Office, and because Mona had gotten yet another even better job, they were moving again, this time to the great slate, I mean state, of Winnesota.

For those of you who don't know your geography, Winnesota is the fifty-first state, located in the upper Midwest, near the Canadian border, between Wisconsin and Minnesota. According to some history books I have read, it was foujnded in 1845 by a branch of renegade Norwegians who bjork, I mean broke, away frjom Norway to protest their religious freedom. Apparently they were being forced to emote, and since all Norwegians, indeed all Scandinavians, consider the expression of emotion a sin against god and snowmobiles, this silent but angry (you could tell they were angry because their faces were red and when they said, "How ya doin'?" they didn't really mean it because their upper lips weren't completely turned upward in a true non-stoic smile) group sailed on rented ships to the new world, where they went North in August and settled where they first found frost, in the land that is now known as the state of Winnesota, as I said, between Minnesota and Wisconsin. Closer to Minnesota, come to think of it. This was where Mona was born and raised. They moved there in the late fall, buying a small house in a supposedly solidly middle class area that always seemed to me on my-yet-to happen visits as being solidly white trash area, right outside of Windiapolis/St. Snore, the twin capital cities of the great state of Winnesota.

~

A few weeks before Christmas, in the Chinese year of the cock, I was going up to New York for a few days to visit my family. As I was talking with Stephen the day before I was to leave, he mentioned that Mona was going to be in New York on business at the same time, and that maybe we could meet for dinner or a drink. He seemed rather cold in his attitude toward her. "Problems," I wondered? "Nothing major," he replied. Usually he was just absurdly analytical about the things she did that he hated, (like her attempted rape of me), and his Freudian philosophical perspective on all things emotional helped him deny, I mean explain, things to himself that a lesser thinker might have been bothered by. So, "nothing major" translated to "something major!" But I figured Stephen was a good man, and that Mona was a good woman, and that they were a good couple, and everything would work out for them and the kid in their new home, her old home. After all, this was Stephen and Mona I was talking about, to me the model couple on earth. If I could be like them, if I could have a wife like her, I would be fine and dandy! Of course Nancy thought they had some problems, based on her first-hand experiences, but what did she know about love anyway?

Mona and I arranged to meet for dinner at a cheap Italian place I knew in the West Village. It was a frigid Sunday night, with a horrible wind blowing off the river, freezing the rats and my testicles in an unborn state of suspension. The city was deserted, just the way I liked it. Over pasta and Chianti, the two of us reminisced and renewed. She told me that Leopold was all right. She told me that Stephen was all right. She told me that she was all right. I told her that I was all right. So, it certainly was an all right night, except for the fact that we both had horrible colds, which made breathing less than all right. Because of our stuffed noses and clogged heads, we decided, upon finishing dinner, to make it an early night. I suggested, however, that before we part, we have one quick beer at Angie's, the place of my aboriginal dreams of a cheap pint.

We arrived at Angie's. We entered Angie's. The place hadn't changed, hasn't changed, won't ever change. The crack in the glass of the front door was still there, is still there, will always be still there. Harold was working. He is still there. He greeted me in Italian, and I responded in English, ordering two pints of McSorley's Dark. Since we were both sick with colds, Mona brought out some Alka Seltzer Plus cold medicine, and as we talked, we alternated a swig of beer, a swig of health, a swig of cheer, a swig of fizz. What a relief it was!

FFS

Under the influence of the beer and Alka Seltzer, Mona started to talk, revealing to me what was going on between her and Stephen. She told me that their marriage was falling apart, and that she was thinking of kicking him out of their house when she returned to Winnesota. Things were not all right! This was of course a great surprise to me, my image of perfect happiness for my two friends falling to pieces, the center not holding, but melting like the last snow in April, or June in Winnesota. I was upset and confused in my head at her unexpected news, but nevertheless was feeling good because of the Alka Seltzer and McSorley's in my blood. As we were still deciding whether or not to make it an early night after our third pint at Angie's, we decided to go to another bar I liked around the corner called Jehovah's Witless.

We walked huddled together around the wind-curdled block, me thinking of their disintegrating marriage, my face feeling like it was wrapped in ice, her smilingly chatting about how it really does get damn cold in New York City. We entered Jehovah's Witless and ordered a couple of beers. I wanted to know what had happened between her and Stephen, what was happening between her and Stephen. Between sips of beer, and one, maybe two but that's all, okay maybe one more, shot of vodka, Mona rattled off a list of problems between her and Stephen, some of which I knew, such as lack of employment and pants, some of which I didn't know, such as Stephen walking around talking to himself out loud in front of her and the kid, and getting food from a homeless shelter. She said they fought a lot, and she had almost left him on several occasions over the past few years. She told me that he hadn't wanted her to have Leopold, and had pushed for an abortion (Cut, pay, metal hanger MD, we're free!), saying that the child would ruin his life, and only relented when she threatened to leave him and have the baby on her own.

Then the talk got strange, as Mona started telling me how she had wanted to have a baby of her own for years, and before meeting Stephen, whom she thought would be an excellent candidate for fatherhood because he was so sweet and passive, had thought about artificial insemination, because she thought her chances for successful motherhood were greater than her chances for a successful relationship. As Mona went on and on, and we drank on and on, my mind began to wander away from her strange ramblings about motherhood, and I began to think about Stephen, and to wonder for the first time about the truth of all the things he had said to me over the years. He always told me that his marriage was fine, that although he and Mona had their share of problems like any other American couple, there were no serious, insurmountable obstacles between the two of them. Now, in front of me in this dive bar, next to the booze and music whirling around my head, was an alternate set of events, a radically different truth told to me by someone I trusted as much as I did my old friend Stephen. What to think?

What to drink, as we moved past the beer, Alka Seltzer, and vodka, onto the bourbon. Shot after shot shot down our gullets. After the fourth or fifth, I felt queasy. After the sixth or seventh I went to the bathroom and threw up. After the eighth or ninth Mona started to nibble on my neck. Hmm, interesting development. After the tenth or so, she put her hand down my pants. Hmm, ejaculating development! I told her to stop, though it felt real fuckin' good! "Stop!" "Okay!" "Don't stop!" "Okay!" I kissed her on the lips. "Stop this," I exclaimed! God, I thought to myself in the race of my mind filled with bourbon, my pants filled with her, she's always loved me, from the dance floor to that time in the bedroom to now, always with her conjugal hand down my pants.

We stopped. We started. We stopped. We

started. We'd started. We continued. It happened so quickly and drunkenly. We were on the subway. All I remember was brown, the color of Mona's pants, and wet, the color of Mona's cunt. The train! It became synonymous with fuck for us. In the future, when one of us said "Do you think we should ride the rails?" it was code for wink, wink, lick, lick, come, cum, and so on.

We got back to her hotel in Midtown. I lifted her shirt up in the hallway and licked her breasts. As big and beautiful as I had always imagined them. We then fell in the hallway in front of her room. We then rolled around in the hallway in front of her room. We then rolled into her room. We then rolled into bed. We then made out. We then passed out. Later I awoke to find her arms around me, so I got out of bed and spent the rest of the night alone on the floor. I must have felt guilt or something. When I awoke the next morning, my eyes paralyzed from vodka, bourbon, and Alka Seltzer, my temples swaying in the still air of the room, I sat in a chair, stunned and silent, while Mona got ready to go to somewhere. I had nowhere to go. I couldn't go anywhere.

When it was time to go, we kissed gently, like we used to when we were friends. It was the last time we would ever kiss like that. We parted.

As I walked along the frozen streets in a daze, the city filled with huddled masses hurdling all around me, I thought about what Mona had told me the previous night about her marriage. Then I thought about Stephen. Then I thought about Mona. Then I thought about Stephen and Mona. Then I thought about the subway and the hotel and the floor. Then I thought about Robert and Mona. Then I didn't want to think anymore.

When I returned home to Philadelphia, Mona and I talked by phone about what had happened. We agreed upon three things. Uno, we would never tell Stephen what we had done. Dos, we would never drink together again. Tres, we would never take a subway ride together again. It was all agreed, in English and Español.

~

Life moved on. I had one last march in the dysfunctional parade with Nancy, at a New Year's party, where, after swallowing half a bottle of Xanax in addition to my usual festive New Year's drinking, I proceeded to threaten the life of every man who looked at or spoke to her. I figured in my little sun-dried raisin of a brain that if reason had never worked with her, it was time for force, for which, being a man, I was eminently qualified. To every man I saw near her that night, to every male in the room who I even thought had a thought about her, it was "get the fuck away from her!" from me, and "why is that guy looking at me like that?" from them. If a guy sat near Nancy, I would pull up a chair real close and look at him threateningly until he departed. At some point, a gay gentleman told me he wanted to have a threesome with Nancy and me. Lesbians only, please! In between these outbursts of psychic violence, I would make out with some girl in the bathroom. Later I tried to take her home with me, telling her that I would fuck her like no other had ever fucked her, but she declined my invitation.

By the time it was past dawn, well into the New Year's morn, I had successfully driven away any and all cumers, so I figured it was safe for me to go home. I stumbled the few blocks to my apartment, blinded by the sun-drenched pre-hangover light. Then morning turned to black.

When I woke up the next afternoon, fully clothed, my head rolling on the floor, I remembered what I had done the previous night, and my first thought was that I had finally succeeded in permanently eliminating Nancy from my life. Vomit emanated from me a few minutes later, from the rich combination of alcohol, Xanax and nerves. After my visit to the treasured bowl, Nancy called and asked me to come over. I told her I was surprised that she still wanted to see

215

me. What about last night, I asked. Well, she agreed that I had been a freak, but she thought I had been real funny and cute in a way, so she still wanted to see me, still wanted our relationship to continue as it always continued. But what about all the guys I drove away from her, I asked? Well, she might have cared if she had liked any of them, but she really didn't, except for the gay guy who she would probably go out with anyway. But that was for another time. Now, she wanted me to come over and celebrate the New Year with her. Happy New Year?

~

A week later I bought a plane ticket to Winnesota to see Stephen and the child, who was now almost three. And to see Mona as well, but I only knew that back then on a subconscious and masturbatory level. They were still having marital problems (as I now well knew), but Stephen told me that they weren't too serious, and that they were trying hard to work them out. Since Mona hadn't thrown him out yet, I assumed that they had reached some kind of truce in their rapidly defrosting marriage.

Little Leopold left a message on my machine a few days before I came, telling me to "come veesit!" How cute! He and Stephen picked me up at the airport. I played hide and seek, front seat, back seat, with the kid—I was immediately a big smash in his eyes, now that he was old enough to know who I was, as he had always been in mine.

We went back to their house, where we hung out, the three of us, and talked about life, love, jobs, and Barney the dinosaur. It got dark. We ate dinner. Mona still wasn't home. In an off-handed manner, I asked Stephen where she was. He informed me that she had gone to the gym after work, but would be home in a little while. Then what, I wondered to myself?

At about seven o'clock, as I was sitting on the couch watching television with the kid, the front door opened, and in she came. We greeted each other with a cool nod of acknowledgement, me on the couch, her in the doorway taking off her snow-covered sneakers. There were no hugs, no kisses. I didn't even get up. However, as she was sitting on the ground removing her sneakers, she suddenly looked up, and our eyes met, quickly and fleetingly, but with the intensity of a whip. I knew at that very moment that we were in big trouble. We always communicated through the eyes. Except when drunk, when we communicated with hands down the pants. As I looked into her eyes, I knew instantly that all of our agreements to be nice were to be canceled in the coming days. The best laid plans of mice and men, of shiksas and Jews, canceled in an instant, in the blink of two sets of eyes.

Nothing happened between us that first night because Stephen was there. The following day, after Mona went to work, Stephen spent the entire morning and afternoon telling me how fucked-up his marriage was. He was agitated, anxious, and angry, as he walked around in circles, telling me how hard it was to live with Mona, how impossible she was to please, and how she never forgave him for anything he did wrong. But he didn't want to live without her! When I asked him if this was really the case, that it was all *her* fault, he told me that, well, everything was probably originally *his* fault, since he had flunked out of school, and then had had difficulty holding a steady job. Still, he asked me, wouldn't a good wife forgive her husband for a few honest mistakes?

I spent the rest of the day trying to help him, trying to give him the best advice I could. I really did! Deep down, I still wanted him and Mona to resolve things, to be the happy couple again that they once had been, despite my obvious intrusion into their situation. When I talked to Stephen that morning, the advice I gave him on how to try and save his marriage was honest

and genuine, even though I knew I would probably be acting carnal with his wife that night.
Strange split in me this was, when I think back
upon it. To act in one's best interest in contradiction to one's impulses, and then to contradict
that. Strange, strange indeed. I watched Stephen
pace furiously on the floor before me that gray
day in Winnesota, the image of his marriage falling apart to dust choking him, confusing him, en-
raging him. I consoled him as best as I could, telling him what I thought he should do, how to win
her back, how things weren't too bad between
them, how they had a wonderful child, etc. I was
his best friend trying to help him repair his tee-
tering marriage. At the same time, I was his worst
enemy, watching him spew and curse and cry,
while thinking in the back of my mind what I
wanted to do with Mona, the kissing and the
sucking, and maybe soon, the fucking. Very
strange split in me this was, when I think back
upon it. I couldn't face myself, couldn't confront
what I was doing, while at the same time I
couldn't deny myself, couldn't deny my inner-
most desires for Mona. I wanted things to stay
the same, to stay the way I knew them—Stephen
and Mona, my best friends, side by side in love,
together, happy, eternal. Yet, I wanted things to
completely change, for Stephen to disappear, for

Mona and I to be together, side by side in love, together, happy, eternal. Strange days indeed—I was hoping for things to be the way they once were, yet at the same time I was determined to destroy them.

That night, after Stephen went out on a temp job, Mona and I sat together in the kitchen, drinking white wine out of one of those cardboard boxes that you just leave in the fridge, put your glass to the spigot, and pour pour pour. Kmart Chardonnay! We chatted easily, as we always did, and drunkenly, as we often did. After awhile, Mona and I moved into the living room and sat on the couch, drinking more wine the whole time. Leopold was watching television in front of us. We sat real close together on the couch, cheek to cheek, wine to groin to groin to wine. Mona asked me what I was thinking. I asked her what she was thinking. She asked me what I was thinking. I asked her what she was thinking. She said she was thinking about fucking me. I said I was thinking very similar thoughts. She started to rub my leg. I rubbed hers back. Just then Stephen came in the door, with pizza for all of us. For all of us! For all there was delicious cheese, spicy sauce, and golden crust. For all! For some, though, there was boiling blood, meaningful glances across the table, and "accidental" bumps into one another that shot electricity through the spine. For some! For all there were full stomachs. For some there were empty hearts, full minds, and organs ready to burst with the sauces of human frailty and human triumph. For some it was getting started; for some it was getting ended.

~

Mona and I spent the next several days, or should I say nights, with one another. By day Stephen continued to rant and curse and pace and quiver and holler and shout and cry and wail and whimper about his marriage. I continued to console him as best as I could, even though I was now less and less interested in his ravings and more and more interested in when he was going to go to work, and when Mona was coming home. The minute he was gone, Mona and I would drop the kid off somewhere with someone, and we were off to start pawing one another, in the backseat of her car, at a bar, at a bookstore, everything anytime all the time! We were having a grand time in our deception, and I must say that we had little guilt over what we were doing. We were like a young couple in love, trying to hide from her husband. It was all a game to us, of how far we could go without being discovered. Of holding hands in public and wondering if anyone who knew Mona could see us. Of touching each other in the house when Stephen had his back turned and laughing at how we were pulling the wool over his eyes. We felt triumphant at what excellent masters of deception we were, and as our egos were stroked by our lying and sneaking around, our behavior in front of Stephen became more and more brazen, especially since he seemed quite willing to turn a blind eye. Or maybe he really couldn't, or wouldn't, see?

The whole situation became completely ridiculous one morning when Leopold woke me up at dawn, wanting to play hide and go seek. Now, I loved the boy as if he was my own son, but I loved my sleep even more, especially at six in the morning in the frozen land of god-fearing adulterers. For a few minutes I tried to keep him entertained, while at the same time keeping my eyes shut. Eventually, he got bored of my feigned interest, and wanted his mommy and daddy. Since Stephen didn't work until evening, he got up to attend to the child, making sure to lock the door to the bedroom so that Mona would not be disturbed, as she had to get up in a few hours to go to work. When I complained that I was tired and also needed to sleep undisturbed, Stephen told me to go into the bedroom and sleep with Mona.

"What are you doing here?" she wanted

to know as I entered their bed, not unhappy in the least to see me. "Well, your husband ordered me in here, and he is guarding the door to make sure that no one disturbs us, especially him!" You can imagine what we did that morning in bed, while Leopold kept Stephen busy outside the locked bedroom door.

~

After a fortnight of fun in the snow and locked bedrooms of Winnesota, it was time for me to go back to Philadelphia. The afternoon of the night of my plane ride came. Mona was to take me to the airport, as Stephen had to engage in his nightly ritual of disturbing the dinners of the inhabitants of Winnesota with credit card pitches. Before going to the airport, we went to a wonderful arboretum in St. Paul, right over the border in Minnesota. It took us a long while to get there, as there was an ice storm in progress. The roads were slick and shiny, the cars were slipping and sliding, and the air was sizzling with the white-hot stench of winter. Eventually we arrived, and rushed our fearful bodies through the mid-winter scream. Inside was another world. It was steamy in the glass enclosure of trees and non-indigenous plants, with a light mist encircling our eyes, like tears falling from the soft light of unnatural indoor nature.

We sat in a quiet corner, speaking softly, kissing tenderly, hugging endlessly. Time passed beautifully, fearfully. Then darkness descended, as the night fell in pieces of uninterrupted slumber, quickly and with a deafening finality. It was time for us to go to the airport, to return me to my home that wasn't a home, far away from this place that I wanted to be home, a home with her. What would happen when I landed in a few hours? What had happened since I landed two weeks ago?

The board said "canceled!" The flight was canceled. Bad weather! In Winnesota! What a shock! Maybe it was the ice storm that messed things up? Whatever the reason, there would be another day for me in this frozen paradise! Mona leapt into my arms at the ticket counter. The agent asked me if I needed a hotel room overnight, then quickly smiled and said it seemed like I probably didn't. Mona and I ran joyously to her car, stopping along the way to make out in some strange blue stairwell at the airport. We then went back to the house, where I called Stephen at work, telling him that I had decided not to go back to Philadelphia, and that I was going to live with him, Mona, and the kid from now on. He replied that I could stay with them for awhile, but that he would have to check with Mona to see how long I could remain. Longer than he was going to remain, I thought to myself. Then I laughed and told him I was kidding. He didn't laugh back.

Mona and I were quite content the rest of that night, finishing off two boxes of that famous Kmart Chardonnay. Unfortunately, we weren't able to do much with each other in the touchy-clutchy department, because Stephen got home only an hour or so after we did. Still, we smiled silently and knowingly throughout the rest of the night, feeling that the gods of weather, love, and adultery were on our side.

When I awoke the next morning, in my extra-added day of frostbitten delight, I looked out the window first thing and saw that the ice storm had abated, and the sun was out. I knew that there would be no more cancellations. It was really time to go.

Stephen and Mona took me to the airport together. During the eternal ride to damnation and Delta Airlines, I sat in the front of the car next to Stephen, while Mona was in the back. I sat sideways so I could get a view of the whole interior of the car, and of her, without turning my head and arousing Stephen's suspicion. The look in Mona's eyes was one of pure sex and misery, pure fucking, pure longing, pure emptiness longing to be filled. I really wanted to fill her, right then, right there, in the car, in front of her husband.

We arrived a few minutes before my flight was to depart. The three of us made empty chit-chat for awhile, killing time as if things were the same as they had always been, as if we were still the friends we no longer were. At the gate, Stephen hugged me and told me he loved me. I hugged him back, and then I hugged Mona, gave her a kiss, and looked her in the eye like I had on a street corner years before. Then I disappeared into the plane.

I immediately wrote her a long love letter that I don't think I ever sent. Then I sat back and tried to rest, to reflect on the past, and dream of the future. As my eyes shut, and after I had thought about how much I would miss Mona, I started to think of Stephen, my longtime friend. I remembered the night before, when I had jokingly told him I was going to live with him and Mona. I had laughed, but he had not. I knew that the reason he didn't laugh was not because he was suspicious of me and Mona, or anything like that. No, the reason he didn't laugh went all the way back through the history of our friendship. Since we were boys, I had always told him little white lies like that, simple, harmless untruths, things that would humor me, keep me entertained, but never hurt him. Little fibs, such as making up a baseball trade, or saying that I had heard on the radio that our favorite rock band was going to reunite and play a show. The simple untruths of childhood!

Of course, as we grew older the lies had to become more intricate, such as the time I called and told him I was going to marry a woman from China for citizenship purposes. Or the time I called him in the middle of the night and told him that I was in jail and needed him to post bail for me. And of course, the time when I was in New Orleans and I told him that me and Nancy were getting kicked out of our house and had no place to go and he might have to come from St. Louis to rescue us (oh yeah, that really happened). This was the type of joke I always played on my gullible friend, because I loved him and therefore loved to tease him. And to make things even better, no matter how many times I did it, he would always fall for it the next time, and the time after that, etc., which I know pissed him off to no end. He was so gullible, so beautifully gullible! (Or maybe I was a good liar?) This was part of what made him my friend, my best friend, his earnest acceptance of what wasn't, for the hope that it would be, one day, what was.

Now, a little white lie to tease affectionately was one thing, but what I was doing with Mona was something quite a bit different. Why did I do it, I wondered to myself, with the whir of the plane engines at 30,000 feet singing in my ears, why, why? I needed this to make sense to me, for my relationship with Mona to have reason and purpose, for my lying to Stephen to have reason and purpose. I had to have something, anything, to clear my already bloodstained conscience.

What I needed was that old psychological term, *rationalization*. As I thought about the love triangle between Mona, Stephen, and myself, my ever-justifying brain was able to come up with what it needed, what I needed, to live, and live right. To justify my own actions, I simply combined two things: my belief in the rightness of my love for Mona, all that destiny and meant-for-each other kind of crap, and an increased dislike for Stephen, even though he had done nothing to me but be my friend. Putting these two elements together allowed me to feel no guilt each time I touched Mona or lied to Stephen. I found it surprisingly easy to convince myself that Stephen was the villain, and that he deserved my anger and contempt, as if he were somehow, through his own actions, forcing me to lie to him about my feelings and actions toward Mona.

While I had always thought him to be the greatest of all people, I had seen on this trip a different side to my old friend, the psychologically fucked-up side of his personality that somehow had never come across during years of long distance phone calls. His self-involvement, his self-denial, his self-fulfilling prophecies of his own doom that somehow he never felt responsible for (though that he would angrily and insincerely admit full responsibility for), all these screwed-up pieces of himself had unraveled before my very eyes over the past two weeks. And when I asked Mona about all this, telling her that I couldn't believe that this was really Stephen, that the disintegrating marriage must be the cause, she told me that he had always been this way, but that I had never been around to see it. And, since I had fallen in love with Mona, any negative thing that I (or she) could find in Stephen made me feel better about what I was doing. I might be wrong, I would think to myself, but so is he, and he was wrong first. And since I didn't want to be bothered by guilt or shame at what I was doing, every bad characteristic that I discovered in Stephen made my behavior with Mona seem not so bad to me. As a matter of fact, there were times that I felt that my actions were admirable, as if I was going to correct the mistakes he had made, undo the misery that I knew he had caused, for which I knew Mona bared no responsibility, of course. I would right his ship, make myself captain, take his wife and child for my own, and it would all be his fault. And then, my conscience would be clear! I closed my eyes, and was able to sleep peacefully for the rest of the plane ride.

It was three in the morning when the plane landed, and I stepped into a taxi to step back into my life alone. Mona was gone, Stephen was gone, and the streets of Philadelphia were wet from rain, and the air was heavy and damp like summer, even though it was the middle of winter. I started to cry in the back of the cab as I thought about Mona sleeping so far away from me, in a land of ice that had frozen our memories in its soul. That ice, that cold, hard tundra that I had walked hand in hand with Mona through, that I had kissed Mona through, that I had loved Mona through—where was it now? It had evaporated, leaving the streets of the foreign city that I lived in stained with the invisible mist of unforgettable reminders! Reminders of her! I was reminded, and as I was reminded, I remembered, yes I remembered, remembered her, remembered me, remembered that she had said yes to me. She had said yes to me! A yes that at that moment I saw in my mind alone, without a body to confirm it, a yes alone as I soared through the horrible imitation summer streets of one of the fucked-up places of my emotional destruction. But, I was reminded, and thus remembered, that she had said yes, that I had said yes, that we had said yes. Yes! Yes to her eyes, yes to her thighs, yes to my body pressed against hers in the midnight freeze. Yes! She had said it, I had said it, we had said it. Yes!

It was almost four when the taxi dropped me off in front of my building. The night was still pitch-black, and the first hints of blue morning wouldn't invade the sky for another hour or so. I was exhausted. I opened my apartment door, but no one was there to greet me. My cat was staying with Nancy—I would have to retrieve her tomorrow. The heat in the apartment was off. I dropped my bag on the floor, removed all my clothes despite the pre-dawn chill, and fell into bed. Within seconds, I must have fallen asleep, because I remember Mona lying beside me, touching my face, and stroking my lips in the dark room. But it was too dark to really see, too dark to really feel anything. Therefore, I must have been asleep, and alone.

~

I awoke early the next morning, alone and

hard, and jerked off first thing as I thought about her. As I moaned with imaginary pleasure, I wondered to myself if the last few weeks had all been a dream? Or, if not a dream, something that wouldn't last, would it last?, as my plane had sailed through the skies, from there to here.

I got up and went to work, where I was naked and alone in front of a room of students. Sit, stand, pose, lay, rest, robe, disrobe, alone, soft, "Notice the gentle curve of his back, and the finely detailed crack of his ass as I spread his buttocks wide and stick my easel deep inside. Ah, that's better—now draw, class, draw, you have twenty minutes to complete this pose before his rectum prolapses, and his ass becomes so painfully enlarged that he can never properly sit on the bowl again. Draw, draw, my little stallions, and all the cute girls should see me afterward during office hours, alone."

When I came home after a day at the orifice, there was a message on my machine. From her! Call her at work. Call her. Now! Hope I had a good flight. She missed me.

I sat down on my bed and listened to the message again, as a smile slowly crossed my face. Then, I pressed the little button again, and listened again, as the smile expanded into a grin. One more time, and I would be convinced. I pressed the little button again, and heard her voice again saying the same thing again. I rose from my bed, leapt into the humid winter air, and screamed, no shouted, to the heavens and earths and hells and everything else that may or may not exist, "SHE LOVES ME!" It wasn't a dream. I was awake and alive, her and I were awake and alive. It had traveled with me here from there, and now it was everywhere!

Suddenly, my entire life made perfect sense. She had been the thing that I had been searching for, through ALP, through Nancy, through all the times when I couldn't understand what I was searching for. With her, it all made total and complete fuckin' sense. I could now see beyond all I had ever seen, see that all truths, all realities, all fantasies in the world pointed to her, pointed so strongly and absolutely to her, like a light through the night. We, us, Robert and Mona, were that event, that happening, that moment in time that divided all moments in time. We were a thing that couldn't happen, shouldn't happen, but yet did. We were all, all undefinable, all untellable, all unintelligible, all that is all all the time. She had called me and proven it wasn't a dream, wasn't a mistake, wasn't a misunderstanding, wasn't a false hope in my hopeful heart. She had called me on the telephone, from a far-away land, over long distance lines, through the life we would lead, and had asked me to join her. And my answer was yes! Yes to her! Yes to us! Yes to it all! Yes, again and again, and a million more yeses that said yes! It was yes, and always would be! I knew, she knew, the universe knew! Yes! I picked up the phone, dialed a few numbers, heard her voice on the other end, and said yes!

~

Now the secrets began. Secret #1: I wanted to tell Stephen everything, to come clean and tell the truth to my longtime friend. I wanted to explain that this had not been done intentionally to hurt him, that it was nothing personal, but I just loved whom I loved, whom he loved, and Mona loved whom she loved, whom he loved, and if we happened to love one another, best friend to best friend's wife, well, what the hell could anyone do about it? Mona said yes, she would like to tell him, but no, we could not. There was the kid to consider. If Stephen found out about us, he could sue for custody of the kid on the grounds of adultery. Surely not, I said, not Stephen. And, even if he did, I said, what judge would give the kid to him, as he was the male parent first off, and only worked sporadically second off, and third off, I wanted to tell him the fuckin' truth!

Sure, all this deception had been a blast, but now that our love was open and declared, wasn't it time to tell Stephen the truth, the whole truth, and nothing but the truth? She told me she agreed in principle, but in reality the divorce laws were very old-fashioned, and thus they frowned mightily on adultery. She could lose her baby! Also, think of the things that Stephen would call us if he found out the truth. "Adulterers, cheaters, liars, deceivers!" Words that made our relationship sound so base and immoral, which while true, was far from what we knew the *real* truth to be. Telling Stephen would bring so much ugliness to our relationship, when in fact what we had was beautiful, despite the adultery, cheating, lies, and deception.

Despite my moderate external, and light internal, protestations to the contrary, I agreed to agree with her. I must admit, deep down I really didn't want to tell Stephen anything. I didn't want to have a big scene, and subsequent big scenes with him, scenes that I could see going on forever and ever, because I knew he would never get over this, and therefore would never let us get over it. And in addition to the desire to avoid the wrath of my best friend, I also knew I wouldn't be able to deal with the guilt if Mona did in fact, somehow, though I knew it wasn't likely, lose her baby. "All right Mona, let's not tell Stephen just yet. I'm sure things will work themselves out."

Now that we had settled that nothing would be settled as regards to telling Stephen the truth, it was time for secret #2: how to plan on seeing one another without Stephen finding out. Especially since he still lived with Mona, and still called me regularly. On this matter, two things were in our favor. One: Mona's job required her to take several business trips around the country each year, on "assignment." Therefore, I could secretly meet her on said "assignments," and as long as Stephen didn't find out, no suspicion would be alerted. Two: Mona liked, even after she had been married, to take vacations by herself, so it was no big deal if she went away under the guise of a self-imposed exile, and if I just happened to meet her at her own personal Elba, well, who was going to know?

Based upon those two facts, it wasn't difficult for us to plan our undercover rendezvous. We visited many places that spring, all under the pretense of business or personal recuperation for Mona, yet in reality filled with the two of us, well, filling each other. We had a grand time. To my surprise, deception was even more fun now that it was on a national scale. It was exciting, it was fun, it was dangerous, it was love! As each secret trip came and went, as time came and went, I felt closer and closer to Mona, closer to a reality with her, closer to a real future, a real us. I started to dream of moving to Winnesota, to live with her and Leopold, and of one day having a child of my own with her. As time passed, and our love grew, what I dreamed of went from hoped-for possibility in my heart, to inevitable probability in my mind.

~

As much as everything seemed perfect to me, there were little seeds of imperfection lying around, items I chose to disregard, or regard as unimportant, but which, in retrospect, were clues to the rest of my time with Mona. One particular area of concern was the way she was handling the situation between Stephen and myself. While on the one hand, she was talking about having a future with me, she was, at the same time, dealing with Stephen as if they still had a possible future together. Her two realities had somehow led her to an unreality. While we were making plans, concrete plans I thought, for me to move out to Winnesota (even though she hadn't told Stephen the truth about us, or mentioned divorce), she was at the same time still working on her marriage with Stephen, to see if they had a future.

Sense a contradiction somewhere in there?

He had finally moved out of their house about two months after our affair began, not because of the affair, which he still (willfully or not) remained in the dark about, but because of the other "problems" they were having in their marriage. But, because they were still hypothetically working on their hypothetical marriage, and because of the kid, which gave him a real reason to be with Mona, he was still over at the house all the time. So even though he had supposedly "moved out," he was nowhere else really than where he had always been, which was where I wanted to be.

In order to deal with my feelings of unease and jealousy, I invoked my favorite instrument of psychological logic—the rationalization! The way I looked at the whole situation was such: that this was the kind of thing one had to put up with if one had an affair with a married woman, particularly a woman married to one's best friend. I could have waited to get involved with Mona, waited until she had gotten divorced, and things between her and Stephen were settled. But that was not the way I worked, not the way Mona and I worked—we were passion, right now, on the dance floor, on the subway, in the bedroom with your husband guarding the door. So while I wished that Stephen would never come over and see Mona, I was understanding of the situation, particularly since Mona assured me that it would be only a temporary situation.

All of this was trivial compared to what I discovered next. One beautiful sunny spring day, I found out that Mona was still on occasion, or maybe more, sleeping with Stephen. Now that was a shotgun blast to the head! I had been aware at the beginning of our tryst that she and Stephen still fucked, but I hadn't really cared back then, as I still had that strange split in me between wanting her and hoping that the two of them would work things out and reconcile. After several months with Mona, my split had healed, and I was no longer in favor of reconciliation. And because of all that Mona and I had been through, after all our expressed declarations of love and forever, I blindly assumed that all activities such as fornication had ceased between her and Stephen.

It was Stephen himself who informed me of this piece of shocking news. He called me late one night, a Friday as I remember. One of our mutual friends from high school, Tony, who had become a Scientologist, and whom Stephen and I just stayed in touch with because of sheer lack of will and misplaced sentimentality, was threatening to kill himself, which was a regular occurrence in the life of Tony. The drill was always the same—a desperate phone call saying that life was not worth living, followed by graphic descriptions of the ways he was going to do himself in, and eventually, after about an hour or so, a request for some money until his next paycheck from the Scientologists arrived. Since I had known Tony for years, I had experienced these calls for years, and, as a result, I was always more annoyed and impatient with him when he called than I was ever concerned for his well-being.

As I was talking Tony out of suicide, I was always hoping for some kind, any kind, of interruption, and on this night, Stephen provided it. "It's my other line, Tony. I'll be right back. Make yourself comfortable on the ledge." By this time, I had grown increasingly uncomfortable lying to Stephen, and thus tried to avoid speaking to him as much as possible, which should have invited suspicion in him, but didn't seem to. On this night however, I was happy to hear his voice, as anything was preferable to trying to talk Tony down from the precipice.

The first thing I tried to do was pawn Tony off on Stephen, but he knew what I was trying to do, and refused. I quickly got rid of Tony, saying Stephen had to talk to me urgently about his failing marriage, but that, if he were still alive tomorrow, we would speak. I started talking with Stephen, and the usual things cropped up, the complaining about and longing for Mona. I had heard it before, and I didn't want to hear it anymore. However, good friend I was, I listened sympathetically. And then he blurted it out. "...And I don't understand, I mean we had sex this afternoon while the kid was asleep, and it was good, but when it's over, everything just goes back to being fucked up again." What? Fuck! This afternoon! Fuck! You and her!

I died, but managed to keep talking for a minute or so. I then got off the phone, under the pretense of having to talk to Tony again. After hanging up, I sat on the edge of my bed for a few minutes, silently spitting hate. Then I got up and paced around the apartment for a few more minutes, the wood floors creaking with each angry step I took. Deceiver! Slut! Bitch! Cunt! Whore! As my eyes seared with the fiery certainty of injustice, I picked up the phone and called the deceiver, slut, bitch, cunt, whore, who I loved.

Besides starting the conversation off with, "So, do you think we should end this charade now?", I don't remember many of the specifics of what I said. I do recall that I wouldn't tell her what I was mad about, and she couldn't, or wouldn't, figure it out on her own. "Something happen this afternoon you might want to share with me?" "I don't understand, tell me what's wrong." "This afternoon, something you might want to share with me, something about fucking your husband." Pause the first. "Well!" Pause another second. She had nothing to say, no defense of her own actions, at least none that would make any sense to me. "Well, you see, we're married, and when you're married, you have to do things sometimes. The whole time I was thinking of you!" That was really helpful, the thought that she was really thinking of me while Stephen's hard dick was inside her, and she came once, twice, three times, who knew, while he shot his load inside her, all over her, or wherever the fuck. Yes, if only it could have been me, then poor Mona wouldn't have had to go through the pure hell that I'm sure fucking Stephen had been. "Damn you," was my response, and then there was silence. Pause the third. And then she asked my favorite question, the one she would always ask whenever she did something fucked up. "What do you think *we* should do now?" Yes, it's all up to me, to absolve you, to curse you, to love you, to hate you. *We!* "How the fuck should I know? Damn you!" (She later told me that whenever I said "Damn you" to her during this conversation, it cut her like a knife to the heart. Cool!)

We talked until dawn. Eventually, I calmed down, and while I never forgave her for what happened, we continued as lovers. I just, of course, rationalized her actions away, rationalized that I deserved this, since she was married to my best friend. The usual! Whatever. It kept us going, and deep down, that is all I wanted, to keep going, somewhere, anywhere, out of the hell I was in, a hell that I knew only she could take me out of. By the next morning, everything was fine again, and I kept my feelings on this matter, which would stir up fire in me at unexpected moments when I was alone, silent for the rest of our time together. She told me a few months later that she hadn't fucked Stephen since the night we had had the conversation. "Good thing we talked then," I said.

~

Despite that little hump in the road, things between us were still in the blissful period of total love and forgiveness and daily letters and wonderful three-hour phone calls. No matter what happened with Mona, however, I had to get out of Philadelphia, the American haven for incest and tri-sided phallus shades tied to the tits of homogenized strippers at the corner of Samson

and Delilah. I loathed and abhorred and generally had unpleasant feelings toward Philadelphia,
the home of Tastee cakes and untastee pussys in
my dry-mouth slumber. I couldn't wait on one
more table, couldn't display my unwashed cock
for one more student. I had to get out, out, out,
of the bootlicking city of premenstrual nausea.

In order to wrench myself out of the city
of brotherly butt-fucking, I had originally, pre-
Mona, thought about returning to New York and
going back to graduate school. But, with my feelings and penis toward Mona on the rise all
throughout that spring, I was becoming more and
more convinced that my true destiny lay out in
the land of the sentimental ice sculpture. Mona
was begging me to come out there, despite the
fact that there was still no talk of divorcing
Stephen, and despite the fact that he continued
to come over her house every single damned day.
When I would bring this unpleasant fact up to
Mona, wondering how would I be able to move
out to Winnesota, to live with her and Leopold
in holy acrimony with Stephen eternally present,
she just avoided the subject, something she was
quite good at doing. Eventually, I got tired of asking, and just avoided the subject myself. So, despite the fact that, in retrospect, it made no sense
whatsoever, I started making concrete plans to

move out to Winnesota.

I figured I would just get any old job when I moved out to Winnesota. I believe it was Mona who one day suggested that I go to library school? Hmm, I thought, library school? Library school? Library school! Libraries are wonderful places, right? Filled with books and knowledge and really cool, yet slightly introverted-type people, right? Bataille had been a librarian, and he had written that nasty book, right? Yes, I would fit in just perfectly in the library world! It was where I rightly belonged, where I had always rightly belonged, among the infinite pages of infinite knowledge! Yes, great idea, my sweet Mona! To library school I would go!

I decided to apply to one school in Winnesota, and one in New York, just in case my foolproof plans with Mona somehow fell apart. But I knew in my heart of hearts and my dick of dicks that I would soon be in Winnesota, the land of 11,000 frozen lakes, and 11,000 frozen smiles, and 11,000 unexplained deaths from exposure, and 11,000 suicidal thoughts in the heads of the 11,000 people every day. I knew that I would soon be living with my gray-eyed lady of the slopes, in the land of snow, progressive thinking, sharply obeyed speed limits, socialized medicine, and socialized emotions. Just a few more months, and the winter of us would begin, an endless winter of endless content and endless white and never-ending endings that begin where beginnings end. Me and her, ice and life, buried beneath the frozen earth, hidden by the permafrost, missing and presumed together. Missing and presumed together! Me and her! By the side of ourselves. Missing and presumed...

~

Mona was in New York on business in June. I was consequently in New York on vacation in June. Summer in New York! Reporting and photographing for her by day, sheet meetings for us by night! It was to be a glorious time. And for a few days, it was! I was confident that this was going to be the last of our secret visits together because I knew I would soon be in Winnesota, once I heard from library school, and that after my acceptance, Mona and I would tell Stephen about everything. He would, of course, be angry at first, yet understanding in the end, and then, Mona and I would live happily ever after in the land of the frozen smile.

One day during this nice early summer trip, Mona and I were fucking in my childhood bed in my childhood room while visiting my childhood parents, when she suddenly felt a sharp pain in her womanly area. Then a few more sharp pains, then a lot more. I wasn't that hung, so we knew something was amiss. We chose to ignore these pains at first, in the hopes that they would go away on their own.

That night, however, as I slept on the couch in the living room, Mona came down from my childhood room where she had been sleeping, and awoke me in agony, asking for a bucket. "A bucket? For what?" "To fuckin' vomit!" Mona was in no mood to have the discussion I wanted us to have at this moment, which was basically about the origin of the bucket. You see when I grew up, if you were sick and had to lose it from your upper hole, you either made it to the bowl, or unfortunately, did it somewhere along the way, and hopefully not on the good carpet. In Mona's world, you were raised with a bucket by the side of your bed, to avoid having to call someone in to clean the rug. I later took a survey of people that I knew in order to determine if the majority were raised pro-bucket, or sans bucket. I found it came out about fifty-fifty, which I believe clearly disproves Mona's postulation that my family was crazy.

I immediately told her to go to the bathroom, which was just a few yards away, or if she couldn't make it, to go in the hallway (tile over cement, very easy to clean). However, she wanted a bucket. I informed her that I didn't know where the damn buckets were, as I didn't live with my parents any longer, and thus didn't know where they kept their buckets, damn or otherwise. Mona declined to regurgitate the evening's meal without a bucket, and went back to sleep nauseous. But, her pain concerned me, concerned us. This late-night-vomit need was not a good thing.

The next morning, as Mona was still in agony, we paid the emergency room a visit. She was admitted, I was admitted. They first thought she had leukemia. Then she didn't. Then they didn't know what was wrong with her. I called Stephen to tell him what was going on. He had finally gotten very suspicious of things between wifely and friendly, so he wasn't very kindly toward me anymore. Mona had requested that I tell him not to let his father, who lived in New York, come to the hospital. Stephen agreed. Stephen hung up. Goodbye.

The following day, bright and early, before I arrived, Stephen's father arrived. A prick of a man. That's all I'll say about him. Since Mona and I wanted to be alone, she played real sick, and said we should both leave so she could get her rest. I left first, hid in the bushes, and when I saw he was gone, snuck back in. Mona and I had a great night together in the hospital. We ordered pizza for the nursing staff on the floor, and chatted amiably with the woman in the next bed who was dying of lung cancer, and was concerned that her husband and boyfriend, each of whom didn't know of the existence of the other, might show up at the hospital at the same time to visit her. Mona and I burst out laughing at this. I stayed the night, even though it was against hospital regulations. In the morning, the nurse left out two toothbrushes.

~

Mona got better, fortunately, and went home to Winnesota, unfortunately. I cried and cursed her, myself, Stephen, cops, judges, god, the universe, and prostitutes, that I was again without her. After she left, rather than returning to the empty dung-hole that was Philadelphia, I stayed at my parents' house for three weeks, sleeping late, eating wrong, and frequently visiting my old college campus, where I had once been happy.

Finally, after my father started to tell me what a good idea it would be for me to move back home again, where I could live in my childhood room and pay rent because it would build character, I returned, quickly, to Philadelphia. I remained in my desolate shit heap for a few days before I flew out to Winnesota. The point of this trip, for the deceptive benefit of Stephen, who was now barely speaking to me, was to visit library school. I had been accepted into library school in both New York and Winnesota, so I had to make my choice, and I used this choice to camouflage my real purpose for this trip which was, of course, what it always was: Monality!

It was not a good time in Winnesota. Stephen was constantly angry with Mona, at the same time hoping that they could somehow resolve their problems and get back together. He stopped by the house all the time, always bringing her little presents and doing things for her, things that I wanted to be doing for her, things that she let him do for her. In his presence I had to stay distant from the woman I loved and had held in my arms so many times over the past several months, lest more suspicion than was already obvious be raised, suspicion that had already been raised to its highest point short of confrontation. It was like waiting at base camp at 20,000 feet, acclimatizing to the airlessness of what had once been so beautiful and frost-free, preparing to climb the summit to the top of the world, where death awaited me. It was hard to breathe.

Stephen was alternately cold and friendly towards me, and I went through the motions of friendship with him, all the time wanting him to just disappear from my life, her life, our life. We both pretended at times as if nothing had happened, nothing had changed; in reality, we both knew the truth. Yet we could not meet each other, either in our hate or our love, so we remained apart as we were together, fragmented like bits of sun through a partially closed blind, revealed, yet unseen.

There was no way I could move to Winnesota, no way I could be with her. Not now, not with things like this. It was killing me. My anxiety came back full bore. Many mornings I would flee the house, and walk through the quiet streets of her neighborhood, muttering to myself, puking by the side of the road or behind a parked car.

"I can't move here, Mona," I told her over lunch the day before I left, "not now, the way things are. It would be bad for me, it would be bad for everyone." I could hardly breathe. "I love you." I could hardly breathe. She took a sip of white wine, tears welling in her eyes, and told me she understood. She hated it, but she understood. She always fuckin' understood!

Stephen wouldn't speak to me the day I left, wouldn't say goodbye to me, would never say goodbye to me. Mona and I got to be alone at the airport at the end. We hugged and kissed as we had so many times before. I told her I would be back, one day, that this would never end, that we would never end. I knew it. I felt death. I felt life. I slipped a poem I had written into her hand. "Feel my life flowing through you, feel my lips upon yours this moment for all moments, until our lips meet again and the moments apart are gone and we are together again in our moment, the moment that will never end." "I love you, Mona!" I said as I kissed her one final time. "Don't forget me," she called as I went up the tarmac. "Never," I replied.

When I got home to Philadelphia, I found a note she had left in my bag, along with a picture of her. "Never!" That night, Stephen called me, said I was a "little prick" among other choicey adjectives, and that was the end for childhood friends. Alone again as if we had never met. I was now alone without him, without her. "Never!"

~

That fall, I left Philadelphia, and moved back to New York to go to library school. Contact between Mona and I became distant and limited. Apparently, Stephen had begun confronting her more and more about our relationship and, as a result, she moved farther and farther away from me, less calls, less letters, less love. She would get so polite when she wished to create distance

between the two of us, a politeness that infuri-
ated me. "Thank you for talking to me," she would
tell me after our more and more infrequent phone
calls, like I was taking time out of my busy schedule to talk to her, like I was doing her a favor,
like I had bought her a cup of coffee or something.
"Well, thanks for letting me lick your nipples, and
hey, for the blow job I owe you one, friend."
(Thank you for reading my book everyone.)

From time to time there would be a burst
of passion from her, maybe a phone call out of
nowhere, maybe a short letter from Winnesota.
One time she sent me a steamy Rosh Hashanah
card after Stephen, her and the child had gone to
Rosh Hashanah services at the local temple. She
wrote me that she had been impressed by the
pageantry of it all, and it had awakened feelings
in her of the pelvic variety toward me. She told
me that as she sat in the synagogue, taking in the
poignant experience of the Jewish New Year, she
had wished that I had been sitting beside her,
instead of Stephen. Just like when you had fucked
him back in the spring, I thought, seeing my face
instead of his!

While she was getting damp from the
reading of the Haftarah that fall, I was trying to
forget her, forget us, trying to concentrate on library school, the closest thing to damnation on

this mortal earth. Despite my best efforts, I could not forget her, would not forget her. I thought of her all the time, through long and boring classes, and long nights spent in front of the television, and long nights spent in front of the telephone hoping each time it rang that it might be her, a phone call out of the nowhere into the here, into my heart, from her mouth over thousands of miles of fiber optic cables. I waited, I wanted, and I had, not.

~

As winter approached, which was, not coincidentally, the next time her mag rag sent her to New York on "assignment," contact from her grew more frequent and intimate, with regular phone calls, regular emails at work, plus a couple of letters in the post to boot. She wanted me, again, wanted to reconnect, to reestablish yet again the ties that blind, to reenter my body as I reentered hers, and to reemerge full and hole, shooting the load of timelessness into the yielding loins of tenderness.

I was ready, and could hardly wait for her plane to land on that cold winter afternoon. We embraced at the airport, our tight kiss blocking the way of the other passengers who were trying to embrace their friends, lovers, and disenfranchised cohorts. As we kissed and touched, I remembered our history, our story, one of steamy subway cars and barroom hands, and immediately felt as if we had never been apart for even a second.

We went down the escalator, hand in hand, to the luggage carousel, to the outside world, to my car, to my home, to my bed, to our bodies, melted and merged again and again like sand and shore swerving against itself. We met, and the blood poured simple and direct into the skins of ecstasy. When I entered her, it felt soft and wet, like moist silk. We were together again, on top of my bed, on top of one another, by the clear light of a winter night. We finished, and then opened the window, and let the cold air refresh our sweat-stained bodies. All was cold, and clear, in the warmest of places...again. Find again. Found again. Finn again. Begin again.

~

This reunion between semi-ruined lovers featured the usual: the handholding, the kissing, the fondling, the fucking...the works! I was so relieved to have her back, to be beside her again, to be loved, touched, and embraced by her loving, touching embrace, that I neglected to question her on the usual subjects, Stephen, divorce, me and her, future, etc. I just let things lay as they were, and allowed her to lay me as she was.

FFS

One night, as we were lying in bed in the major Manhattan hotel at which she was staying, I started to rub my chest against her breasts, and grind my pelvic region against her pelvic region. In the swollen hypothalamic regions of my mind, I figured that we were seconds away from a scream-and-cream session. Right before the moment of infiltration, she suddenly stiffened up and told me to stop. As I unstiffend up, I asked her what was wrong, did she feel okay, the usual-type questions at this most unusual type of moment. She told me to be quiet and listen. I lay quiet and listened. I heard the sounds of a honking car, and a loud radio thumping, thumping, thumping, until the thump thumped away. I heard nothing else. I told Mona, "I don't hear anything." She told me to sssh, and listen. I ssshed and listened, and all I heard was the sound of my brain asking me why I was ssshing and listening. "Mona, I don't hear anything. Is something wrong?" After a few more seconds of silence, she informed me that she could hear the voices of the people in the next room. I listened hard, but all I could hear were the voices of the people in *this* room. "Mona, I still can't hear anything!" She whispered that if we could hear the people in the next room, then undoubtedly they could hear us. "So what?" I replied. Well, she replied, if they could hear us, then we couldn't fuck. But, I replied, I'm sure they can't hear us. And if they can, well, who the hell cares? No, no, she said, we must be quiet. "Yes, but..." I was cut off as she told me she loved me, kissed me good night, and turned over and went to sleep. Time to sleep in the land of thin walls and thick heads. I lay awake for awhile, staring at the white ceiling, holding my hard dick in my hand, listening to the sounds of the hotel. All I could hear was the soft breathing of a woman beside me, quietly sleeping.

The following night, as we were lying in bed in the same bed, in the same hotel, with I presume the same nosy neighbors, Mona mentioned how much she wanted to have a baby with me. What a sweet thought, I thought. I touched her cheek, gave her a big hug, a tender kiss, and told her how much I loved her. "One day, Mona, when I move out to Winnesota and we are together, we will have a child of our own. I hope it's a girl!" However, she thought we should conceive a child that night, tonight! My first thought, my first excuse, was to remind her of what she had said the previous night. "Well, Mona, ah, well, what about the fact that you said you didn't want to fuck last night. Remember, the whole thing about disturbing everyone in the next rooms?" "It would be different if we were trying to make a baby!" "Yes, that is true, but, ah, um, what about the fact that, ah, um, well, that you are still married, and that, ah, we live a thousand miles apart?" "I think we should have a baby, and you should stay in New York, and I'll raise it in Winnesota. You can visit it whenever you want!" Hmm, I thought. What to say to this? What in the world to say to this! "Well, Mona, sweetheart, don't you think that is a little, well, ridiculous?" "No, I think it is wonderful. Because even if our relationship doesn't work out, we'll always have something beautiful between us, like Stephen and I do!" We made out that night, but didn't have sex.

Later, as I was about to doze off into the Freudian wasteland, I started to think to myself of the other times that Mona had acted "funny" since I had met her. There was the time in the dance hall that night we met. And the time she attacked me at my parents' house. And her continuing hot and cold, up and down ways toward me. And last night's fear of disturbing the neighbors, and, tonight's idea for us to have a baby, while I remained a thousand miles away from her in New York! Hmm, I thought to myself, if you put these things together in a list, they do sound a bit different, a bit strange, a bit offbeat...and just plain nuts!

As I thought some more, however, and delved deeper into rationalization land, I came to the conclusion that all her supposedly "strange" behavior was just an expression of how much she loved me, how much she wanted me, how much she wanted a union of some permanence between us. She just expressed things a bit differently than I did. She was from Winnesota, I was from New York. It was all just a bit of cultural confusion, which we could easily fix when we lived together.

I turned and at looked at her sleeping face, observing her light, gentle breathing, her soft red locks framing her angular white face. God, I loved her so! Immediately, I felt better about things, better about us. When I woke up the next day beside her, her large breasts resting on my back, I had forgotten any weirdness from the previous night, the previous years. I started to vibrate my ass against her midsection, and she started to vibrate back. I put my hand behind myself, between her legs, and she grabbed my swollen cock from behind and...everything was back to normal!

~

The secret trips resumed within the pseudo-adulterous universe, and they were better than ever. A quickie before Christmas in Winnesota, when Stephen and the kid were out of town for a few days. An incredible two-day romanceathon in a bed-and-breakfast in Wisconsin, possibly the two most perfect days we ever spent together (weirdness quotient: zero!). After that trip, Mona wrote me a postcard, wondering aloud in writing why I couldn't be part of her life, now! Well, there was that divorce thing, I thought to myself, but only slightly. I was delighted, enthralled, in love, in lust, in want, in any and all things she wanted or needed.

Finally, late in the winter, she mentioned divorce. She sought out a lawyer. She got a lawyer. She filed for divorce. Stephen more or less went along with it. Their day in court came. Their day in court went. She was now a free woman, free to marry me, the man of her dreams. Things were perfect, right? Things were imperfect, right! Though our love had shone brightly through the winter and spring, feelings (hers) started to change as the first steps of summer were taken.

During one of our rendezvous sometime in June, I casually asked her over dinner one night about our future. Expecting a positive answer filled with plans and talk of life together, she instead told me that she couldn't offer me anything more than the long distance thing we had. But, she was divorced, wasn't she, I asked? Surely, after all the waiting, our time had finally come? Well, she replied, she still had many issues to work through, Stephen was still upset about the divorce, and her job was very busy at the present time. According to her, it wasn't the right time for us yet.

After a few glasses of wine, she blurted out that she didn't think she would ever be able to live with anyone again except for Leopold. She had come to realize that she didn't get along well enough with other people to actually live with them. She needed her space, or something. This comment was not directed at me at all, no, it was just an observation on things as they were. Reality in a plastic bag! She went on to inform me that summer was a bad season for her, a time to stay indoors and meditate alone, and therefore, she did not like to speak to people in the summer. Seasonal Insanity Disorder (SID), I think they call it. I lived 1000 miles from her, and I felt like I was 10,000 miles from her at that moment.

As I sat there, eating my meal, drinking my wine, and staring at her, I thought about the past few years between us, trying to get things in order in my own head, trying to make some sense of the things, one thing, anything, that she had said. I couldn't. It seemed that when things were "wrong" for me, they were "right" for her. When she was married, she wanted us to be together. Now that she was no longer married, it was the "wrong" time for us, as she had a lot of issues to deal with, things to think about, things that apparently didn't bother her when she was married. I thought about the long distance baby thing, which she had mentioned again the previous night while we were in bed. I thought about her SID. I thought about her saying she no longer could live with another human being except for her son. Then I thought it best not to think anymore. I ordered one last glass of wine and asked for the check.

It was over again, as suddenly as it had begun, again. Her passion turned off in a moment like the push of a button on the remote control. I asked her in September, since I was finishing library school in December, if I should consider trying to find employment in Winnesota in January, so we could be together now that she could talk to people again. After much hesitation, and much conversation about how it was my life, my decision and she didn't want to feel responsible for me, she told me no. It was over.

~

The seasons changed. Fall crashed winter as the leaves burnt and the trees flew away.

Divorce decrees were approved in ice-strewn courtrooms. Joint custodies were established jointly. I got a job as a medical librarian. The dead remained deceased. The living remained erased. My long distance phone bills dropped. I went out to bars all the time. I thought less about Mona, though I thought about her all the time (that paradox thing). I didn't need her—yes I did! But, it was over—no it couldn't be! I didn't love her anymore—I wanted her all the time. I was all right without her—I loved her desperately! I didn't think about her much—I dreamt about her every night! I didn't talk about her much with friends—I bored my friends with talk about her. I was fine—no I wasn't. Really I was—really I wasn't. I didn't need Mona anymore—I hoped we'd still get married somehow. It was good to be free of her—why didn't she call? I felt great all the time—I puked in the toilet. I hoped Mona had a good life—without me I hoped she would die. I didn't care anymore—without her I was dying. I didn't love—yes I did—I didn't need her—yes I did—I didn't want her—yes I did. Yes I did!

Then it came, again, like clockwork. No, not Christmas. No, not the fourth of July. No, not the running of the bulls. No, not the invasion of encephalitis-strained mosquitoes in Queens. It was Mona's next business trip to New York, for the American Society of Photojournalists and Peeping Toms convention, scheduled for that December. From this simple act of scheduling, several chains of events were unchained. First, starting about two months prior, around October, Mona started to initiate contact with me. A phone call once a week, a few emails. Then, phone calls twice a week, and a few more emails. Then, letters started arriving in my postbox. Then, a little romantic gift or two. Phone calls three, four times a week. Emails every day. Phone calls every day. Phone sex every night. Times to be picked up at the airport. Many things planned that we would do together when she was in New York that we would never actually do when she was in New York.

The day came. It was sunny and cold, a classic mid-December day. It had been six months since I had last seen her. Unlike my usual trips to the airport to pick her up, I was calm this time. This time. Whatever, whatever, I thought. Maybe we'd really break up for once and for all. Maybe we'd get back together, once and for all. No need to hope one way or another. Too much had happened for hope, the most innocent and stupid of all notions. Hope for life in a world of death. I wonder if the Jews in Auschwitz had hope, not knowing the history of what would happen to them. So, I felt calm, peaceful, and was not hopeful or hopeless. Just there. With a new haircut she hadn't seen. I wondered if she'd like it. Short hair for the first time since I was born bald.

After a few minutes, I spotted her. That's her..no..yes, no...Yes! That walk, yes, the hips moving in just that way. Yes, yes, that was her! I could already taste her on the tip of my dick. Closer she came, step by step, inch by inch. I tried not to smile. I never did when she arrived, as the emotion would so overwhelm me that I would retreat into dignified stoicism, or whatever I called it.

I met her eyes. She was smiling. They're so friendly out there in the land of frozen death and mid-summer ice knishing. Her hair was shorter; she had cut hers too.

I moved back. She came closer to me. I didn't know what to expect. A handshake, a pat on the back, a punch in the stomach, a little jig and a twist of lime? She grabbed me wordlessly, and threw me up against a wall, as people trying to move around us ran into each other, disrupted at this sudden interruption of the human exiting flow. The domino theory of walking, the chain of events broken, reconnected, reemerged, really quick, right now, into my mouth. Against the wall and into my mouth. No words, no names, just lips, and breasts wrapped in a black turtleneck against my black sweater. No words, just soft lips against surprised lips and hard bulges in the crotch vicinity. No words, just minutes flying by like months disappearing in her embrace, her arms holding me tight against her, her lips righting my tilted soul, battered by the past half-year's indifference.

It should have ended there, in a never-ending embrace. Instead there was luggage and a walk to the car. I was smiling in the cold winter sun. The flight was good, no. I like your hair, yes. Well, should we go straight to your midtown hotel, or to my apartment for a few minutes, to see my cat, my new computer, my dick inside you? Pick one. In the car, on the road, in my bed, my head in her hole, her screams, my shooting cum, our quivering bodies shaking the walls, the ceiling, the sewers, all of humanity. Pick all.

I drove her to the city afterward. She checked into her hotel, while I went to some library school class. Then I came back, and we had dinner, and some wine, before going back to her room. As we closed the door, she opened her legs, and rode me with her beautiful breasts shaking in the pre-Christmas air. The respective orgasms were completed, and completed well, I might add.

We then fell off in each other's arms to dream about being in each other's arms. We woke up in the middle night and fucked hard, and then fell off in each other's arms again to dream about being in each other's arms again. We woke up the next morning, alive, tired, and a-humming. She was happy, I was happy. Then, we kissed goodbye to go our separate ways for the daily business day. However, before we were out the door, our kiss turned into a caress that turned into a no-clothes-barred situation. Fifteen minutes later, I left to go to work with a big smile on my face, and I left her to go to work with a big smile on her face. I got to work late, but I was smiling for my quarter hour of tardiness. I worked, she worked, and then we met that night again, went to dinner, had some wine, went back to the hotel room, followed by kisses, caresses, hands down pants...etc.

All in all, it was a wunderbar trip, except when she got weird. This time is was the night I was supposed to meet her after some business-related cocktail party she "had" to go to. I was waiting for her outside the hotel where the party was being held at, pacing back and fourth in front of the glass doors, waiting for a glimpse of her. No glimpse. She was late, ten minutes, twenty minutes, half an hour late. I was beside myself, as well as under and atop. I hated waiting. I hated that she lived so far from me, and that now, to-day, though she was here, I still had to wait, wait like she was still a thousand miles away, wait like I waited every day, for her, waiting and wanting and never getting.

Finally, as I was pacing in front of the window to the hotel bar, I looked in and saw her sitting with a group of people. She immediately made eye contact with me and came out into the street. "Baby (or something like that—she never actually called me baby), why don't you come in and join us?" "I thought you said that we would go back to the hotel alone after your little party. You're half an hour late, and now you want me to go in and hang with these people?" I was not in a swell mood, and as usual for me, I was altogether unreasonable, as I think back on it. However unreasonable I was, she could always top me. "But I want to be with you. We'll just have one drink with them." "You can go if you want. I'll go home and meet you later or tomorrow." "But, I want to be with you!" "Well, I don't want to drink with these people. I hate them." "But, I want you to be with me. It's my career on the line!" Whatever the hell that meant, I went with her into the bar.

I sat in the corner and refused to talk to anyone, while watching several disgusting men buy her drinks. It's her career! When it was time to go, some guy hugged Mona goodbye for far too long, right in front of me. To this day I have never forgotten the jealousy I felt—the anger still wells up inside my gut like an imploding blender. Her "career!"

When we had finally left the hotel and were alone in the street, she thanked me for being so patient. "Thank you, Robert. It was great of you to wait! You were very understanding!" My response was to tell her to go fuck herself, which triggered a fun and expletive-filled ten-minute row in the street, me jealous and enraged, her drunk and aggrieved. After an "I'm leaving, no I'm leaving, no I'm not leaving, no I don't care what you do" time, we went back to her hotel, where we passed out after fucking, dead to the world for twelve hours.

The next morning we awoke to a cold, gray Sunday, our love renewed again, our anger forgotten. We had a leisurely breakfast at a Greek diner, followed by a romantic handholding walk across town. We ended our afternoon with some pastries and tea at an old-world Italian cafe I knew on First Avenue. We were happy again, the night before just a mere bump in our bliss, not even a bump, but more like a trip over the cat when you go to the bathroom in the middle of the night.

That night we continued our romantic ways with an intimate dinner at a small candle-light-type place in the Village. I had a good steak, the second best thing to have on a winter night, next to Chinese. After a late-night cocktail, we went back to the hotel, where we had some cock and tail. We were happy, we were full, she was filled, I was empty, and the universe, so corrupted, erupted, and disrupted twenty-four hours previously, was back in perfect order as Mona's tender red locks rested upon my hairy chest. I stroked her hair, then her face, then her arm, then her breasts, and I felt whole with my girl at my side.

~

Now that we had reemerged, reawakened, reformed, and were reborn, things were better than they had ever been before. Mona told me during one of our post-fuck evenings in bed (the only time two people can really talk without trepidation, at least in my experience) that she was ready. Ready for me, ready for us, ready for *it*. What was *it*? *It* was that I could make phone calls to her house, and if she wasn't home, I could leave a message on her answering machine! That was it? Well, yes, I know that that doesn't sound like much to those of you who inhabit the fairly sane realm of existence, but Mona, fearful as ever of losing her child to the irrepressible (or was it irresponsible?) Stephen, had always informed me that I could not leave messages on her machine at home, because even though Stephen no longer lived with her, and hadn't for almost two years by now, he had a nasty little habit of checking the messages whenever he visited. If he heard my voice, Mona felt there would be trouble in her stable land of milk and snow. I thought it would be funny if Stephen heard my voice, ha, ha, but Mona, lacking my gift for the humor of self-destruction in this case, did not share in my Marx Brothers-like belief in good dirty fun. So if I wanted to call Mona out of the blue, to say, I don't know, that I loved her, wanted her, was dying without her, well, I couldn't leave a message to that extent, or any to any extent except silence. And Mona would rarely pick up the phone unscreened. So, it created a bit of a contact problem at times for me. The times that I had hung up on Stephen over the years must have been in the high teens or low twenties. At times, if I was real confident that Mona was at home alone, I would cough into the machine, and a few seconds later, a laughing Mona would pick up at the other end. Happy times in the land of deception (or was it self-deception?).

Now that Mona had made the big commitment to let me use her answering machine, I felt confident enough, during my next "visit" to Winnesota, to "confront" her about the rest of our relationship. "Since we are now embarking on the third year of this relationship," I told her, "and since I believe we only have one life to live on this earth, I feel it is time for us to make the big decision—to be together or not to be together!" That was the only question. Simple and clear and unwrapped for her inspection! I didn't want to hope anymore, to pray, to conjole, to plead, to infer—I wanted to know, once and for all, what was in her mind, what her intentions toward me, her intentions for us, were. I wanted to finally and fuckin' know! No more wasting time, no more secret visits, no more lying, no more weirdness, no more ambiguity!

"I need to know Mona! Please!" This time it was an easy decision for her—the answer was yes! She was ready for us to come out as a couple, to come out of the snow into the sun, out of the adulterated into the unadulterated.

After all was said by me, listened to by Mona, and for once it seemed actually heard by Mona, things between us were elevated to a rather high level of lust and trust. She became tender towards me all the time, often calling me three, four times a day, just to tell me that she loved me, missed me, wanted me. It was like the early days between us again. Even the few secret trips we engineered because she wasn't quite ready to tell Stephen had a deep strain of nostalgia about them, a pleasant feeling of innocent deception, rather than the gut-wrenching hidden-prisoner syndrome that had permeated all of our recent rendezvous.

Then, as spring arrived, stirring the dull roots, Mona said it was time for my grand unveiling to her world. That's right, an open trip to Winnesota, free and clear for Stephen and everyone's inspection. I could see her family, meet her friends, and we could hold hands in public without wearing plastic glasses and fake moustaches. And, I was looking forward to seeing my one-step-away stepson Leopold again, as I hadn't seen him through all the years of secrecy and deception.

On a cool spring night, my plane left New York City, bound for Winnesota. A very pleasant fellow sat next to me on the flight, telling me about his job (I can't remember what he did), how he was soon getting married in Hawaii, and how he himself had once dated a woman who had a little kid. Whenever he would sleep over, the little kid, a girl I think, would come into the bedroom early in the morning, and announce loudly and proudly to mother and boyfriend, "When is he going to leave?" He told me that this woman wasn't the woman he was going to marry. I told him that little Leopold and I got along well, and I skipped over the little adultery stuff in our conversation.

Then the plane landed, as they luckily usually did when I was on them. Leopold was there with Mona to greet me at the airport, just as he had been there with Stephen, many eons ago, when he was younger, and Stephen was still my friend. Both were happy to see me. I was happy to see them. We were all happy!

Leopold and I played hide and seek, front seat, back seat, during the car ride home. Back at the house, while he played with a toy that I had brought him from New York, Mona and I went into the bedroom to play with one another. I felt her wetness, and she felt mine at the end of my tip tip tip. I think I even put it in for a moment or two. Then, before we had a chance to have a chance, Leopold shouted for us to come out of the bedroom, because he wasn't comfortable with the thought of mommy and Robert doing things like mommy and daddy used to.

As we came back into the living room, rearranging our rearranged clothes, he asked us if we were going to have sex. "We're not going to have sex, Leopold." "Yes, you are!" "Why do you think we're going to have sex Leopold?" "Because you like it!" I laughed so hard my eyes teared up, while Mona stood by silent and horrified. "Can't argue with you there, Leopold!" Ah, the purity of a child's mind, and the truth of the childhood utterance!

As this trip progressed, there was very little weirdness from Mona, but plenty of wetness, which I took as a positive sign for our future. She was talking about us living together in an active sense (i.e. where to put furniture and such), and even hinted that we could get married, which had been a big taboo to her before, after her experience with Stephen.

Speaking of Stephen, I avoided seeing him on this trip, or more accurately, he avoided seeing me. Whenever there was need for a child exchange between him and Mona, it was either done at the car, by the side of the road, or at his home, far away from my peering eyes. With him consciously absent from the picture, Mona and I, for the first time, felt like a real loving couple. And, not just in a spiritual, I'll love you forever and ever in this world and the next ultimate bullshit but nice to say and think about kind of way, but in a real his-and-hers towels kind of way.

As spring spread into summer, our love

seemed to be spreading into eternity. With cheap airfares abounding, we were able to make several trips to see one another. At some point, I think we saw each other on four consecutive weekends. Mona would call the time I spent in New York my "business trips" and would tell me when I visited her that I was "coming home." I felt the same way! We even agreed that once I found a job in Winnesota, I would move out there, and we would be together. I told her that I would give myself six months to look, and after that time, even if I had found nothing, I would move out there. Love came first, everything else came second, and we would never come second again! All the painful years apart were about to yield a perfect summer together, followed by a perfect forever together. The loneliness, the isolation afar, the longing, the deception, the resentment, the jealousy, the sins against friend and husband, were being washed away, as the sands of deliverance were smoothed over by the rejuvenating waters of awakening. Our togetherness was being affirmed, finally and grandly. I knew that soon, so soon, in no more than the turning of two seasons, our distance would become translucent, and we would walk through the holes in the clear molten earth into the arms of the other, to die, die, the death of a thousand rebirths. As Mona wrote to me in a card at this time, "if I could move the earth, so that I was standing by your side." I know, baby, oh yes, I know! At least I thought I knew, I was sure I knew! But, as usual, something was happening in her head. What *was* happening in her head? I wish I knew...I wish I knew!

~

The fourth of July, the time for America to get stoned on fireworks, patriotism, and Budweiser. A long trip for me to Winnesota was planned and executed. I was to stay a whole week, an eternity in the vortex of long distance one-partner married relationships. Coming home after one of those dang "business trips." Mona called me the night before I was supposed to arrive. Everything was hunky-dory, lovey-dovey, moon, stars, and sun kind of talk. I couldn't wait to see her. Only 173 days till the Xmas of my life began, and I was living in a sub-zero clime with my warm and wet baby. It was only a matter of time!

Airport, plane, delay, depart, apart. Land, deplane, delivered, together. The usual story. Mona and Leopold met me at the airport. Mona and I hugged instead of kissed, as our rampant affections still made the kid uncomfortable. Leopold hugged me too. Everything seemed normal at first, just an average American couple at

the airport, with an average American story behind us.

We drove back to *our* home. We talked in
the car, we chatted, the three of us, about love,
plane rides, the weather, and Barney the dinosaur. Things were not weird per se, but they were
not okay, if I do say. Mona was kind of, well, to
put it gently, but succinctly, nasty as a fuckin'
bitch with a hot fork up her ass. We hadn't fought,
we hadn't yelled, nothing had happened between
us, yet she was all a-scowl. I asked her what the
matter was, and she said nothing, that she was
fine. Maybe she was just in a bad mood. I decided
to try and make whatever the hell was wrong or
not wrong with her better. "How about a barbecue?" I suggested. Something to take her mind
off of whatever had taken her mind.

I cooked, we ate. Good food, bad human.
There was no change in her mood. One day, bad,
two days, worse, three days, horror, four days,
what the hell was I doing here! It was amazing
how the best-laid plans of mice, men, and me
could be changed by the ill will of one beautifully
twisted babe. And, to top it off, we had the kid
with us everyday, which meant we could never
talk privately, which meant that I could never ask
her what the hell was going on, which also meant
that I had to sleep on the couch, with Mona's dog

(the love of my life for this week) every night, which meant that there was no humpty grunty for us any night, not that she seemed the least bit interested. I was trapped in a hell of her own making, for no reason I could discern or comprehend.

After several summer days of suffering, on the next to last day of the trip, Stephen finally took the kid off our hands for a night (what had happened to joint custody?). Mona and I were finally alone. Thus, it was time for the great confrontation! If she thought she was getting away with this crap, well, she hadn't dealt with Robert Lasner. She would feel the acid of my wrathful tongue! The time for reckoning was at hand!

But first the time for fucking was at hand! "I want to fuck, Mona." "I don't want to!" "I think we should fuck, Mona." "Fine, we can, but I won't enjoy it," she said with a smile. "Well, fake it then!" We fucked like we always did; it was good, like it always was. Mona didn't have to fake it.

Now that the preliminary necessities were out of the way, it was time for Mona to face the music of this angry Jew. "What the hell has been your problem this week? Do you want to talk about something, anything? I love you!" Pause. Tick, tock. Dog barked. Car started. Oxygen moved. "I just remembered, I have to call my mother. I'll be right back." Mona hurried out of the bedroom. One potato, two potato. One minute, two minutes, ten minutes, twenty. I got out of bed and went into the kitchen. Mona was scrubbing the kitchen counter, getting the white even whiter. Look, she can see herself in it! I decided that the time for conversation had come to an end. I said nothing more to Mona about her behavior.

The next night, I flew back to New York. When the plane landed, I smiled to myself, happy to be away from her. This had never happened before. Usually, I was halfway between suicidal and psychotic on the plane trips back from Winnesota, the interior of the cabin like a prison, trapping my mind and body in compressed indifference. This time I felt liberated to be away from her. What the fuck had happened? How had perfection turned into destruction? Why? Why? I asked myself this question over and over again, and once you start asking that question, it is over. Why? We had traveled a million years in this relationship, from the beginning of nothing, to the end of everything. Why? She had no reasons—I could not ask, she could not tell. Yes, there had always been problems, those little whiffs of weirdness were always drifting about, waiting to pounce and annoy. But, to destroy? Never! Even after it had all happened, my response was "Never!" Not to me and her! Not to me!

At first Mona ignored everything, emailing me in a manner of extreme ordinariness. As time passed, her actions during the course of that week we were together became *our* actions, and thus *our* problems, as if somehow I was responsible for half of all that had gone on. She would grudgingly admit, when I pushed her, that she had some problems, everyone does, but always in the context that nothing that could be done about them, that that was just who she was. Nothing!

At the end of summer, after a month or so of back and forth nothingness, I decided to confront her. During the course of a two-day email argumentathon, I laid out my concerns heartily and courageously. She responded, a bit lost, a bit scared, a bit loving. At the end of the two days, after I had aired out all my concerns, we concluded that she was leaving it up to me to decide whether or not I wished to continue the relationship. Of course I wished it to continue, because I had never wished it to end. I figured in my little sundried tomato of a brain that if I could just ignore all her bad points, and concentrate on her good points, then things would turn out fine and dandy. That was the philosophy I had always followed into destruction and damn if I was going to stop now!

~

As the summer ended, Mona's seasonal reflux affective syndrome passed with the autumnal equinox, and she became fairly "normal" to deal with again. However, she had developed many "doubts" about us again, so she said we had to proceed cautiously in order to see where things would go. Despite this need to proceed with caution, she wanted to see me again, badly and immediately, so it was deemed time yet again for me to visit the land of the infinite Dairy Queen.

There was one major problem, however: airline strike! The one airline that flew directly to Winnesota International Airport, Iceway, was on strike. Something about wages and rights. So, Mona wondered, what were *we* going to do? After a summer of delicious indifference, she had to see me again, soon, couldn't wait, must see me NOW! When I suggested that maybe we wait a few more weeks, to see if they settle the strike, 'cause it was damn expensive to fly at the present time, Mona said she wanted me to come, NOW! So, I managed to book a flight, at a few hundred dollars more than usual. In two weeks we would be together again.

As I usual, I counted the days until my departure. Two weeks to go. Ten days to go. One week to go. Six days to go. Five days to go, Four days to go...

However, this time the countdown stopped with "three days to go." That morning at work, out of email nowheretown, I received a missive from Mona:

Robert,

I have changed my mind about seeing you. I do not wish you to fly out here. My feelings about you have changed. I am hopeful that we can somehow remain friends, but I believe it would be best for you not to come and visit me.

Love,

Mona

Interlude for Lite Reading While The Author Freaks Out

Ma: Pa, I feels that the author is gonna get real angry and bitter toward his lover over this here plane thang, don't you think?

Pa: I reckon you're right, Ma.

Ma: Maybe he needs some of that there anger counselin, just like cousin Jesse got after he shot up the Kmart.

Pa: I reckon you're right, Ma.

Ma: I'll send him the number of good ole Doc Moonshine. He cured Jesse, and got three years cut from his sentence.

Pa: I'm lucky to have a wife like you, Ma.

Ma: Oh, Pa, come here and rock me, you old horse you.

What do you want me to say at this point? What should I write? The end? I walked into Central Park, across from where I worked, and threw up in the bushes. I tried to get into contact with Mona, but was unable to, as she had apparently sent me the email and disappeared. Finally, after trying, crying, puking, and other general hysterics, I succeeded in getting touch with her by phone the next afternoon. She was as nasty on the phone as she had been in her email, refusing to discuss what had happened, refusing to tell me what was wrong. No explanations, no reasons, just "leave me the hell alone." It was as if I was bothering her, as if I had done something to her! I told her maybe I would come to Winnesota anyway, whether she liked it or not. She told she might pull an ALP if I came. (To those of you who are skimming through this tale in a bookstore, deciding whether or not to buy, pulling an "ALP" meant that she would treat me the way ALP had treated me on my visit to Arkansas (chapter one), meaning to ignore, abuse, threaten, and treat me with various other forms of total indifference and hate. I don't know if she had it in mind to start bringing home women as well.) I told her that this plane thing was the worst thing anyone had ever done to me. She told me the only reason I cared so much was because of the money I had spent on the non-refundable plane ticket. Well, yeah, that too baby! Our conversation went nowhere fast, and each time I heard her distant, smug, "I'm busy so why are you bothering me" voice, I wanted to kill her. This was the woman I had fallen in love with, the woman I had pledged my life to? This ugly, non-communicative, cold, miserable, cruel bitch!

After a few more days of me talking, pleading, yelling, begging, crying, etc., and her saying that she had to go and would talk to me later if she could, something finally hit me, as if an electrode had exploded in my brain. Or maybe some sense had finally gone through the hole in my soul. Whatever the deep-seated psychological reason, I stopped talking to her, stopped even trying to talk to her. I didn't call, I didn't email, I didn't try to communicate with her on any level. Something inside of me told me that I had nothing left to say to her, and that she had nothing left to say to me, so I stopped saying anything. For the next few weeks, I made no attempt to get in touch with her (or her with me). I went straight home after work each day, and went right to sleep, and when I awoke, which I tried never to do, I would either cry and hate the world for ever existing, or sit on the couch and stare numbly at the television.

After this initial period of shock passed, the next logical stop was alcohol. I built a still directly from my mouth to my brain, running along my cerebral cortex. This worked for awhile, but as in all things alcoholic, the pain remains, it's just that stealing a police car and driving across country in the middle of night seems like a worthwhile and fun idea. "No one will notice you at four a.m., right occifer?"

Finally, after a few weeks of drinking, I started to feel better, an almost physical reaction to the trauma, an "I can't fuckin' deal with this, so it is time for me to feel good and live in denial" kind of reaction. I may have been in denial, but for the first time in weeks, maybe months, maybe even years, I had some level of peace of mind. I stopped worrying about Mona, stopped wondering where she was, what she was doing, when she would call. For a little while, I had my life back, and if I wasn't wholly whole and complete, at least I wasn't as shattered and scattered as I had been. For awhile I was almost maybe possibly happy. For awhile.

~

Late on a rainy and cold Saturday night, I was watching a biography of Eric Clapton on the telly when the phone rang. I picked it up. It was her. I could immediately tell by the tone in her voice that the lust was back in her loins. I could feel her juices shooting through the receiver, into my ear, down my stomach, through my balls, out into my dick. We spoke for a few minutes about nothing in particular—I was friendly, if a bit rigid. She just wanted to know how I was doing, and to tell me that she missed me. After a few minutes, she told me she had to go. We agreed to talk again, soon.

I hung up the phone and jumped for joy! We were alive! As there was still breath in me, as there was still blood in my veins, as there was still cum in my pants, and come in my mind, I would never rest without her. We were back, me a little poorer in the pocket, with a plane ticket to nowhere, Mona a little poorer in the emotional stability department. But what was most important was that we were back. America's first couple of dysfunction was together again, and more fucked up than ever! The "healing" that I had

undergone over the past several weeks was undone by one ten-minute phone call from the land
of the smiling psychopath. Even after all that had
happened, I still loved her, still wanted her back,
still wanted things to correct themselves somehow, still wanted her to correct herself somehow.
I wanted her, and I had never stopped, and after
that phone call, I realized I never would stop
wanting her.

~

We resumed our regular schedule of
phone calls and emails. In addition to
reawakening my old feelings of love and depen-
dence, speaking to her again brought out a brand
new feeling in me: hatred. Part of me hated her
now. The plane thing had pushed part of me off
of part of an edge. During the previous years of
our affair, she had never done anything actively
to hurt me, anything thought out, premeditated,
direct and right through the gut. Not that there
wasn't plenty of indirect shit, which hurt just as
much. But I was able to successfully rationalize
that stuff away, someway. I could not successfully
rationalize this. She had been so anxious for me
to come to Winnesota this time; it had been her
idea more than mine, and then this. Why, why,
why, I wondered, questioning her, imploring her.
I used all the action verbs trying to get an an-

swer from her. I asked her why she asked me to come and visit her if she really didn't want me to come at all? I mean, I told her that she could have just hemmed and hawed like she usually did when faced with making any kind of decision, instead of being forthright for once. She told me that when she wasn't sure of something, she would just vacillate back and forth until she couldn't stand it anymore, before finally reaching a decision at the last minute. Well, goody gum drops for me, I thought, and all those who love you and rely upon you. And since her reality always reigned supreme to her, fuck me, fuck my plane ticket, fuck my money, and, again, fuck me!

~

Another Interval of Lite Reading, While the Author Smashes his Fist through a Window

Ma: Now Pa the boy seems real angry again, don't you think?

Pa: I reckon again Ma that ya are right.

Ma: Maybee he needs to go on that Pruzac stuff— I hears it makes the upset reel darn happy.

Pa: Oh, Ma, you still got all the smarts in the family—you's even smarter than Wilbur the pig.

The result of all of this was that my feelings towards Mona changed on a day-to-day, hour-to-hour, sometimes minute-to-minute ba-sis. I would stop speaking to her, then resume, then stop, then resume, again and again, and then again. It was very unstable, even within our usual specter of instability. The ups and downs had ups and downs. To illustrate:

R   M

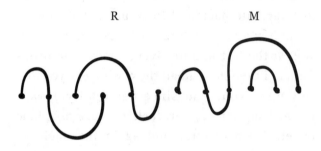

The intersection of m (instability quotient), and r pro-duces an irregular curve of fuckability, which inter-acts as a prime number with the cosign of the isosce-les aspect of the invariability of the dysfunctional ele-ment of our relationship times pi to the x power, which of course equals screw. Multiply by three to obtain the ideal median range of rational numbers versus irra-tional actions, then subtract one, and add none as well.

~

Finally, after a few more weeks of on-again, off-again contact, and on-again, off-again caring, we decided that it was time for us to meet again, face to face. Mona thought that we should meet at a neutral site, not Winnesota, not New York. However, we couldn't decide on a neutral site she approved of, so she came to New York.

Anticipation of a strange variety, lust and love mixed with hate and indifference, ensnared me as I started the countdown to her arrival. As the days moved to zero, it was time for yet another trip to the airport, yet another meeting at the airport, and yet another series of weird dreams inside the Hitler oven of relationships. She walked down the tarmac and into my arms, this time with a deep hug and a gentle kiss on the lips. She felt as hot to my touch as usual, and just as odd to my mind. I wanted, at that moment, to take her in my arms and shake the brain out of her head, to fix the tiny blood vessels that had to deal with judgment, and then reinsert it, brand spanking new and perfectly functioning, into that lovely red head. Then she would operate according to my specs, and our relationship could continue, as beautiful as before, as beautiful as before fall, before summer, before the plane thing and her few months of insanity. Instead, we just chatted politely, about Leopold and work, and got into the car and went to lunch.

The trip was rather uneventful, for us.

FFS

We fucked a lot, not particularly passionately, the weather was nice, she was friendly, etc. One day we took a long walk on the beach, and talked about having a talk about what had happened over the past few months. However, our talk about talking went nowhere, as I wasn't ready to talk to her yet about all that had happened, because I was scared of talking to her and finding out what a big part of me already knew, which was that we had no future. Mona was relieved, of course, to have any opportunity not to have to talk. We therefore agreed to say nothing of consequence for the rest of the day, and just to enjoy the sun, sand, and surf. In a word it was: Ignoreland. Nothing was said, nothing was unsaid, the rest of the trip was fine, decent and upstanding, and when Mona went back to Winnesota a few days later, things were no different than when she had arrived, nothing settled, nothing agreed, nothing more than nothing more.

~

There was one ointment in my fly. It looked like I might have a job in Winnesota, a well-paying, powerful library position. I had applied for the position months before, during one of the good days during the unstable period of our relationship, and forgotten about it, until low and below, I received a phone call one day. They were interested in me. Very interested!

First, there was the phone interview, which went well. This was followed by the in-person interview, which meant that it was time for "A Trip to Winnesota," part XX (I counted). I flew out for the interview about two weeks before Christmas. It was the date of our third anniversary together, or at least the third anniversary of the night we messed around in the bar, in the subway, and on the floor of the hotel room. We always dated that as the start of our relationship. How appropriate, really. We should have stayed on the floor, flat on our backs—it was where we were at our best.

Mona said she wanted to celebrate our anniversary when I came, but when I arrived in Winnesota, there was no celebration. It was much like our previous trip, ordinary in every respect, for us, except for the first night, when Mona was as horny as an unfixed kitten. When she greeted me at the airport, I knew. She had that old look of lust her in the eyes. In the car I massaged her crotch through her jeans while she attempted to drive within the white lines. I knew. She had that old feel of wet in her pants. We went for a couple of drinks, then back to her house for some incredible ridin' and glidin'.

While we were resting in bed after our fuckfest, I dug in a little at her, because I was still mad about everything, and because I felt quite secure to criticize her after my pecker had been emptied. I wanted an explanation from her about why she had done the whole plane thing, an explanation that I still hadn't gotten. I got a little nasty as we laid there in bed, our chests heaving, our bodies covered in the sweet sweat of fuck. I'm not sure if she registered what I was saying or not, after the drinky drinky and the bonky bonky, but by the next morning, things were back to being real ordinary 'tween us.

~

The job interview was pure Winnesota. The people were pleasant, too pleasant. They wondered why I would want to leave New York. Why does anyone ever want to leave New York? They told me that Winnesota had wonderful theater. I wondered why people always say that culturally bereft locales have "wonderful theater," as if that makes up for the intellectual and artistic void.

For lunch, we had ham and cheese sandwiches in a room with no windows. The lunchtime conversation consisted of talking about nothing. "What did you do last week?" "Nothing." "You know, tonight my husband and I are going to do nothing." "Really!" "And this weekend we're going to do nothing again." "Really!" "And, for Christmas we're going to my parents' house to do nothing." "Really! Well, I still have to finish my Christmas shopping, as I have nothing left to buy." "Look at the weather we're having, it's like nothing we've ever had before. Robert, do they have this kind of weather in New York?" "Nothing doing," I replied.

After lunch, they introduced me to a million different people who were the same, except for one girl who stood out because she was Jewish. I saw a puppet show that they put on over closed-circuit television for the sick kids since this was a hospital or something (to make them well, or make them sick?). Then, since they kept saying how flexible the hours of my job would be, I asked what "flexible" meant in terms of my livelong workday. They told me that everyone had to work at least forty hours a week, and sometimes evenings as well if there was a special event, and that the library opened at eight in the morning, when it was still dark outside (it doesn't get light in the winter in Minnesota until noon). Other than that, it was all real flexible, as long as I worked until I dropped dead in the snow.

The day came and went, nowhere. They practically offered me the job on the spot (since

I had expressed interest, they said they would love to see me on the puppet show, so I knew that was a positive sign), and said they would call me in four days. I immediately went to visit Mona at work. She had gone, in the space of our relationship, from being a photojournalust with a high powered magazine, to being the office manager of a company that published books on hunting and fishing—another part of her delicious free fall from the top of her head to the bottom of her mind. It was much less pressure, she told me. She seemed pleased with what I told her about the interview, but not ecstatic. Things were real normal.

That night, we got drunk together while watching awful Saturday night non-cable television while Mona forced me to intentionally lose games of Go Fish to Leopold in order to build his self-esteem. What about my self-esteem? At nine it was time for them to go to bed (nobody stays up late in the land of the permanent time capsule), and Mona and Leopold went to the bedroom they shared because he was still afraid to sleep without his mommy. (Or was his mommy afraid to sleep without him?) I was to sleep on the couch, on the floor, under the sink, anywhere I wanted to go.

"Good night" wafted from the bedroom,

and then all was quiet, all was peaceful, all was still, Saturday night, at 9:15, in the great state of windburn. However, I was drunk, not tired, and more than a bit agitated. God, I thought, back in New Orleans, I would sometimes *wake up* at nine in the evening! What should I do, what was there to do, this night, in the silent land of nocturnal thunder and treasured galoshes?

After a few minutes of contemplation, I knew what I had to do. I had many plans, many plans, indeed. You see, I wasn't feeling too...sane. Maybe it was the two bottles of wine. Maybe it was the time (nine). Maybe it was me out here, my baby and her baby in there. Whatever it was, I felt isolated, trapped, and angry.

My first thought was to go to a bar. This was wondrous, I thought. Here I was with the woman I love, whom I never get to see, and I am alone Saturday night at nine o'clock, thinking about going to a bar. This relationship was getting better by the minute!

After I dismissed the bar plan because I was too drunk and didn't want to risk crashing Mona's car, my next plan was to sleep in the garage. Boy, I figured, wouldn't that show Mona, me sleeping in the garage, all cold and stiff on the concrete floor, covered in dust and lawn-mowers and trash bags. That would show her.

The garage thought stayed in my head for awhile, as paced back and forth in Mona's basement, muttering curses against her under my breath, her dog staring at me in disbelief and hopeful for food of some sort. "Maybe I'll just sleep right here in the basement. Yeah, that's it!" But it was cold in the basement, and I imagined it was even colder in the garage. My feet were frozen, even with the wine. Sure, I could wrap myself up, like Washington at Valley Forge, and that would show her, but maybe there was a better way to show her. Hmm, what could I do? What to do?

It suddenly came to me, like a tornado to a trailer park! Why, of course, it was so obvious, so simple, so perfect! I would go right to the heart of the cow, right to the most forbidden zone in all of Winnesota—Mona's bedroom! Right where she was, and the kid was. They'd wake up in the morning, see me on the floor, Mona would freak, the kid would cry, and I'd show them that they couldn't keep me down. Yes, now that was a plan! And much warmer too!

I gathered my blanket and my pillow and crept up the stairs, followed by the dog, and entered the forbidden boudoir. There I laid myself down on the floor right at the foot of the bed. It was done! The dog jumped up and went to sleep on the bed. I laid there, basking in my triumph.

I'd shown them who was boss!

I tried to fall asleep. I turned to the left. I turned to the right. I lay on my stomach. I lay on my back. Slowly, I began to have serious doubts about all this. Maybe it was the unwelcome intrusion of sobriety reawakening my fears of conflict, but now I couldn't face the prospect of waking up on the floor, and upsetting Mona and the kid. My triumph of spirit was short-lived as I trudged out into the living room, pillow and blanket in hand, dog in tow.

At least I didn't sleep on the couch. As my final act of defiance, I slept in Leopold's room on a daybed. Actually, Mona had told me I should sleep there, as it was more comfortable than the couch. And she was right. It was much more comfortable than the couch, much more comfortable than the garage, much more comfortable than the basement, much more comfortable than the bedroom floor, and much more comfortable than my bed at home, alone.

I curled up in the daybed, surrounded by the toys of Leopold's childhood, some that I had given to him, many that I had not. The dog jumped into the bed beside me, exhaled loudly, and put its head down, to sleep. I pulled the covers up to my head, and looked up at the universe, up at the ceiling, then at the wall, beyond which was the bed where my love and her child were asleep, oblivious to the madness of my evening. I faced the white wall shining in the silent night blackness, shed a small tear of finality, and closed my eyes to sleep.

That night snow fell all over Winnesota, all over the living souls drenched in bars, all over the dead souls drenched in empty hours. It was falling all over Winnesota. On every part of the dark frozen tundra, all over the carless highways and deserted farmhouses, all over the stoic thoughts and silent conversations. It was falling, too, upon the house where Robert Lasner lay alone, below the surface of the earth, below the life of his lover, as he wept alone with a sleeping dog as his warm company, his tears falling as lonely snow all over the living and the dead.

~

I was offered the library job two days after I returned home. I asked them how long I had to decide, and they said about a week or so, but that it was not set in stone. I had no idea what to do. Six months before, it would have been an easy decision—go to Winnesota. Three months before, it would have been an easy decision—no way was I going to Winnesota. Now, it was in the middle of the middle, in the uncertain portion of uncertainty, as in who the fuck knew what the hell I should do? I certainly didn't know what I should do. Mona certainly didn't know what I should do. Friends who I asked were certain that they certainly had no idea for certain what I should do, but I should certainly go, but not for certain.

I was scared to make a decision either way. On one hand, I was lonely and miserable in New York and the thought of spending an endless time stream there sent me straight to the toilet with mouth open. On the other hand, I had seen what bad times with Mona were like up close, and the thought of being alone in the land of frozen death didn't really appeal to me either. The scales of justice were balanced in favor of nothing, and there was nothing for me to do, except suffer in indecision.

Tick tock went the clock. Flip flop went my brain. Patter splatter went the rain. Ding dong went my shlong. A week went by, then two. I asked the people in Winnesota for more time to decide; they said ya. Since the holidays were coming up, they didn't seem to care about me making a decision in the immediate sense. "Merry Xmas, and take all the time you need!" That was just what I needed, if extending this indecision and suffering was what I needed. At least I was certain that I could be uncertain for a while and it certainly wouldn't matter. So I just didn't think about it anymore, Mona style. Though, of course, I thought about it all the time, Rob style.

In order to help myself not make a decision, it was decided that a trip to Winnesota, part XXI, was in order. This time, however, I would travel not by air, but by land, driving alone across the mid-winter empty. Nothing better than a thousand-mile journey in winter through the Northern tundra to clear the mind in order to make an important life-changing decision.

I wanted to come for Christmas, to be with Mona for the holidays, kind of a middle class fantasy of mine, of home, hearth, carols, mistletoe and eggnog spiked with whiskey. But Mona decided that it would be too stressful, that too many questions would be asked (Of whom? By whom?) if I came on the anointed day, so it was determined unilaterally, and I went along with it, that I would come a few days later.

~

I left the day after Christmas, a clear cold day in New York. As I set off, I began thinking of the other times in my life when I had undertaken such long journeys by automobile. There was of course the trip to New Orleans. But what entered my mind most were trips I had taken many years before, when I was a boy and my family and I used to drive down to Florida every summer to visit my grandparents.

The anticipation was exhilarating as we pulled out of our driveway late on a Sunday night. We always left late on a Sunday night because my father had it all figured out so that we would miss the evening rush in New York, as well as the morning rush in Washington D.C.

He was usually in a good mood during the long state-to-state drive. I would always sit in the front of the car with him, as the "navigator" of the trip. My mother and sister would sit in the back, their job to portion out the food we brought with us so we didn't have to pay for, as Dad told us, "the overpriced crap they sold on the highway."

It was always exciting to ride through New York City, my father driving like a maniac. He would speed along the bumpy and pothole-strewn streets of the city, occasionally yelling curses at the cabdrivers who cut him off. We would always leave the city through the Holland Tunnel, where my father knew all the toll takers by name, which to this day either blows me away or frightens me, I'm not sure which.

Once we crossed the tunnel, we went from the exhilarating no-potholes-barred part of the trip to the eight-state quest of endurance. The world passed by my window as we zoomed in a rented car through the summer night air and mosquitoes hitting the windshield. New Jersey was so long and boring. Delaware was so short and boring. I don't remember Maryland much, except for the big tunnel going to Baltimore. We never went through Washington D.C. because my father said there were too many jungle bunnies there. One year I asked my mother what a jungle bunny was, and she said it was a black person. The thought of black people hopping around our nation's capitol with bunny suits on seemed strange to me, even at that age, but, if my father said it, it must be so. For me the trip really got going in Virginia, the tobacco pickin' South. We always needed to get gas for the first time in Virginia, and it was fun for me, to get out of the car and be walking in the deep dark South, even if it was a gas station.

After the first refuel, the stay-awake nineteen-cups-of-coffee part of the journey began, as we went through the Carolinas and Georgia. My father, being a loyal Republican, always made fun of Georgia, with many jokes about someone named Jimmy, and a lot of stuff about peanuts which I didn't understand at the age of nine. By the time we got to Florida, we had been on the road at least sixteen hours, and still had eight more hours to go, so Florida, which seemed like the end, was really just the beginning of the end, the very beginning. It was always long, hot, and populated, compared to the Carolinas and Georgia, which were long, hot, and unpopulated.

Every year, as navigator, I tried to stay awake for the entire trip, but never succeeded. It was wonderful though, trying to stay awake with my father throughout the long night of miles and white lines on the highway, my mother and sister fast asleep in the back. The two of us together, in the middle of the night, in the midst of the blackness of nowhere, trying to find baseball games on the radio from crazy cities like Pittsburgh or Cleveland, or heaven forbid, a game involving my beloved Dodgers. Best of all, except for the occasional freak out, my father would never yell during the long ride down the coast.

~

With all those happy memories of traveling down South as a boy to accompany me, I headed north along borders framed by snow-filled skies. I left New York in early evening. The first state, Pennsylvania, was a long snore on my disembodied subconscious. Been there, lived there, nowhere. After Pennsylvania, I stopped at the Ohio welcome station, where some yokel informed me that gas was real cheap, right down the road. Thank you. After gassing up, I headed

305

down the straight and narrow, the flatness and darkness under and around me, like a flake of frost on the last autumn leaf dying. "Four dead in Ohio" I sang as I whizzed past Kent, past the past that I had nothing to do with, except for knowing a song from the radio.

After passing through the rest of Ohio without incident or interest, I got off the road to get food in Indiana, and found myself not accidentally near the former hometown of Stephen and Mona. It was past midnight, the wind was hitting my face like an ice whip, and the skies were black and clear except for the smoke rising from random chimneys, from random homes where Stephen and Mona used to live. I looked at these houses, quiet and dark in the midnight chill, and up at the sky, clear and cloudless, the wafts of smoke disappearing into the stars. I thought of Stephen and Mona, smoke coming out of their chimney, their life together starting here, before they knew it would end elsewhere. I thought of the way things used to be, for all of us, and of ALP, and the warmth of New Orleans.

I put my cold hands into my warm pockets, and stood staring into the sky for a little while longer, until my pockets could no longer provide protection. Then I got back into my car to drive away from this place, a place where Stephen and

Mona used to live, toward a place where I didn't know if I could live, a place where Mona lived, where Stephen lived, apart and alone, with a child between them, separating them, bringing them together. I was now on my way towards her, his Mona, my Mona, no man's Mona, hoping to see in the look in her eye, and the yielding of her body, the woman I loved, whom he had once loved. And I prayed that when I got there, I would no longer feel alone like I didn't belong. Please god, I asked, let me belong! Then I hit the accelerator and left the place where I had never belonged, to continue on towards a place I didn't belong, to be granted the right to belong. It was so far, so cold, and so long.

It was now the middle of the night, three a.m., the lights of my car the only lights on this night after Christmas, except for the occasional convoy of trucks, and the lonely car going somewhere else, as I was. A man could die out here, I thought. No help, no friend, just a road, unyielding and eternal, and then, death, unyielding and eternal. Mona told me that in the spring, they would find the bodies of people all over Winnesota, people who had frozen to death over the winter, usually drunk and passed out in the night air, their bodies covered by snow and ice until the spring thaw came to pass.

Indiana ended, and I never knew it. Illinois began, and I never knew it. But then I saw the sign. A few miles later there was Chicago at the blue-black end of night, an empty steel city on the verge of dawn. I wanted to go to the bathroom, but the McDonald's was locked, so I drove right through the rest of Chicago, to some place called Lake Forest, or River Forest, or Lake River, or Liver River, or River O' Forest in the Lakes of Liver. Whatever.

I stopped at a rest stop. It was about six in the morning. Exhaustion had crept in. I phoned and left a message on Mona's machine, telling her where I was and when to expect me. I didn't know where I was or when to expect me. In the rest room, the warm piss felt good coming out of my cold dick. There were a lot of well-dressed men milling about, peering, staring, and looking away longingly. Ah, good, I was in the resthole of Sodom and gonorrhea. Yummy yum asshole ping shoot cum. If only I had a taste for my own kind. Mmm delicious! I thought of Joe Orton. "Sorry boys, but I have to go. I have miles to go before I cum, on my baby's tits in the far away land of churned desire and frostbitten nipples." Miles to go.

I left, feeling kind of blue in the dawn. Blue tired I was! But I couldn't stop, must go on!

The midwinter's night dream continued. Sleep...sleep. No...no...! Then, bang, light! Then, Wisconsin in the morning! America's Dairyland! They weren't kidding. Isolated farmhouses isolated from other isolated farmhouses. Nice looking country, though—from what I could see out of my half-shut eyes.

The morning crept into my night-strained eyes, wide, shut. Open! Shut! Open! Shutting. Shut. Sleep...sleep. No, no...yes...no...nes...yo. Then swerve. Then median. Then awake. I staggered off the highway at sixty, and pulled into the parking lot of a hotel, where I laid down on the back seat, and dreamt of Mona's big boobs, until the cold of the unheated car woke me. Why didn't I leave the car running with the heat on?

I was now mad with exhaustion, but I knew I must keep going, keep going, as my destination was in sight. Sleep...sleep...fucking soon. Must get to fucking, soon! I passed through Minnesota, just crossing the southeastern corner, and then, bang, yawn, Winnesota! "Welcome to Winnesota! Land of 11,000 Degrees Below Celsius!" I was here, I was not queer, and I was finally home, in the gray morning light of Winnesota.

I saw the snowline, I mean skyline, of the Frozen Cities, Windiapolis, and St. Snore!

Winnesota in winter! I knew this place, my dis-
associated homeland. I knew these roads in my
sleep! However, I get lost for awhile in the Frozen Cities from lack of sleep. Eventually, I righted
my ship and sailed on the smooth black ice right
into Mona's arms, who was waiting for me in her
bed, alone, no kid, thank god. I jumped in,
rambled incoherently, hugged her tight, felt her
body loosen and yield, felt her nightgown come
off, felt my dick come out, and as I came in, we
screamed, smiled, and then slept. A reward for
all at the end of a thousand-mile journey. And, I
hoped, a good start to my week of decision making.

~

In addition to making up my mind about
the job, I had decided to do something else on
this trip to the land of the permanent frost. I was
going to write again, something I hadn't done in
years, since before I had met ALP. I decided, in
grand tribute to *Dubliners*, to write stories about
my Queens childhood, my boring and utterly
meaningless Jewish existence in "bayou Bayside."
The nights of rejection spent in big-hair bars,
rejected because I could think and didn't have
muscles ripping through my skin. The endless
insameness of every holiday, eat too much, turn
on the TV, fall asleep on the couch, Dad's pro-

310

truding belly spilling out over undone pants. A few hours each day in this worthless tundra, and I would have my beginnings on paper, my childhood like an eggshell, exposed and sharp.

So I wrote for the week, spending my time in a coffee shop right next to Mona's office, since she had to work, and couldn't take time off. After my day spent with pen and paper, Mona and I would go home together, sometimes with Leopoold, sometimes without. Things between us were friendly and polite. There was little fucking, little fighting, a lot of writing, and in short, a lot of good, clean ordinary behavior between two loving lovers such as Mona and myself.

However, I had yet to make a decision on the job, and Mona was not helping the matter. She refused to be more than an impartial mediator, which is exactly what I wanted out of my longtime lover. She would help me make out pro/con lists of whether I should take the job, as they had helped her in the past. With what? (Remember: "I vacillate back and forth until I can't stand it anymore.") So I made meaningless lists, all the time hoping that Mona would one day grab me in her arms and tell me she wanted me, and that I should come, come, come! However, whenever I would directly confront Mona about the job, I would get a sharp "it's up to you." Exactly what I wanted out of my longtime lover!

Finally, the week passed, and it was time for me to go. We had sex one last time about an hour before I left. It was good; it was always good with her. Then it was really time for me to go. As we hugged at the front door, I told her that I hadn't reached a decision about the job yet. She told me it was up to me, but she would support whatever decision I made. Then she cried, and told me to come visit her again, even if I turned the job down. I told her I loved her. She told me she loved me. Then I got into my car and drove away down the highway so white with winter that I couldn't see the white lines any longer.

~

For the first part of the trip back, I was all right. I called Mona from somewhere in Indiana or Ohio, I don't remember or couldn't tell which, and I pulled off the road to jerk off in, I do remember, Indiana. As night fell, and I drove through Pennsylvania, my old companions, the vaudeville team of anxiety and dread, returned to my gut in full force. I drove over the dull and dark road, across the nothingness and carbon copy straightness of the key-stoned state, and I thought of the life ahead of me without her, alone in my apartment, no her, each day, the next day, all days. My heart pounded nervously, and I could feel the terror in my stomach, rising through my throat, into my silent mouth. I didn't want to go home. I didn't want to go back. I didn't want to go. I think if at that moment I had lost control of the car and perished in a ditch, my body never found, it would have been the best of all the miserable worlds I contemplated.

Past Pittsburgh, and towards Harrisburg, I shook with the fear of no choice and no chance. I thought of my bed at home, empty and alone, my pale figure twisting and turning on the nocturnal mattress, to the left, to the right, and then looking up, to face the white ceiling, above which she didn't lie, but where the souls of remembrance resided. No, I couldn't do this! I couldn't be without her! I would say yes to the job, yes to her, even if she had said no to me. Even if I had to be without her, I would still be close to her. I could drive by and see her light on at night. Or, if I was lucky, I could glimpse her going in the morning, or coming home in the evening. At least I would have a glimpse! I would see her red hair, her voluptuous shape, her exquisite walk, and I could take those images home with me, to a shack somewhere in Winnesota, where I would live with her eternal image in my memory. I would go to sleep each night alone, content that a small piece of her form resided in my snow-drenched brain.

Yes, I would be with her. I would come, and even her indifference would not stop me.

I felt better as I approached Philadelphia, my old former hell of a home. "Hello, fucked-up city of cock-sucking indifference. How are you doing tonight? Let me send my regards, or more accurately, burn baby burn!" Nancy still lived there, and worked as a nurse in a prison. We had stayed in touch over the years, speaking on the phone every few months, talking about her latest man, or her latest woman. When discussing our relationship, she often told me we were just "friends who happened to fuck!"

As I drove past Philadelphia, into New Jersey, my emotions completely reversed themselves. No, I couldn't do this! I couldn't take the job! I couldn't be near her! I must just forget her, forget, FORGET! She would destroy me, nothing would ever change, we would continue down the same path, ever forward to nowhere. No, I must say no. It would hurt for awhile, for always maybe, but it must be no, NO! The capitalization didn't help.

I saw the first signs for New York City. Fifty miles to go. The highway was empty and surrounded by a dense forest. It looked like I was in the middle of nowhere. I could have been any-where. The signs said New Jersey; my mind, for an instant, said New Orleans. I still had one photograph of ALP, stuffed in a drawer somewhere at my parents' house. In it, she was costumed as a floozy of the Old West, wearing a gun and a feather boa, with a bottle of Cuervo in her hand. She was wearing a short skirt, and I could see her thin bare legs. On her face she wore a mischievous smirk. It was a staged photograph that she had made for me in a portrait shop, as a surprise. She told me that it had cost her fifty dollars.

I thought about a day in the future, the day after my death. They would be going through my things, throwing most of it away, giving my clothes to charity, when they would stumble upon a yellowing photograph of a strange woman with a gun. They would wonder who she was, what she had meant to me, and why I had kept this photograph for all these years. Who was she, what had she meant to me, and why I had kept her photograph for all these years?

I thought about Mona. I had many pictures of her, some with me, some with Leopold, some with Stephen. Some with Stephen! I had pictures of him too, from when we were kids, together, young boys smiling, with our arms around one another's shoulders. Pictures of the past! In the past! I had a lot of memories, memories of my childhood, memories of my friends; some were gone, some remained.

The sign said "New York City—40 Miles!" I thought of the life ahead of me in New York, alone and without her. I pulled over to the side of the road, opened the car door, and forced my fingers down my throat. Nothing came out.

I got back on the road. I quickly accelerated to ninety on the empty highway, then ninety-five. Then I hit one hundred. Could I go any faster? Suddenly, I took my foot of the petal, and let the car slow to sixty, fifty, forty, thirty... to nothing. Then I stopped. There was no one on the road, nothing behind me, nothing ahead of me. It didn't matter how fast or how slow I went. It didn't matter where I went. The sign said "New York City—35 miles!" There was nowhere else to go. Years ahead of me, years behind me, it didn't matter.

.

Other titles from
Ig Publishing

Sinners in Summertime
by Sigurd Hoel
Afterword by Sverre Lyngstad

~

Cloud 8
by Grant Bailie

~

In Wonderland
by Knut Hamsun
Translated by Sverre Lyngstad

~

Careful!
by Richard Madelin
Spring 2004